IN PLAIN SIGHT

BROKEN BOW

BOOK THREE

ASHLEY A QUINN

TCA PUBLISHING LLC

ISBN is 9781733160063
Library of Congress Control Number: 2021903662

PROLOGUE

A bitter wind bit into Rayna Nydert's face as she hurried up the walk to her boyfriend's house, a casserole carrier in her gloved hands. Thomas had been out working in this cold all day with a local vet. He deserved a hot, home cooked meal.

She twisted the doorknob and walked inside, shuddering as she finally stepped out of the wind. It might be sunny, but the temperature was brutal.

"Thomas?"

"I'll be out in a minute!" he called from down the hall.

Rayna walked through the living room to the kitchen and set the casserole down on the bar separating the two rooms. She took off her hat and gloves, shoving them into her pockets, then shrugged out of her coat and laid it over a barstool.

"Hey, babe." Thomas walked in, his dark hair damp from the shower. Water droplets dotted his forehead, and his t-shirt clung to his well-muscled chest.

Heat licked Rayna's belly as she drank him in. All these years and she still thought he was the most handsome man she'd ever met.

He leaned down and pressed a quick kiss to her mouth. "What's in the carrier?"

She grinned and unzipped it. "Ziti. And garlic bread."

"That sounds great."

She stood on her toes to kiss him again, then moved around the bar into the kitchen to grab some plates. "I figured you'd want something hot after being out in this cold all day."

He sat on one of the stools and watched her work. "Yeah. It was nasty. Dr. Adelson hates this weather, so I did most of the work while he huddled in his giant parka and supervised."

She giggled. "Can you blame him? He's like seventy and his assistant is a strapping, intelligent young man in his early twenties."

Thomas sighed. "I know. And I appreciate the experience." He grinned. "It's paying off, finally." He lifted a hip and pulled a folded piece of paper from his back pocket, holding it out to her. "I got into vet school."

"What?" She snatched the paper from his fingers. "Thomas, this is great!" She unfolded the letter.

"There's only one bad part."

"The University of California?" she said, cutting him off as she read the letter.

He sighed. "Yeah. That's the bad part. *But* it's the best vet school in the country."

"What happened to Colorado State?"

He shrugged. "Their letter came today too. I got accepted. But UC's program is better."

"Marginally."

"Not marginally. They built a new research facility last year that's better than any other in the country. Rayna, this is my chance to study with the best."

"Yeah, but what does it mean for us? California's a long way away."

"I know. But I'll be home on holidays, and you could fly out every once in a while."

She straightened, frowning. "You want to do a long-distance thing?"

He nodded.

"For four years?"

He ran a hand through his hair. "Yeah, that sounds like a long time now that you say it out loud."

"You think?"

"I know it's a long time, but I really want this, Ray."

Rayna's mind whirled. She couldn't imagine four years of only seeing him a few times a year, limiting their relationship to phone calls and texts. She thought about all her plans here for the little farm her parents granted her on their property when she graduated high school. She'd already started building her produce business, but she had a long way to go to get where she wanted to be. But was it more important than Thomas?

She stared into his dark eyes. She wasn't sure she wanted a life without him. "What if I go with you?"

Shock made his mouth drop. "You want to leave Silver Gap? What about your farm and all your plans?"

"No. But I love you more than my farm."

"So, just like that, you're going to move to Sacramento with me? What will you do there?"

She pursed her lips and shrugged. "I don't know. Probably try to get a job at a nursery or at one of the state parks. I might even take some botany classes." She reached across the bar and took his hands in hers. "I just know I don't want to have a long-distance relationship. Not for four years."

He sighed and turned his hands over to hold hers. "Your parents are going to flip."

"Not too much. We'll be married, so—"

Thomas jerked his hands away and stood, a deer-in-headlights look on his face. "Whoa, hold on a second. Who said anything about marriage?"

She frowned, an ache forming in her chest. "You... don't want to marry me?"

"Not now."

Rayna reeled back as though he slapped her.

Thomas swiped a hand over his face. "That didn't come out right. Yes, I want to marry you. Just not right now. I'm not ready to have a family yet, Rayna. I want to focus on building my career."

"Who says we need to have a family right away?"

"Then why do we need to be married?"

"You think the only reason to get married is to have kids? How about the commitment to each other it represents? We've already been dating five years. And if I'm moving a thousand miles for you, I expect that kind of commitment. I'm not going as just your girlfriend, no matter how much I love you."

"Okay, say we get married. I know you. You're going to want kids. I'm not ready for kids."

"I know you're not now, but you won't be that way forever."

"But are you willing to wait another five or six years until I'm established?"

That ache building in her chest blossomed into a crushing pain. "So, even if we don't get married now, are you saying it still wouldn't happen until we're nearly thirty?"

He hesitated, but she could see by the look in his eyes that was exactly his plan. "Rayna—"

She held out a hand to stop him. "Don't." She broke off a piece of the garlic bread and set it on a plate, then picked up a large spoon and heaped a portion of the ziti next to it before putting the foil back over the dish and zipping it back into the carrier.

"Don't 'don't' me," he said, his expression hardening. "Never once have I said I wanted to get married anytime soon."

"So this is my fault? Yeah, okay."

He huffed and put his hands on his hips, looking at the ceiling. "I didn't say that."

"Sure you did. Just not in so many words."

"I don't want to argue semantics with you. I don't want to argue with you at all. All I want is to not get married!"

"Yeah? Well, you're getting your wish." She took a fork from the silverware drawer and slammed it onto the counter. "There's your dinner." She picked up the carrier, walking around the bar to put her coat on.

"Wait. You're leaving?"

She scoffed, sarcasm dripping from the sound. "No. I'm just eating on the porch."

He took hold of her arm to stop her as she walked past. "Are we breaking up?"

Rayna stared straight ahead, knowing if she looked at him, she'd start blubbering incessantly. "Seeing as we're at an impasse, I think that's probably best, don't you? We want different things from life. I'm ready to get married and start a family in the next couple years. You, obviously, are not. And who knows if you'll ever be. All I know, is I can't live the life you want."

"Well, I guess we are, then. Because I most definitely don't want a wife and kids right now."

Her vision swam as she shook her arm loose from his grasp. Standing on her toes, she pressed a kiss to his cheek. "Goodbye." Her voice broke, and a tear leaked out as she walked away.

As she closed the door behind her, her heart shattered into a million pieces.

ONE

Twelve years later...

A cool wind whispered over Rayna Nydert's face and through her hair as she cut the engine on her utility vehicle. She glanced back at the wagon she towed. It was full of a dozen different kinds of tomatoes and peppers, and she still had more to pick. She needed to hurry, though. There was only about an hour of daylight left before the sun dipped behind the mountain and cast the valley into deep shadow.

Hopping out of the vehicle, she unhitched the wagon, leaving it parked next to the shed she used to store her harvest. She would unload all the crates later. Right now, she just wanted to get as much of the field picked as she could before it got too dark to see.

Rayna climbed back into the vehicle and backed it up to a second wagon parked behind the building, already loaded with empty crates. She made quick work of hitching it up, then set off for the field. Once back in the rows of pepper plants, she cut the UTV's engine and climbed out. She took a crate from the wagon and got to work.

For twenty minutes, she made her way down the line of

plants, the snip of her clippers the only sound other than the wind and the chirp of the evening birds. The peace was nice. It took the edge off the restlessness in her mind.

The last few weeks since the disaster with her most recent ex-boyfriend, Derrick Thorpe-slash-Jared Fetter had been rough. It had been a couple months since she found out the man she'd started to fall for was a lying, manipulative psycho who killed her best friend's husband years ago when they were both part of the same SEAL team deployed in Afghanistan. Since then, Rayna carried a hefty amount of guilt that she'd allowed him to get close to Tara. That she'd put her friend's life in danger by unknowingly supplying him with information. It had put a strain on her relationship with her friend. Tara kept telling her she didn't blame her, but Rayna blamed herself, and it was much harder to gain her own forgiveness. She'd always been hard on herself.

She glanced at the sky as she filled a crate, lifting it to carry it back to the wagon. One more row and she would have to head back in.

A muffled grunt made her pause just before she reached the back of the wagon. She glanced toward the rows of beans, where the sound came from, trying to see through the dense foliage and growing darkness. Something scuffed the dirt and she heard another low grunt.

What the hell?

Setting the crate on the ground, she withdrew a shovel from the back of the UTV, mindful of all the craziness that had gone on lately. Between the serial killer who abducted one of her best friends and the crazy ex-soldier who lied to her about who he was so he could get close to another one of her best friends, she wasn't taking any chances.

Heart thumping, Rayna moved through the rows of peppers toward the beans. She rounded the end of the row where she thought the noise came from, brandishing the shovel. Shock rounded her eyes.

She dropped the shovel and hurried toward the young man curled up on the ground. Small, circular wounds dotted his arms, one of his eyes was swollen shut, and he cradled his dislocated left arm against his bare chest. Bruises discolored the skin around his wrists and marred his naked torso.

As she got closer, he scrabbled backward.

"I'm sorry! I'll pay for what I ate. I don't want any trouble." He backed further from her, struggling to get his feet under him.

Rayna stopped and held her hands out. "Wait! Don't go. Please. You can eat whatever you want. I just want to help you. My name's Rayna. What's yours?"

He stared up at her through his good eye. "I'm sorry," he mumbled again. He crumpled into the dirt, as though his muscles couldn't hold him up anymore, and curled up on his right side in a fetal position. His dirty, blonde hair hung in hanks over his face.

Her mind whirled as she stared down at him. She'd never seen him before, she was sure of that, so where did he come from?

His eyes closed, and he moaned. Taking a chance, she took a few more steps toward him, then crouched near his middle. She reached out and laid a gentle hand on his thigh.

He jerked and started to scramble up, but pain from his dislocated arm made him fall back to the ground, moaning.

"I'm not going to hurt you," she said softly. "Let me help you up. I'll get you to the hospital."

His good eye snapped open, the whites showing with his fear. "No! They'll find me and make me go back. I just need to rest for a bit. I'll be fine."

"You need a doctor." *And a police officer, from the sound of things*, she couldn't help but think. "Your shoulder is dislocated."

"No hospitals."

His voice carried a strength that surprised Rayna. She stared down at him again, debating what to do. She couldn't leave him out here, but if she tried to take him to the hospital, he'd bolt.

Kind, dark eyes and a mischievous smile flashed through her mind.

Did she dare call Thomas? Would he even answer the phone if he saw her calling?

The boy moaned again, wincing. A fine shiver ran through him, making up her mind for her.

"Hang on. I have an idea." She stood and hurried back to the UTV, grabbing her jacket and her phone. Running back to the young man, she draped the jacket over him before pulling up Thomas's name in her cell.

"Please answer," she muttered to herself as she lifted the phone to her ear. It rang five times before it rolled to voicemail.

"Dammit." She sighed and tried again. And again, it went to voicemail.

Muttering curses under her breath, her thumb hovered over the home button, but she decided to try one last time. She touched the green phone icon once more and lifted the phone.

He picked up on the third ring. "I'm busy, Rayna."

"Thomas, please don't hang up. I know you don't want to talk to me, but I need your help."

There was a pause, and she could almost see his face as he processed that. A little crease would form between his brows, and he'd get a slight purse to his lips.

"Is one of your animals sick?"

"No. Look, I don't really want to explain this over the

phone. It'll be easier if you just come over and see for yourself."

"Rayna…" The hesitation in his voice rang through the line.

"Please, Thomas. I wouldn't ask if it wasn't important." She glanced down at the man again, who looked like he'd fallen asleep. He looked so young!

Thomas sighed. "Fine. I'll be there in a few minutes." He hung up without saying goodbye.

Rayna released the breath she didn't know she'd been holding and turned off the phone's screen, putting the cell in her back pocket. She bent down and gently poked the man—more of a boy, really—on the hip.

"Hey. I have help coming, but you need to get up."

His eyes cracked open. "I told you, no hospitals."

"It's not a hospital. It's just a friend who can help. Can you get up? I have a utility vehicle parked a few rows over."

"You swear you won't take me to the hospital?"

"I promise. Unless my friend says you could suffer serious, permanent damage. Then, all bets are off."

He stared up at her, weighing her words.

Rayna decided to sweeten the pot. "I have vegetable soup waiting in the slow cooker back at the house. Fresh baked bread, too. I think I might even be able to scrounge up some homemade chocolate chip cookies."

His eyes widened imperceptibly and his tongue darted out to wet his lips. "With milk?"

She smiled and nodded. "Of course."

Indecision lit his face for only another moment before he shifted and stood on wobbly legs. Rayna reached out to steady him and helped him toward the UTV. Once she had him settled in the passenger seat, she put the crate of peppers in the wagon, then hurried around to the driver's side and climbed in, starting it up.

She tried to make the drive back to the house as smoothly as she could, but she knew the terrain jostled his injured arm by the pinch to his face. Even with his eyes closed and relaxed against the seat, he looked like he was in a tremendous amount of pain.

They came to a halt at the back door of her little log cabin, which was a few hundred yards from her parents' two-story, white farmhouse. She'd had the cabin built a few years ago after her produce business took off. She loved her mom and dad, but she needed her own space.

Rayna shut off the UTV's engine, then hurried around to help the young man out. She led him to the door, giving the knob a twist. Figuring he would be more comfortable in a chair he didn't sink into, she helped him to the dining table.

"I'm going to get you some water."

"Milk. Please," he said. "I'm so hungry."

She hesitated. "How about we let my friend look at you first? If you need surgery, I don't want to put any food in your stomach."

She could see the protest brewing, so she headed him off. "I meant what I said in the field. If he thinks your condition is serious enough you need a hospital, you're going. We'll figure out the rest later."

He glared at her, but said nothing.

Rayna walked to the sink and got a glass from the cupboard, filling it with water, then took it to him. He nodded his thanks and took a hearty gulp.

She heard the front door open and turned to look. Thomas walked in, his large frame filling the doorway. Her heart skipped a beat at the sight of him, like it had since they were sixteen.

His eyes landed on hers, and he stared at her for a moment, before they shifted to the disheveled man sitting at her kitchen table. He walked further into the house, closing the door, a deep frown marring his handsome face.

"Rayna? What's going on? Who is that?"

She walked toward him, casting a glance at the boy before looking up at Thomas. "I'm not sure who he is. I found him in my field." She lowered her voice. "He's been beaten and burned. I think his left shoulder is dislocated. I also think he's dehydrated."

Alarm widened his eyes. He stared at the young man for a second, then looked down at her again. "Why did you call me instead of taking him to the hospital?"

"He wouldn't let me take him. Said *they* would find him there and make him go back."

"Who's they?"

She shrugged. "I don't know. He wouldn't tell me his name, either. But he's in a lot of pain, Thomas. I did tell him if you thought he needed serious medical attention, he was going to the hospital whether he wanted to or not, though." She laid a hand on his forearm. "Please, just take a quick look at him. I know you're a vet, but you have some EMT training, and I didn't know who else to call. He's scared and in pain."

Those lovely lips pursed as he regarded her. He nodded and stepped toward the stranger. "I'll look at him, but he probably really does need a doctor."

Thomas stepped toward the young man at Rayna's table. His blonde hair hung limp over his dirt-streaked face. Even from fifteen feet away, he could see the burn marks on the man's arms and torso, not to mention the wicked bruises on his left arm and ribcage. Someone had used him as a punching bag.

Anger burned in his gut that someone could do such a

thing to another human being, but he pushed those thoughts away so his expression didn't scare the man.

"Hi. I'm Thomas," he said, crouching down. "Can you tell me your name?"

The man looked up at him, weariness in the one light blue eye he could see. Thomas tamped down the shock as he got a good look at his face. If he was over eighteen, Thomas would eat his boots.

The kid studied him for a moment before replying. "Mason."

"Good to meet you, Mason." He gestured to the arm hanging at a funny angle at the boy's side. "Can you tell me what happened?"

Mason swallowed hard and shook his head.

Thomas bobbed his head. "How about these?" He pointed to the burn marks—which looked an awful lot like cigarette burns.

Again, Mason shook his head. "I don't want any trouble."

"Kid, I think you're knee-deep in it whether you want to be or not." He rose. "I need to take a look at your shoulder. It's not going to feel good, but if I can pop it back into place and there's no obvious fracture, you won't need to go to the ER. Okay?"

Mason nodded and sat straighter.

Thomas looked back at Rayna. "Do you have a towel or something he can bite on?"

She walked over to a drawer by the stove and pulled out a dish towel, passing it to him. He rolled it into a log and handed it to the kid.

"Here. Bite on this so you don't break a molar."

The kid took the towel and put it between his teeth.

"All right, let's see what we have here." Thomas put his hands on the boy's shoulder, pushing lightly around the joint.

The kid grunted, but stayed still.

"I'm sorry. I need to see if there's a fracture." He probed the end of the humerus as well as the clavicle, but didn't feel anything move that shouldn't.

"Well, the good news is, I don't think anything is broken, and it feels like it's only a partial dislocation. But we need to put that shoulder back into place."

The young man nodded and took the towel out of his mouth so he could speak. "Do it."

"I can try, but this works a lot better if you've got pain killers onboard. They help relax you and your muscles. How long has it been out of place?"

Mason looked down. "Three days," he mumbled.

Thomas crouched back in front of him. "You walked around with your arm like that for three days?" he said, his voice soft with concern.

The kid nodded, giving Thomas a brief glance before looking away again.

Thomas looked at Rayna in surprise. She wore a shocked expression as she stared at the young man in her kitchen. Tears shimmered in her violet eyes.

He turned back to Mason. "Why didn't you go to the authorities for help?"

The kid tried to shrug, but winced. "They don't help. I end up back where I started."

"Mason, how old are you?" Rayna asked, coming to stand beside them.

He looked at her through his lashes, then turned his gaze to the floor. "I don't know," he mumbled.

"What do you mean, you don't know?" Thomas asked, his voice low.

Mason looked at him, a wealth of sadness in his eyes. "What's the date?"

"September thirteenth," Thomas said.

"Of what year?"

Shock rendered Thomas speechless for a moment. What had this kid been through that he didn't even know what year it was? He cleared his throat and croaked out the year.

The boy gave them his first genuine smile. "Then I'm eighteen."

"Does that mean I can take you to the hospital?" he asked, hopeful. This kid could have a lot of underlying issues if he'd been held captive.

Mason's smile disappeared and some of the fear crept back into his eyes. "No. I'd still rather not go."

Rayna crouched beside them. "Mason, who did this to you?"

"I don't want any trouble," he repeated. "Please, just fix my arm and let me go on my way."

Thomas shared another glance with Rayna. Her eyes pleaded with him to help.

Dammit. He never could say no to her.

Taking a deep breath, he nodded. "Okay." He patted the boy on his leg. "Let's see what we can do about that shoulder. We'll talk about the rest later."

The young man nodded.

"Ray, I need a piece of cloth we can fashion a sling out of."

She nodded and stood, hurrying off to another part of the house.

"You some kind of doctor?" Mason asked when she disappeared.

Thomas smiled and stood. "Sort of. I'm a vet. But I have some EMT training. Yours won't be the first shoulder I've popped back into place. My brothers have had their fair share." He pointed to the dish towel the kid clutched. "Put that back in your mouth and do your best to relax. This will feel much better after I get it back in the socket." He prayed he could pop it back in. With as long as it had been out, there was a chance the muscles had seized around it and it would take some heavy sedation to get it back into place.

He put one hand back on Mason's shoulder, feeling for the ends of the joint. Rayna returned with a long scarf in her hands as he picked up the kid's arm.

"Okay, here we go."

He lifted his arm higher, and the young man let out a moan. Thomas applied some pressure, feeling the muscles resist. He massaged the muscle going over the joint, then pulled up and twisted Mason's arm. The kid's shout was muffled by the towel, then cut short as the joint slid back into the socket with a soft pop, bringing him some relief.

Mason pulled the towel from his mouth and slumped in the chair. "Thank you," he murmured.

"You're welcome." Thomas stepped aside, so Rayna could tie a sling around the boy's arm.

"Thomas, grab the bottle of ibuprofen out of the drawer by the fridge," she told him. "And pour him a glass of milk."

He did as he was told and set four tablets and the milk on the table in front of Mason. The kid scooped them up and downed them with one big gulp.

"Do you want some food now?" Rayna asked the young man, patting him on his good shoulder.

Mason nodded. "Yes, please."

She looked at Thomas. "Have you eaten?"

He shook his head.

She walked around the half wall separating the dining area from the kitchen and went to the cabinet by the fridge, taking down three bowls. Stepping over to the slow cooker, she removed the lid. Thomas walked up to stand next to her.

"What do you want to do about him?" he asked in a low whisper, glancing back at Mason, who sat on the other side of the half wall, eyes closed as he slouched in the dining chair.

"I'm not sure, but I know we can't turn him out. He's got

no money, and he's injured. We might as well give him back to whoever he ran away from."

"Agreed."

"I guess he could stay here for a few days. I have a spare room."

Alarm bells clanged in Thomas's head. "I don't know if that's such a good idea. You don't know anything about him."

"Oh, come on, Thomas. He's just a frightened child." Her whisper was harsh, and she glared up at him.

"That may be, but he's still a stranger."

"What do you want me to do, then? You can't take him home; there are too many people on the Broken Bow. Someone will wonder who he is and start asking questions. Until we know who he ran from, it's probably best he stays somewhere out of the way." She ladled soup into the three bowls, passing them to him as she went.

"I think so, too, but I still don't like the idea of you being here with him alone." He grabbed the last bowl and went to the silverware drawer.

Rayna took a loaf of homemade bread from the bread box and set it on a cutting board. Thomas took a butter knife from the drawer along with three spoons, then retrieved the butter from the fridge.

She sliced off several pieces of the bread and handed them to him to be buttered.

"Unless you know of a better place for him, I'm inviting him to stay," she said, setting the buttered bread on a small plate.

He took hold of her arm to stop her from walking away. "If he's staying, then I am too."

Two

Rayna's eyes widened as she looked up at her ex-boyfriend. He was serious.

No. Nope. He could not stay here with her. He could barely stand the sight of her anymore. Thomas had been abundantly clear he was over her. Leading his brother-in-law's killer to his sister's doorstep had taken care of anything he might have felt for her.

"What? No. You can't stay here. I don't have room for both of you."

It was a testament to how much their friendship had changed in the last couple months when he didn't crack a joke about staying in her room with her. Instead, he just stared down at her.

"I'll sleep on the couch," he said, completely serious.

"Thomas, we'll be fine. You know I can defend myself, if necessary." Like most kids who grew up in these parts, she'd been taught to use a firearm at a young age. And after their break-up, she'd thrown herself into the jiu-jitsu lessons she started months earlier after Seb showed her a few moves. The activity helped her deal with her rioting emotions. She still practiced it to this day.

She opened her mouth to protest again, but he cut her off.

"Humor me." His mouth flattened, and he glanced at the boy again. "With all the weird shit that's happened this summer, I just want to make sure you're safe."

She frowned up at him and put her balled up fists on her hips. "Really? Is that why you didn't want to answer your phone when I called? Why you avoid me like I have some deadly plague?"

He rolled his eyes, which only fanned the flames of her indignation.

"You want to get into that now?"

"Well, it's a valid argument, Thomas. You can't stand to be around me. Why should I let you stay in my house?"

He sighed and pinched the bridge of his nose. "I don't want to argue. Can we just please come to a truce for now?"

She stared up at him, still hesitating. It wasn't just the hostility he'd shown her lately she was worried about. It was her own muddled feelings for the man. She had thought herself over him, but his anger toward her had her heart all twisted up to the point she wasn't sure anymore how she felt about him.

"Don't make me sleep in my truck, Ray."

It was her turn to roll her eyes. He would do just that. "Fine," she conceded. She picked up two bowls and headed for the table, leaving him to grab the silverware, bread, and his own bowl.

Pasting a smile on her face, she set one dish down in front of Mason, then took the chair to his right. Thomas sat on the boy's left and put the bread plate down in the middle of the table before passing out the spoons.

"Dig in," she said to the young man.

She didn't have to tell him twice. The boy ate with gusto.

She studied his lean form as she ate, noting the lack of fat on his ribs. The poor kid probably hadn't had a decent meal in a long time. Not for the first time, she wondered where he'd come from.

Only the sound of spoons clinking against the ceramic bowls broke the silence as they ate. The boy was too hungry to speak, and the adults had too much baggage between them to carry on a comfortable conversation.

Rayna took the opportunity to study Mason a little closer. He was so thin. And dirty. His tall, lanky form was coated in a fine layer of grime. Several days of stubble dusted his jaw and his greasy hair needed a good trim—after it was washed. And he needed clothes. She doubted anything she owned would fit him. He could probably get into her pants, he was so thin, but they would likely hit him mid-calf. While the kid was skinny, he was close to Thomas's six-foot-four.

She noticed both Thomas and Mason had finished their soup. "Would you like more?" she asked the boy.

He nodded, eyes downcast. "Yes, please."

She reached for his bowl, and he flinched away. Her heart lurched for the pain this child must have been through in his life. Offering him a sunny smile, she took his dish and pushed back from the table, motioning Thomas toward the kitchen with the tip of her head. He picked up his bowl and followed her.

Taking the lid off the slow cooker, she filled Mason's bowl. "Do you think you can bring him some clean clothes? There's nothing on the ranch that will fit him." Even her dad's stuff would be too short on him. "And maybe some toiletries so he can clean up a bit? He can use my shampoo and body wash for now, but he needs the basics like a toothbrush and deodorant."

He nodded and set his bowl in the sink. "I need to pack a

bag of my own, anyway. I'll see what I can dig up and be back soon."

She replaced the slow cooker's lid and gave him a soft smile. "Thanks. I know this is the last place you want to be."

His mouth flattened as he stared at her. "It doesn't matter. That kid needs help." He took a step back, turning. "I'll be back."

She watched him walk away, her eyes straying to his tight butt, before giving herself a sharp mental slap. Ogling Thomas Archer would help nothing. It would only string her tighter than a bowstring and make her as frustrated as a bull separated from his herd.

Sighing, she went back to the table and set the bowl of soup down in front of Mason. He dug in straight away, but with a little less hurry than before, his hunger satiated a bit. He eyed Thomas's retreating figure with a frown as the cabin door closed behind him.

"He'll be back," she told him. "He went to find you some clothes. I don't have anything that will fit you."

The spoonful of soup in the kid's hand paused on the way to his mouth for a second before he nodded. Satisfied she was telling the truth, and Thomas wasn't going to summon the authorities, he bowed his head over his food and concentrated on eating.

Rayna blew out a breath and watched him eat. He wasn't going to talk anymore tonight.

~

Thomas muttered under his breath about his own stupidity as he tossed a duffel bag onto the passenger seat of his truck and climbed inside. What the hell was he thinking, offering to stay at Rayna's? That kid couldn't hurt a flea in his condition.

But the wounds and injuries he sported didn't get there by

themselves. Someone did that to him. And as scared as the kid was of his captors, Thomas had a bad feeling they might be looking for him. He didn't want to leave Rayna and Mason by themselves should the people who abused him show up.

Cranking the truck's engine, he pulled away from his house and headed into town to buy Mason some clothes. He bypassed the general store downtown where he usually bought clothes for himself and headed to the big box store on the outskirts of town, preferring the anonymity of the chain retailer for this particular purchase. Keeping the kid a secret felt vital until they knew more about what was going on. Something about the situation made him want to stay mum about the boy. He just couldn't put his finger on what.

He angled his pickup into a space and hopped out, striding inside and grabbing a cart. Thomas made a beeline for the men's department, where he snagged several long-sleeve work shirts in muted colors from a rack before moving toward the wall of jeans. He could only guess at the kid's size, but went with the slimmest and longest they had. Mason was nearly as tall as Thomas, but at least sixty pounds lighter. There wasn't any fat on the boy's lanky frame. His thoughts strayed to Rayna. She'd fix that if Mason stayed with her long enough.

Thomas looked around the department, stopping in the underwear aisle to grab a package each of boxers, socks, and t-shirts. Thankfully, he noticed the boy's shoes hadn't been in terrible shape, so he didn't have to guess on shoe size. He'd buy him a pair of boots later if need be. He also tossed a pair of flannel pajama pants into the cart.

On his way to the checkout stands, he spotted the pharmacy section and decided to get more pain medicine and a better sling for the boy's shoulder. Rayna had also asked him to bring the kid some toiletries.

Back out in the main aisle, he saw the overhead signs for

the grocery and frowned. Rayna shouldn't have to feed all three of them on her own. He hadn't even thought to pack some food from his house.

Sighing, he headed for the other side of the store. He wandered the aisles at a quick clip, throwing in what he needed and what he thought Rayna and Mason would like. He even grabbed a container of Rayna's favorite ice cream, blackberry chip, as well as a couple other flavors, then headed for the registers. At the self-checkout, he scanned through his purchases, thankful no one would be the wiser about what he bought. He didn't want anyone to know about Mason until they got some answers.

The machine spit out his receipt, and Thomas stuffed it into a sack before pushing the cart toward the exit. He hooked the bags over his hand and left the cart in the cart bay. Back at his truck, he threw the bags into the backseat next to his duffel and climbed inside, quickly pulling out of the lot.

On his way through town, he passed the police station and debated stopping to talk to his sister's fiancé about the boy. Jace would keep it quiet if he asked. He slowed, but something stopped him. They needed more information from the kid first before they involved the authorities, even if the police were family. He was glad Seb was out of town on his honeymoon. Hiding this from him would be a lot harder.

The miles zipped by as he drove back to the Double Moon. He pulled up behind Rayna's cabin and parked, doubting she wanted her parents to know he was staying. That would bring another set of questions they didn't want to answer.

Climbing from the vehicle, he slung his duffel over his shoulder and looped the grocery bags on his hand and headed for the back door. He twisted the knob, but it was locked, so he kicked it softly with one foot. Rayna came around the half wall from the living area and let him in.

"What all did you buy?" she asked as he set his loot on the counter. "I thought you were just going to bring him some of your clothes."

Thomas shrugged. "My pants won't fit him except in length, and he needed underwear and socks, so I went shopping. I bought food too; I don't expect you to buy all the groceries while I'm here."

She started looking through what he bought, putting things away as she emptied the sacks. She pulled out the ice cream and let out a little laugh. "This ice cream is for you?"

He looked over in time to see her roll her eyes at him as she held up the blackberry chip.

"You don't like this kind."

One side of his mouth tilted. "Call it a peace offering for forcing my way onto your couch."

"Sure." Her voice dripped with sarcasm, but she stowed the frozen treat in the freezer.

"There's vanilla and mint chip in there too. I figured maybe Mason would like some later." He glanced up, realizing the boy wasn't in sight. "Where is he, anyway?"

"In the bathroom, taking a shower. I figured you would be back soon, so I sent him in to clean up."

He nodded. "I'll set some of this stuff on the bed in the spare room and let him know." He ripped the tags off several items and scooped them up along with the new sling and the bag of toiletries.

Walking down the hallway, he entered the spare bedroom as Mason emerged from the bathroom. Tendrils of steam followed him as he stepped into the room with a towel wrapped around his waist.

His eyes went wide with fear as he spotted Thomas, and he froze.

Thomas paused at the sight of the boy's fear and lifted the

items in his arms. "I brought you some clean clothes and a new sling for your shoulder."

Mason gave him a hesitant nod, resignation tightening his features. "I don't have any money. How do you want me?"

Confusion lit Thomas's face, but it was quickly replaced by horror as Mason's hand went to the knot on his towel.

"No!"

The young man jerked at his shout, and he backed against the wall.

Thomas swallowed the bile that rose in his throat, and he forced himself to speak calmly. "Mason, I don't want *anything* for the clothes. You're safe here. One hundred percent. We will never ask that of you. Ever."

Mason looked down, shame on his face. Thomas felt a lump form in his throat and the slow burn of anger in his gut. Someone needed to pay for what they'd done to this young man.

Taking a deep breath through his nose to still his emotions, he stepped toward the bed and set the items down. "There are a few other things in the kitchen, but that should get you started. Feel free to lie down if you'd like. Rayna and I will be in the living room if you need anything."

Still staring at the floor, Mason nodded.

Thomas turned and strode from the room, his anger growing.

Rayna looked up as he walked back in the kitchen, frowning when she saw the hard set to his face.

"What? Is he okay?"

He scoffed. "Define okay." He sighed and stepped over to help her with the remaining groceries. "He just offered himself to me to 'pay' for the clothes I bought."

"What?" she breathed, her eyes wide.

He nodded. "I think once he gets some rest, we need to try to get some answers out of him. Find out where he came from and who held him captive. Someone exploited and trafficked that kid. There might be others."

Her hands shook as she shut the cabinet. "Who around here would do such a thing?" Horror made her voice hoarse.

"I don't know, but we need to find out."

Thomas's mind whirled as he helped Rayna clean up the remnants of his shopping. *Just what the hell had they stumbled over?*

THREE

"That smells good."

Rayna looked up from the frying pan as Thomas walked into the kitchen the next morning, bleary-eyed. His dark hair was mussed and black stubble dusted his jaw. His white t-shirt outlined his muscular torso, and the gray sweats hanging low on his hips left little to the imagination. She bit the inside of her cheek and turned her attention back to the bacon. Why couldn't he have gotten dressed first?

"There's coffee in the pot." She pointed to the carafe on her right with her tongs. "I'm going to make pancakes too."

He walked toward the counter and took down a mug. "Is Mason awake yet?"

She shook her head. "I haven't heard him, no."

"Are we sure he's still here?"

That was a valid question. He'd been skittish enough she wondered if he would try to leave while they slept. She didn't think he had, though.

She motioned to the back door and the pair of dirty tennis shoes beside it. "His shoes are still here, so I don't think he left."

"I didn't leave."

They both whirled at the sound of Mason's voice. He stood in the doorway to the kitchen in the flannel pajama pants Thomas bought and a black t-shirt. He'd also put on the new sling.

Rayna smiled at him. "You're awake. Good. Just in time for breakfast. Do you like coffee? I have orange juice too. Or milk."

He pushed his long blonde bangs back from his eyes. "Um, orange juice is fine."

She looked up at Thomas, silently asking him to pour the boy a glass of juice. Without a word, he reached for the cabinet where she kept the drinking glasses.

"So, did you sleep well?" she asked.

"Better than I have the last few nights."

Her heart lurched. The idea that he'd spent several nights in the cold, especially in his injured condition, had her fighting back tears.

She swallowed around the lump in her throat. "Good. I'm glad. Do you like anything in your pancakes? I have blueberries and chocolate chips."

"Whichever is fine. I can't remember the last time I had pancakes."

Rayna tried not to let the sadness color her voice or her face. "What do you normally eat for breakfast?"

He shrugged with his good shoulder. "If they gave me breakfast, it was usually cereal or a piece of fruit."

That's what she'd been afraid of. "Well, around here, we eat a hearty breakfast because we work hard. That doesn't always mean bacon and pancakes, but it does today. And before you say anything, I don't expect you to work. Your job right now is to heal. Good food is part of that."

Thomas handed him the glass of juice he requested, and he took a sip, watching her thoughtfully. She suspected he was trying to decide if the kindness they showed him was genuine or if it would come back to bite him later.

"Why don't you help Thomas set the table while I make the pancakes? I'll make both kinds. Thomas likes the chocolate chip ones, but I like blueberry."

Thomas opened another cupboard and motioned the boy forward. "We'll make quick work of this and maybe go sit out on the porch then while we wait for everything to finish cooking. There isn't much like watching the sun rise and listening to the birds on a crisp morning like this. Grab some silverware." He pointed to a drawer next to the sink.

Rayna got out the ingredients for the pancakes while the two of them gathered what they needed for the table. By the time they had it set, she had the first batch on the griddle.

Thomas pushed his feet into his boots and shrugged into his jacket, then handed Mason the sweatshirt he'd pulled from Rayna's closet. It was a bit short on him, but it would do the job for now. He made a mental note to check his closets at home. There might be a coat floating around there he didn't wear anymore.

He picked up his coffee mug. "Ready?"

Mason nodded, and Thomas led him outside to the front porch. He knew he was taking a risk that Rayna's parents, John and Izzy, would see them, but it was still early for them to be up and about. The sun hadn't even crested the mountain yet. He pulled a blanket from the box that doubled as a table and handed it to Mason before they sat in the rockers flanking the chest.

For several minutes, the only sound was the chirp of the birds waking up with the rising sun. Thomas smothered a yawn with his hand, then took a sip of his coffee to clear the cobwebs. He glanced over at the boy who sat huddled under the blanket, taking sips of his juice as they watched the sun come up.

"Mason."

The young man looked over.

"I know you don't want to talk about it, but I need you to tell me where you came from. We need to find who did this to you."

Mason stared down at his glass. "It doesn't matter. I'm not ever going back, and no one can make me now that I'm eighteen."

"What if they find you again, though, and force you to go with them? Wouldn't it be better if they were locked up so they couldn't ever get to you again?"

He shook his head. "I'll die before I go back."

Thomas looked out over the ranch and ran a hand over the stubble on his jaw as he took in Mason's words. He couldn't imagine the horrors this kid had seen to make him want to end his life rather than go back to where he'd been.

"What about others? Are there others there like you who you could help by telling us where you came from?"

The kid shifted in his seat, and Thomas knew he'd hit the nail on the head.

"How many others, Mason?"

"Five," he muttered.

Thomas's gut clenched. He put one foot on the railing and tried to keep the rage building in him banked.

"I'd love to tell you how to find them, but I don't know. The... man they left me with got drunk and stoned after he was done with me. I put up a fight, and it made him tired. Between that and all the stuff he took, he passed out. Normally, they're more careful, but I think he thought I was too injured to move off the bed. When I realized he was hitting the drugs pretty hard, I pretended I was too hurt to escape.

Once he was out of it, I slipped away. It was dark, so I couldn't really see much except the house and other mini cabins the guests stayed in when they came for their visits. Any time I left the property for any reason, I was blindfolded. I just know it was deep in the mountains. This place is the first house I saw, and I walked for two days."

Disgust and anger churned in Thomas's belly as he listened to Mason's story. "Do you know the names of your captors, or the man you were with when you escaped?"

"I don't know his name, no. But it was a man and a woman who held me captive. They said their names were Jim and Anne Smith."

Thomas couldn't stop the scoff that burst past his lips. That was one of the most common surnames on the planet.

"Yeah. I know now they probably lied about that. But when I met them, I was desperate to get off the street."

"How old were you?"

"Eleven."

Thomas uttered a string of curses. "You've been captive since you were eleven?"

The young man nodded.

Jesus. Thomas couldn't help but think about what he'd been doing at eleven. He'd been running around the ranch, causing havoc with his brothers and picking on his twin sister.

He scrubbed a hand over his face. "I know you aren't keen on going to the authorities, but we need to find these people so we can rescue the other kids you were with. My brother, Seb, is the sheriff, and he—"

Mason leaped from his chair, the blanket falling to the porch at his feet. Fear made the whites of his eyes gleam in the growing daylight. "I knew I should have left last night! You're going to turn me over to the cops!"

"Whoa, there." Thomas rose more slowly. He set his mug down and held out his hands, attempting to placate the boy.

"I'm not turning you over to anyone. You're legally an adult. But my brother can help. He's a good investigator."

Mason shook his head and started pacing. "No. The cops never help. I always end up back with the Smiths."

Thomas stepped into his path. "Mason. No one is going to send you back to the Smiths. You have my word. Even if Seb tries—which he won't—I will help you leave town and start a new life before that happens. You will *never* have to go back there."

He laid a gentle hand on the kid's good shoulder, stilling his furtive eyes. "I need you to trust me. And Rayna. We will do everything we can to help you. And we don't expect anything in return. Ever." He arched a brow and let his hand fall. "Okay? Not everyone is like the Smiths."

The boy held his gaze for a long moment before nodding.

Thomas offered him a smile. Relieved he hadn't scared him away, he dropped the subject for now. "Come on. Let's go see if Rayna has breakfast ready."

Four

With a sigh born from a bone-deep fatigue, Rayna locked the produce shed, then headed for the house, glad she got the rest of her summer plants picked. They were forecasting some heavy frost tonight. This year's weather had been strange. Summer started off hot and stayed that way. There'd been very little in the way of fall. They'd had one light frost so far, and now it was going to dip into the freezer. Thankfully, her pumpkin and squash patches would take the cooler temps well. The fall farmer's market she ran on the property was a big hit locally.

Pocketing her keys, she walked across the grass to her house. Lights shone in the windows, beckoning her home. Mason had promised to stay out of sight and rest today while she and Thomas went to work. She'd left him with her laptop and told him to explore the world he'd missed in the last several years.

Lights lit up the yard and the low growl of a truck's engine drew her attention to the drive. Thomas's black pickup rolled toward her. He pulled around behind the house and parked.

She changed direction and met him as he climbed from the vehicle.

"Hi." She drank in his long, muscular body. He'd been devilishly handsome when they dated in high school and their early twenties, but in the intervening years he'd morphed into a spectacular example of the male form. His shoulders were broader, and he'd packed a substantial amount of muscle on his frame just from the hard work that came with being a rancher and a large animal vet. The years had also added a maturity to his features she found extraordinarily sexy. The little crinkles around his dark eyes only added to his allure. Having him so near and not being able to touch—to have the easy camaraderie they'd worked so hard to cultivate after their break-up missing—was more difficult than she imagined.

He glanced over at her greeting and nodded. Reaching into the truck, he withdrew his heavy coat and another jacket she hadn't seen him wear in years.

"I'm glad I caught you out here. We didn't get a chance to talk this morning before I left."

She strolled closer, curious now. She just thought he hadn't wanted to talk. He'd hardly said a handful of words to her after he and Mason came back inside.

"I got Mason to talk some while we were on the porch. He said there are five other kids where he was held. But he doesn't know how to get back there. Only that it was a man and a woman who 'rescued' him from the streets when he was eleven."

Her hand flew up to cover her mouth at the mention of Mason's age when he was taken. Tears welled in her eyes. "Oh! He was so young. Those people are monsters."

"Agreed." Thomas stepped closer. He held up a hand like he wanted to touch her face, but hesitated, then let it drop back to his side. "At least he's safe now. We can't change what happened to him, but we can make sure he has a brighter future."

"And those other kids too, if we can find them." She chewed on her lip and stared off into the darkness for a moment before looking back up at him. "Do you think we should call Jace? Have him come over and talk to Mason?"

Thomas's mouth flattened into a thin line, and he stared past her shoulder for a moment, thinking. "Not yet. Seb will be back Sunday, so I think we should wait for him. He knows more about the county than Jace. Maybe he's heard rumors of something. I don't want to waste Jace's time and possibly have him learn nothing when Seb might be able to point us in the right direction from the get-go. It'll also give us time to gain more of Mason's trust. I think if we brought Jace over now, he'd clam up and maybe run when we're asleep. He's got a deep distrust for the authorities, and that came from somewhere. I hate to say it, but I think we stand a better chance of finding those other kids if we wait."

She knew he was right, but it didn't stop the pain lancing her heart or the churning in her gut as she thought about what those children might be experiencing. If she thought too hard, it would make her sick.

Letting out a sigh, she nodded. "Okay. Let's go in and just try to be his friend."

He nodded and motioned her to go first. As she turned toward the house, headlights split the night.

"Are you expecting someone?" he asked, glancing down at her.

She groaned and looked up to the heavens. "Yes. It's Macy. I was going to start the alterations tonight on her bridesmaid's dress for Tara's wedding. I completely forgot." She headed for the front of the house. "Maybe I can head her off. Tell her I'm tired and have a headache from being in the field all day, or something."

The SUV's headlights swept over them.

"Too late for that. She's seen me," Thomas said.

Rayna moaned. "I'm sorry," she whispered. There was no way Macy would believe he was here just for a visit. Not with as pissed as he'd been at her about the whole Derrick-slash-Jared nightmare.

"Let me handle this, okay?" He didn't give her a chance to answer before he strode away from her and toward Macy, who had parked and was climbing out of her car.

"Thomas? What are you doing here?"

Rayna could make out the confusion on Macy's pretty face, even in the waning light. She couldn't wait to hear what tale Thomas spun.

"I came for dinner."

Macy stared at them for a moment over the open driver's door, mouth agape. She stepped back and shut the door. "What?"

Rayna's eyes met his as he glanced back, and he smiled. That impish grin that showed off his dimples brightened his face, and her breath caught. It had been a long time since she'd seen him direct that smile at her. He had done little more than glare at her for the last several months.

He turned back to Macy. "I came for dinner," he repeated. "Rayna and I decided it was past time we buried the hatchet."

What?

Rayna tried to keep the surprise off her face. That was the last thing she expected him to say.

He held his hand out to her. Aware they had an audience, and a young man inside who depended on them for his protection, she took his hand and let him pull her to his side. When he wrapped an arm around her waist, she did her best not to stiffen. Not because she didn't like it, but because she liked it too much. As soon as Macy left, he would push her away like she had a communicable disease.

Macy's mouth dropped open further before a radiant smile split her face. "What? This is amazing!" She ran around the front of the car to pull Rayna from his side and wrap her in a tight hug.

"Why didn't you say something?" she whispered, her tone fierce.

Rayna pulled back and shrugged. "It just kind of happened."

The other woman squealed softly. "I'm so happy for you."

"Thanks." She fought to keep her smile genuine. She hated lying to her friends. "I don't suppose you'd mind rescheduling your dress fitting, would you? We both just got done with work for the day, so I haven't even started cooking yet."

Macy stepped back, still grinning. "Of course not." She bounced on her toes and whirled, heading back to her car. "Call me tomorrow and we'll set something else up." She pulled open the car door and waggled her eyebrows, her smile turning naughty. "Have fun." Sliding inside, she closed the door and started the car, quickly turning around and driving back the way she'd come.

As soon as her car was out of sight, Rayna's shoulders fell and she groaned. "I can't believe you let her think we were together again. How are we going to explain this away?"

"Relax. It's only for a few days. It was the only way to get her to leave without a bunch of questions."

"We could have told her, you know. If there's anyone who would protect an abused kid, it's Macy."

He gave a curt nod. "I know, but I don't want her to have to keep secrets from Declan. In his position, he'd be obligated to report the situation." He turned and started for the house.

"But still—argh! This is a nightmare. It's going to be all over town by morning that we're back together. Are you ready for that? You can't even give me a real smile you hate me so much."

He stopped short, shoulders stiff, and spun to face her. The soft look on his face took her by surprise.

"Ray, I don't hate you."

She frowned. He didn't?

She opened her mouth to reply, but he sighed and shook his head. "But I don't expect you to believe that." He shook his head and whirled on his heel, striding toward the house.

Rayna bit back a groan of frustration. Why couldn't he just talk to her? She hurried after him, catching up as he pulled open the front door.

"Thomas, we should t—" She broke off as she followed him inside. To an empty cabin.

"Where's Mason?"

She stepped around him, heading for the bedrooms. "Maybe he took a nap or is in the bathroom." Moving down the hall, she passed the open bathroom door, her stomach sinking as she rounded the corner to his bedroom to find it empty. She spun around to look at Thomas, who stood behind her in the doorway.

"He's gone," she whispered. Fear kicked her heart into overdrive. Whether he left on his own or someone took him, the young man was in grave danger.

"When was the last time you saw him?"

"Lunch. He seemed fine then. A little quiet, maybe, but I just thought he was still tired from his ordeal." She stared at Thomas, her eyes wide.

Thomas walked in the room and looked around. "His clothes are gone. Go check and see if his toiletries are still in the bathroom."

Rayna dashed through the door that led to the bathroom and scanned the counter. It was empty.

"All his stuff is gone," she said, coming back out into the bedroom.

"Okay. He left on his own. Dammit! He probably got spooked by our conversation this morning. We need to find him. Before he ends up back in the hands of the people he ran from. Or worse."

"Agreed. But if we chase after him, he might feel like we're no different than the people who kept him prisoner."

"So, what do you suggest?"

"We wait and see if he comes back on his own."

Thomas's eyebrows shot up. "What? Ray, if he doesn't, then he could end up anywhere and we'll never find him."

"I know, but if we ever want him to trust us, he needs to come back by himself."

"But why would he come back? He'd never know we weren't out looking for him if he keeps running."

"Actually, he might. While you had him outside this morning, I hid some notes in some of his belongings."

He frowned. "What kinds of notes?"

"Just stuff telling him we understand why he ran, but the door is always open to him if he ever wants to come back."

He ran his hands through his hair, his head bobbing as he thought about what she said. "Okay. So, we're just going to do nothing?"

"I think we have to." It went against the grain to leave that kid out there by himself with only the clothes on his back, but she knew she was right. The decision on where he went was Mason's. He needed that control after so many years of being forced to do what others wanted.

Thomas paced to the window and back, still clutching his hair. He looked at Rayna. "Did he take anything besides the clothes and toiletries?"

Her eyes widened. "Maybe. My purse was inside all day.

It's in the kitchen." She whirled around and ran out the door. He was close on her heels.

She found her purse where she left it in the kitchen on the counter and dug out her wallet. All her cash and credit cards were still in it. Tears formed in her eyes. Why didn't he take it? "It's all still here." Her voice broke, and she sniffed.

"What about food?" He stepped to the pantry cabinets and opened them.

She put her wallet away and turned to peruse the contents with him. "There are things missing. At least he took some food with him."

"Yeah, but how long is it going to last?"

Rayna poked through the items on the shelves. "Based on what's missing, a few days."

Thomas sighed. "That's not very long. What's he going to do once he runs out?"

"I think he's used to trading favors for things." She took a deep breath, trying to put a leash on her galloping heart. "I hate the thought that he's going back to that kind of lifestyle." She covered her face, pressing her fingers to her eyes. What Mason would have to do to survive was not something she wanted to think about.

His expression fell, and he spun away, covering his eyes for a moment before swiping his hand down his face and over the stubble darkening his jaw. "Dammit, Rayna. We need to go after him."

She stepped closer and took his hands in hers, holding them between their chests as tears welled in her eyes. "We can't," she whispered. "I want to. So much. But think about it, Thomas. If we track him down, he's going to see us as no better than his captors. We have to wait and pray my notes get through to him and he comes back."

He filled his lungs and stared at a point over her head for a moment before looking back down at her. "Okay. We'll do it your way. But if he hasn't come back in a couple days, I'm calling Jace, trust be damned. We can't leave him out there."

She nodded. "Okay." Her voice was barely audible. She tipped her head forward to lean it against his chest. Emotion clogged her throat, and she fought a sob. She prayed they were doing the right thing and that Mason would come back.

Thomas stared out at the darkness. Rayna had gone to bed hours ago. He'd tried, but he couldn't get his brain to shut off, so he'd come outside. He kept thinking about Mason being out there in the wild. Cold and scared. The kid had gotten under his skin at a remarkable pace. He itched to go find him. The ranch had a drone with thermal imaging and night vision he could borrow. With a little thought about where the boy might go, Thomas could probably make an educated guess on his direction and find him.

But as much as he hated it, Rayna was right. If they tracked him down now, Mason might run again, fearing they were just trying to keep him around for other reasons. He had to be willing to be here. It had to be Mason's choice.

Turning up the collar on his coat and adjusting the blanket covering his lower half, he leaned his head back against the chair and tried to get some sleep.

He must have dozed because the next thing he knew, the chirp of birds and the cluck of the chickens as they came out of their coop brought him out of a restless dream. He and Rayna were in the woods, searching for Mason, both of them feeling more desperate with each passing minute.

The porch creaked and Thomas opened his eyes, expecting to see Rayna. He shot to his feet, boots thudding against the wood as he saw Mason standing on the steps.

The boy backed up a step and Thomas held out a hand. "Sorry. Didn't mean to startle you."

Mason watched him for a moment, then walked up the steps to join him. "Did you sleep out here?"

Thomas nodded. "It felt wrong to sleep inside while you were out there in the cold."

Mason swallowed hard and looked away.

"You came back," Thomas said, taking a step toward him. He wanted to grab the young man and hug him, but was afraid to touch him and scare him away.

"Yeah." Mason looked away for a moment. "I found Rayna's note." His blue eyes connected with Thomas's dark ones. "Did she—did you—mean it?"

"Yes," he replied without hesitation. "Every word. You're welcome here—and to come and go—for as long as you want. We just want to help you."

"Why?" he whispered.

Emotion clogged Thomas's throat as he thought about how to put what he felt into words. "Because you deserve a chance. What you went through—I don't know how you survived all these years—and stayed sane. I think you're amazing, and I respect your resiliency. Rayna and I—we just want to be there to help you build a life you can be proud of."

The door opened and Rayna stood there, still in her pajamas, which she'd covered with a heavy robe in deference to the morning chill.

"Mason," she breathed.

A tear tracked down the kid's face as he looked at her. "I found your note."

A smile lit up her face, and she held her arms out without a word. He stepped into them, wrapping his good arm around her. Thomas walked over and put a hand on the boy's back, taking a deep breath and blinking fast several times to keep the tears away as feelings of relief and gratefulness overwhelmed him.

"I'm so sorry," Mason muttered against Rayna's shoulder.

She pulled away and took his bruised face in her hands. "You have *nothing* to be sorry for. You hear me? Not a damned thing. I'm just glad you came back."

He nodded.

She smiled at him again and let him go. "Now. I bet you're starving. How do omelets sound?"

Mason swiped at his face, his head bobbing. "They sound good."

"Perfect. Go put your stuff away in your room. I'll come start breakfast in a minute."

He gave her a short nod and stepped around her to enter the house. As soon as the screen door banged shut, she spun around and pressed her face to Thomas's chest, gripping his waist. Her body shook as she let her emotions have free rein. Thomas wrapped his arms around her and pressed a kiss to the top of her head.

"You were right," he murmured against the silky strands. "He came back."

She nodded against his chest, then lifted her head to look at him. "He did." A beautiful smile lit up her pretty face.

Thomas's heart stuttered. He pushed a lock of her hair back. He wanted to kiss her, but knew it would open a can of worms he wasn't ready to deal with. Instead, he offered her a smile of his own. "Come on. Let's go make breakfast and figure out what's next."

She bit her lip, her eyes lingering on his mouth a moment before nodding and stepping back. He held the door open so she could enter ahead of him, taking a deep breath to clear his head. If he didn't know better, he'd say she was struggling with how she felt about him as much as he was struggling with how he felt about her.

Five

"You doing okay?" Rayna looked across the cab of the pickup at her young charge as she pulled up to her stall at the farmer's market in Pueblo.

His features were tight as he stared out the windshield at all the people bustling around, setting up their spaces. "Yeah. Are you sure this is going to be okay?"

"Yes. The risk is minimal. You were pretty sure you came from the north, and Pueblo is southeast of my place. You look a lot different too."

They'd had quite the debate last night about what they were going to do today. Thomas had farm calls all day instead of clinic, and she had the Pueblo farmer's market. It was the last week of the season, and she had too much crop left to skip it. Neither of them had wanted to leave Mason alone without someone close by, and he wasn't keen on staying by himself, either, so they'd come up with a plan. She'd chopped off his hair and colored it a deep brown. He looked more like one of the Archer siblings now than some stranger. Except for his light blue eyes. They couldn't disguise those without colored contacts, but the other changes were enough unless someone looked really closely. He was also wearing a ball cap, had left his scruffy beard, and she had covered the bruise on his face with makeup. Her cover-up job wasn't great, but with the hat, it wasn't that noticeable. Thankfully, the swelling had receded. He'd also foregone the sling, so he didn't draw attention to himself.

She opened her door. "Come on. Let's get setup."

Rayna led him to the back of the truck and lowered the tailgate. She handed him a bag with table cloths. "Go cover the tables while I start unloading the crates." He nodded and walked toward the stall, his back ramrod straight and his head on a swivel.

She hoped they'd done the right thing, having him come with her. He looked uncomfortable with the crowd, but at the same time, there was a determined set in his eyes that said while he was down, he was not out. It gave her hope he would recover from his captivity and thrive. Once they talked to Seb, she intended to find a good psychologist who specialized in cases like his. She wanted to do everything she could to help him.

Pulling a folded dolly from along the side wall of the truck bed, she opened it up and piled four crates on it. She wheeled them over to her tables, then went back for more, repeating the process four more times before she had all the produce out of the pickup.

"Can you go get the displays and signs while I start arranging these?"

He nodded and moved toward the truck.

"Don't overtax your shoulder, though. If it hurts, put it down."

Again, he nodded.

It took him several trips, but even one-handed, he still could carry more than she could. She was set up in less than half the time it normally took her to do it by herself.

"Now what?" he asked once they finished.

She opened a folding metal chair. It grated over the asphalt as she scooted it toward him. "Now, we just sit and wait. Although, I think we need some coffee." She motioned toward the coffee kiosk set up at the edge of the market. It was already open for business.

"I've never had coffee."

"Really?"

He shook his head. "No. If they wanted me to stay awake, they gave me uppers."

She swallowed hard at the reminder this normal-looking kid was anything but. "Do you want to try it? It's not just about staying awake. Coffee is delicious. At least it is to me, anyway. Some people don't like the taste. You can get decaf, too, if you don't want the stimulant effect."

He pursed his lips, staring at the kiosk. "I think I'd like to try it. But maybe decaf first? I didn't like the jittery feeling I got from the drugs."

She gave a quick nod. "Absolutely. Come on."

They walked over to the small shed that served as the kiosk, and she ordered a toasted marshmallow and caramel latte for herself and a vanilla decaf latte for Mason.

"Why all the stuff in it?" he asked as he took the drink from her.

"Coffee has a rather strong taste black. I figured we'd ease you into it. You hang around Thomas long enough, though, and you'll learn to like it black."

He frowned, a thoughtful look on his face, and took a sip. His expression brightened as he got a mouthful of the sweet brew. "This is good."

She smiled. "I'm glad you like it. You'll have to experiment with flavors."

Mason nodded and took another sip as they headed back to their stall.

"Rayna, can I ask you something?"

She looked over at him. "Of course."

A frown marred his face, and he hesitated a moment before speaking. "I couldn't help but notice the tension between you and Thomas the other day. But you still seem to trust him. Why?"

Rayna let out a long breath. "It's complicated. We used to date. A long, long time ago. I've known him and his siblings my entire life. Things fell apart in our twenties, but we ended up becoming friends—hard not to when his twin sister is one of my best friends. A few months ago, though, some stuff happened that strained our relationship. Thomas might be mad at me, but I will *always* trust him. He's a good man."

She glanced over at him to see he was mulling over her words and took the opportunity to ask some questions of her own. "Where are you from? Thomas said you told him you were on the street at eleven."

His faced turned stony. "Yes. I'm from Denver. My parents died when I was ten. I ran away from my foster home because they had an older son who liked to use me as a punching bag. But he never got in trouble. They usually blamed me for the situation and locked me in my room afterward. I thought if I ran away, eventually, some cop somewhere would catch me and send me to a different home, but the Smiths found me first." He looked out over the crowd, but she could tell his eyes saw nothing around them.

"Do you have any brothers or sisters?"

His face took on a softer look and he smiled. "I have a sister somewhere. She was younger. Only six. I don't know what happened to her. We got sent to separate foster homes."

"Were you close?"

He nodded. "Yeah. She could be a brat, but I loved her. I miss her—and my parents—everyday."

Rayna swallowed around the lump in her throat. She

couldn't imagine being all alone in the world. She was an only child, but she had her parents and all her friends. "What's her name?" she asked, making a mental note to ask Seb to look for her when he looked into Mason's story. Maybe they could locate her and reunite the two siblings.

"Emma. Emma Jane Lund."

"Lund. Is that your last name?"

He nodded.

She held out a hand to the boy. "It's very nice to meet you, Mason Lund. I'm Rayna Nydert."

He looked down at her hand for a moment before glancing back up into her eyes. Ever so slowly, a smile bloomed, showing her just how handsome he was. It was so nice to see a smile on his face.

"It's nice to meet you too." He took her hand and shook it.

They reached their stall, and Rayna went to the truck to fetch her change apron. On impulse, she'd grabbed a second one this morning.

"Here," she passed Mason the other apron.

He frowned as he took it. "What's this for?"

"Change." She counted out some ones, fives, and tens and handed them to him.

The dumbstruck look on his face made her laugh.

"You're here to work, right?"

He frowned. "I guess."

"There's no guessing about it. I didn't bring you here to babysit you."

He arched a brow at her.

She rolled her eyes. "Okay, that's not the only reason. We were worried you might need something, and neither of us would be close enough to help. You're an adult and don't need babysitting. But I really could use an extra hand. Today is the last market day of the year here, and it's always busy. Having an extra set of hands to complete orders will really help take the pressure off me."

"You aren't worried I'll steal from you?"

She shook her head. "No. You could have cleaned out my wallet when you ran away, but you didn't. I don't think you want to run anymore. And I never thought you were a thief."

He bit the inside of his cheek and looked away. She could see the gears turning as he thought about what she said.

"I don't trust easily. Not anymore. But I feel safe with you. And Thomas. You've shown me nothing but kindness." His voice dropped to a pained whisper. "Please don't make me regret that."

Rayna curled her nails into her hand to stem the tears that threatened. "Never," she whispered back. Blinking hard, she motioned to his apron. "Put that on."

He sniffed and did as she said.

Rayna turned away and rubbed at the ache in her chest. It would be a cold day in hell before she betrayed this kid.

～

"I heard a rumor today."

Thomas looked over at his sister, Tara, who stood in the doorway to Elbert's stall in the horse barn on the Broken Bow.

He stifled a groan. *I should have gone straight to Rayna's.*

If it hadn't been for Brady's call earlier saying Elbert was showing a bit of lameness, he would have. But he'd wanted to check the horse out as soon as possible.

Doing his best to keep his expression ambivalent, he looked over at her. "What's that?"

She strolled toward him, a cheeky smile lighting her face. "That you and Rayna were back together."

"Is that right?" He bent to run his hands down Elbert's

front left leg, feeling for abnormalities, pausing on a bit of swelling near his hoof.

"Mmm-hmm. Macy said you were at her house last night when she showed up for her dress fitting."

"Yep."

He heard her sigh, frustrated by his curt responses.

"You're not going to make this easy, are you?"

He straightened and looked at her. "Make what easy, T? What happens between me and Rayna isn't anyone's business but ours."

Her smile dropped, and the look she gave him implied she thought he was a little daft. "She's one of my best friends. You've already hurt her once—twice if you count the way you've treated her in the last couple months—so you're a little touched if you think I'm going to stand by and watch you do it again."

A sharp pang went through his heart. He knew he'd hurt Rayna when they broke up a decade ago. He'd been an idiot. But what she'd wanted—he just hadn't been ready for that. His anger with her now—well, that was a little more complicated.

"I have no intention of hurting Rayna again. I still beat myself up for doing it the first time."

"Which is why your anger at her over Fetter didn't make much sense to me. I'm glad you've finally let it go. I just can't believe it took you so long. He lied to her from the beginning. She had no way of knowing who he really was."

Logically, Thomas knew that, but emotionally? The man nearly killed the woman standing in front of him, and Rayna had given him knowledge and access to her, no matter how unwittingly. He might tease his twin mercilessly, but he loved her to distraction.

He reached into his medical bag and withdrew a wrap. Elbert had a minor sprain in his fetlock. Knowing Elbert, he'd probably been goofing around and put the brakes on too fast or turned too hard. The horse didn't know the meaning of slow.

"I understand that," he said, wrapping the bandage around the horse's lower leg with practiced efficiency. "I just don't like that she brought danger into your life. You've had enough bad shit happen to you."

Tara scoffed. "That particular danger was coming whether Rayna was part of it or not. Look, all I'm saying is to be careful. You two—I always hoped you would work things out, but I'm not so sure you're right for her anymore."

Anger burned in his gut, even though he knew she wasn't wrong. It wasn't so much that he was wrong for Rayna, but that he didn't deserve her. Not after the way he'd treated her, both when they broke up and more recently.

It didn't matter anyway, since they weren't really together. Not that he could clue Tara in on that. Not yet. He had to keep up the ruse to protect Mason. Somehow, that young man's safety had become his number one priority.

"I guess we'll find out." He tore off a piece of Coban and wrapped it around the bandage to secure it, then stood, tossing the roll into his bag.

She narrowed her eyes at him, but kept quiet. Her eyes went to the silver horse munching on hay.

"What's wrong with Elbert?"

"He's got a mild sprain."

She rolled her eyes. "I'm honestly surprised he doesn't hurt himself more often. He's always acting a fool in the pasture."

Thomas grinned. "His spirit is unmatched."

Tara stepped forward to run a hand down Elbert's neck. "I'll have to tell Jace his buddy needs some extra attention."

He shook his head in exasperation. "He already spoils him."

She laughed. "Wouldn't you if he saved your life and that of the woman you love?"

Rayna's face flashed in his mind. Yeah. He'd spoil the horse too if he saved her.

"Where is Jace, anyway?"

She sighed, scratching Elbert's ears. The horse turned his head to give her better access. "Still at work. He took a couple hours this afternoon to go to my doctor's appointment with me. Which reminds me…" She let her hand drop and pulled a rolled-up paper from her back pocket. "You get to be an uncle twice."

Thomas's eyes widened as he stared down at the black and white ultrasound pictures she unfurled. Two small blobs floated next to each other in their watery balloons.

"Oh my God. You're having twins?"

Her smile stretched from ear to ear. "Yep. I thought Jace was going to faint."

Thomas laughed. He hooked an arm around her neck and pulled her into his chest for a hug. "I'm happy for you, T. You deserve this." After the devastation of losing her first husband and her late-miscarriage, if anyone deserved a happily ever after, it was his twin.

She tipped her head back and smiled at him, pushing out of his embrace. "Thanks."

He ruffled her hair, then bent to pick up his bag. "I better get going."

Tara turned serious eyes on him. "I meant what I said. Don't hurt her."

Thomas leaned in and pecked a kiss on her cheek. "I won't." And he wouldn't, because they weren't actually dating. He gave her a small wave and left the stall. Sadness made his heart ache. He wished they were.

Six

Rayna pushed open the back door to her parents' house and carried the crate of produce inside, hefting it onto the counter.

"Hi, honey."

She looked over at the sound of her mom's voice. Izzy Nydert stood in the kitchen doorway, her silver-streaked dark hair twisted into a knot on the back of her head.

"Hi. I brought you guys some stuff." She gestured to the crate.

Izzy walked closer to look inside. "How did the market go today?"

"Good. I didn't have much left. I kept enough to can some stuff. The rest I donated to the food pantry."

"That's wonderful." She looked through the crate. "Ooo, you saved me some beans. Good. I'll roast them for supper tonight." She glanced up at Rayna. "Are you staying, or is Thomas coming over again?"

Rayna's eyes widened. "What—why would you think he's coming over?"

Izzy arched a brow, a knowing look in her eyes. "Because we've seen his truck come up the drive the last two nights."

Rayna bit back a groan and closed her eyes for a moment.

"I'm glad you two have worked things out. I just don't understand why it's a secret."

"It's not." She rubbed her forehead. She couldn't lie to her parents. Her friends were one thing, but her mom and dad were another matter. "Thomas and I aren't back together. Things haven't really changed."

Izzy frowned. "I don't understand. Why has he been here, then? None of the animals are sick."

Rayna sighed and took her mother's hand, leading her to the dining table on the other side of the large room. "I need to tell you something, but you have to keep it quiet. You can tell Dad, but no one else."

Her frown intensified. "What's going on?"

Rayna sat next to her and took a deep breath. "The other night, I found a young man in the field. He'd been beaten. Badly."

Izzy gasped.

"But he refused to let me take him to the hospital, so I called Thomas. Mason—that's the young man's name—is staying at my house. Thomas didn't like the idea of us being alone, because the boy was held captive before he ran away, so he's staying until we figure out who did this."

Her look turned quizzical. "Why didn't you call Jace? Or did you?"

She shook her head. "Not yet. Mason is extremely distrustful of cops. He's dealt with them before and been sent back to the same situation. We didn't want to scare him off. He actually ran away the other night, but came back thanks to some notes I left in his stuff, anticipating he might run."

"We also thought it might be a good idea to wait until Seb gets back. He knows more about what's going on in the county. We didn't want Jace spinning his wheels or stirring up suspicion unwittingly by asking questions around town. Seb may be able to find answers much more quietly."

Izzy sat back in her seat, eyes wide as she mulled over what Rayna told her. "Okay. What can we do to help?"

Rayna patted her mother's hand. "Just keep his presence a secret. As far as anyone else is concerned, he doesn't exist. People think Thomas and I are back together, thanks to Macy's appearance here the other night. We didn't want to put her in a position where she had to lie to her brother, so Thomas told her we were dating."

A smile quirked one side of Izzy's mouth. "Oh, he did, did he?"

"We're not." She gave her a stern look. Her mother had been trying to get them back together for years.

Izzy shrugged. "A mother can dream. I still think you two need to sit down and talk. Really talk."

"Mom..."

She held her hands up. "I know. You've been very clear that your relationship ended years ago. But it doesn't change the fact I think you're perfect together. Until I know you're in love with someone else, I will continue to hold out hope for Thomas."

Rayna rolled her eyes and stood. She would hold on to that for a long time, then. "I need to get back to the house and start dinner. I just came to drop off that crate."

Izzy nodded. "Okay. Well, tell Thomas we said hello. If there's anything your dad and I can do for that young man, let us know?"

Rayna nodded. "I will. Just keep an eye out for anything suspicious for now. And don't tell anyone about him."

Izzy mimed zipping her mouth closed. "Not a peep."

"Thanks, Mom." She smiled and walked out the door.

Rayna tiptoed from her bedroom and into the kitchen, trying not to disturb Thomas, who snored softly on the couch. She didn't see how he got any sleep on that couch. It was comfortable to sit on, but he was about a foot too tall to lie down on it without his feet hanging over the end. She would have offered him her bed and taken the couch herself, but she knew there was no way he would ever take her up on that. He would sleep on the floor before he would turn her out of her bed.

Turning on the light over the stove, she took a mug from the cupboard and filled it with water before setting it in the microwave. She hoped some tea would help her sleep. She'd been lying in bed staring at the wall for two hours. Morning was going to hurt at this rate.

She took a tea bag from the box in the pantry cabinet while the water heated and grabbed the milk from the fridge. As she waited for the microwave to finish, she covered a yawn. She was tired, but her mind didn't want to shut down. Thomas's presence in her house was messing with her equilibrium. He dominated her thoughts and made her body go on high alert anytime he was near. The magnetic pull he had over her hadn't changed, even if their relationship had. Her body never got the memo he wasn't hers to touch anymore. Having him so close all the time now was making it harder for her to resist the urge to reach out and just lay her hand on his arm or brush up against him.

The microwave ticked down to one second, and she pushed the button to shut it off before it could ding and wake Thomas up. The last thing she needed was to have him come in here while she was exhausted and her defenses were down. Especially in those gray sweats he favored. Why did men wear those things? Did they not know how they outlined *everything*?

Tearing open the tea packet, she dunked the bag in the hot water as she rolled her eyes. Knowing Thomas, he knew exactly what they did and that's why he wore them. She poured a bit of milk in the cup, then reached for the silverware drawer to get a spoon. Her robe snagged on the milk carton and pulled it off the counter. She made a frantic grab for it, slamming it between her body and the lower cabinets. Milk sloshed out, dribbling over her hand and onto the floor.

Swearing under her breath, she set the carton back on the counter and pulled off several paper towels from the roll.

"Ray?"

She shrieked and spun around, laying a hand over her pounding heart.

"Good lord, don't sneak up on me like that!" She swiped at the milk on her hand and tried not to look at him. Even in the low light, she could still see well enough to know his pants weren't hiding anything and that he wasn't wearing a shirt.

"What are you doing up?"

"I couldn't sleep, so I decided to make myself some tea. I'm sorry I woke you. I dropped the milk."

He walked closer and grabbed a handful of paper towels from the roll, bending down to wipe up the floor.

Rayna swallowed hard at his gleaming skin, shifting over his taught muscles as he cleaned up her mess. *Dammit.* She fought to keep a lid on her suddenly raging hormones, clenching her fists.

He stood and tossed the towels in the garbage, then faced her. His dark hair fell over his forehead in a messy wave and sleep gave his face a soft look. She swallowed again and looked down at her tea.

"Why can't you sleep?"

You.

She bit her tongue and shrugged. "Just can't."

He leaned a hip on the counter, only a couple feet away. "I know you're worried about Mason, but he's doing okay."

She nodded and kept stirring her tea.

"Is it the other kids?"

"Yes." She latched on to that excuse. They *had* been on her mind, so she wasn't lying. Not completely.

His hand snaked out to wrap around the base of her neck under her hair. A shiver went down her spine and the spoon clanked against the side of her mug as her coordination faltered.

"We'll find them. As soon as Seb gets home, we'll sit down and hash out a plan."

She swayed into his touch, unable to help herself. His fingers broke down all her defenses against him. She looked at him in the dim light. Their eyes connected and awareness sent goosebumps rippling over her skin.

His hand trailed over her shoulder and down her arm to settle onto her hip. She felt his fingers dig into the flesh there, subtly tugging her closer. His breath fanned over her face, hot and sweet as he leaned closer. Was he really going to kiss her? She wanted that so much!

She reached out with one hand, resting her fingertips on his chest, the skin warm beneath her touch. His muscles flexed in response. She let her eyes drift closed and tipped her face up to his, eager to feel his lips pressed to hers again after all these years.

Cool air wafted over her as he stepped away. Her hand dropped back to her side and her eyes snapped open. His were wide in the low light, regret shining bright.

"I hope the tea helps. Goodnight." He spun on his heel and retreated to the living room, leaving Rayna staring after him, wondering what the hell just happened.

SEVEN

Arms full, Rayna used her foot to knock on Macy's front door. They'd rescheduled her dress fitting, and Rayna asked if they could do it here instead of on the ranch.

The door swung open to reveal Declan Briggs, Macy's older brother. At thirty-six, he was two years older, but his mischievous personality, which showed through with the smile on his face now, made him look much younger.

"Hey, Rayna." He reached out and took the sewing basket from her and held the door open.

"Hi, Deck." She smiled at him and walked inside, not surprised to see him. Macy and Declan were close and spent a lot of their free time together. He was also a lousy cook, so Macy took pity on him several nights a week and made him supper.

"Macy's in the kitchen. I'll set this stuff in the living room."

She nodded. "Thanks."

Rayna walked through the foyer and down a short hall-way, turning left into the kitchen. She stopped short when she saw Tara leaning against the island. She hadn't expected her to be here.

"Hi."

One corner of Tara's mouth tilted in a sly smile. "Hi."

Rayna swallowed hard. She had a feeling she'd been set up. "You come to watch me try not to stab Macy with pins?"

Tara's smile widened. "That, and we figured it would be a nice night for us all to get together and toast your new relationship."

A knock on the front door and the sound of male voices as Declan answered it, reached her ears. One of the voices sounded like Thomas.

But why would he be here? He knew she was coming over here this evening. He said he was going to check on a couple animals on the Broken Bow, then go back to her place. She'd left a batch of shredded chicken in the slow cooker for him and Mason to eat.

She looked back as Declan walked in, followed by Jace and Thomas. Her eyes met his, and she could tell he wasn't any happier with the situation than she was.

Oh, this was a nightmare! She knew Thomas's lie was going to come back to bite them.

She smiled sweetly up at him as he stopped beside her. "Hi. What are you doing here?"

"Jace found me in the horse barn, checking on Elbert. Invited me out for a drink for taking care of his buddy and wouldn't take no for an answer. I didn't realize it was at Macy's house until he pulled in."

Tara pushed away from the island, grinning. "We wanted to celebrate." She motioned to Macy, who pulled two bottles of champagne and a bottle of sparkling cider from the fridge. "We've been waiting a long time for the two of you to get your heads out of your asses."

Jace patted Thomas on the shoulder. "Sorry. Tara threatened to kick me out of the bedroom if I didn't bring you here."

Thomas lifted an eyebrow at his twin, and she shrugged.

"You could have just asked me to come," he told her.

She held her hands out, palms up. "But then I wouldn't get to pick on Jace."

Thomas looked at his soon-to-be brother-in-law. "You sure you want to marry her?"

Jace grinned, his deep blue eyes twinkling as he walked over to his fiancée and planted a kiss on her cheek. He rested a hand on the growing swell of her belly. "I'm sure."

Tara looked at her brother askance. "And would you really have come if we asked you? Either of you?"

She had a point. But not for the reason she thought.

"Mmm-hmm," Tara hummed. She looked at her fiancé. "Open the bubbly."

"I have snacks too," Macy said, pulling a container forward. "They aren't London's macarons, but I make a mean chocolate chip cookie."

Rayna laughed. She loved her friends. The situation might be awkward for her and Thomas, but the others only wanted to celebrate what should be a happy occasion.

Jace popped the cork on one of the bottles, pouring it into the flutes Macy and Tara held out.

Rayna stepped closer to Thomas. "So, are we running with this?" she whispered.

"Yep." He looked down at her. "Unless you want to pop their bubble."

She frowned up at him. "You started this." But, no, she did not want to be the one to clue them in to their deception. She hated that they'd lied in the first place. It just compounded the guilt she already had about what happened in July.

"You know why we had to. It's safer for everyone."

"Oh, look, guys," Macy cooed. "They're being all lovey-dovey."

Rayna's first instinct was to jerk away, but Thomas wrapped an arm around her waist and pulled her into his side.

"Relax," he whispered out the side of his mouth.

She was going to kill him later.

Pasting a bright smile on her face, she took the champagne flute Macy held out to her.

"To my brother," Tara said, raising her glass. "For finally realizing what an idiot he's been and doing something about it."

Rayna raised her glass and took a quick sip to hide her smile. The one saving grace was when the truth came out, Tara would blame Thomas because she always blamed Thomas. It was the hallmark of their relationship.

"But for real, we're happy for you two. You guys belong together, and it's nice to finally see it."

She could feel the redness creep into her cheeks at Tara's speech. Shame filled her, and the pact she, Macy, and London made to not keep secrets from each other roared through her mind.

With a shaky hand, she set her champagne flute down on the counter beside her. "I can't do this."

"Ray." Thomas's voice was a low growl.

"I'm sorry, Thomas. I think you're wrong. They can help even in an unofficial capacity."

"What's going on?" Jace asked, authority ringing in his deep voice.

She looked at him, pushing out of Thomas's grip. "Thomas and I aren't dating. We only told Macy that so she wouldn't come inside the other night."

Thomas groaned and looked at the ceiling.

She ignored him and continued. "Monday evening, I

found a young man in my field, beaten. He said he fled from some people who'd held him captive since he was a child."

A gasp went through the room.

"He was terrified. Refused to let me take him to the hospital for fear he'd be sent back to the people who hurt him, even though he's technically an adult. But he needed medical attention, so I called Thomas. We've been hiding him at my house since then, waiting for Seb to get back. Mason—the young man—was trafficked, and there are others like him at the house he came from."

An angry frown marred Jace's features. "Why didn't you come to me? I know I'm not Seb, but I'm not Barney Fife."

"It had nothing to do with your investigative abilities," Thomas said. "We were afraid you might inadvertently tip off the people who held him captive by asking questions. That, and the boy is very distrustful of the authorities. He's already run off once. We also wanted to know if Seb had heard any rumors before you guys launched an official investigation. Someone, somewhere, has to know about these people. The way Mason talks, he's been sent back to them after receiving medical treatment, which means someone in the system is on the take."

"I'm sorry we lied to you. We were just trying to keep him safe. He was so scared. He still is, but he's starting to trust us."

"Wait. I stopped by *Tuesday*, and you were there," Macy said, nodding at Thomas.

"I've been staying at night in case whoever held him retraces his steps. I didn't want Rayna and Mason to be alone if they showed up on the ranch."

"Which is why you should have called *me*," Jace growled.

"He's barely eighteen and has a deep distrust of cops. He ran away after I mentioned my brother was the sheriff. He only came back because Rayna anticipated he would run and left him some encouraging notes, leaving the decision about whether he stayed or not up to him. As it is, I still don't want you coming out to talk to him."

Jace's frown deepened. Thomas cut him off before he could protest.

"Not until he's ready to talk. I'm serious. We can't take the chance he'll run again. Not just because we lose the connection to the other kids, but because he has no resources to survive." He glanced down at Rayna. "I think the plan is to give him a job on the Double Moon through the fall season and see how it goes."

She nodded. She hadn't voiced that yet, but then, she wasn't surprised he'd come to that conclusion. Mason had done great at the market, and today, since her parents were now aware of his presence, she had him help her start setting up for the fall market on the ranch. They opened in a week and she wasn't even close to ready. Having him there to help would be a blessing.

Jace ran his hands through his golden hair and sighed. "What is it with this town? I wanted a change of pace from Haskell, but not this kind." He pinned them both with a look Rayna was sure put the fear of God into any criminal. "You need to convince him to let me interview him. I'll hold off on asking questions around town or running background on him until Seb returns. But if there are other lives in danger, we need to move."

Thomas looked down at her, worry in his eyes. The same worry gnawing in her gut. She had a feeling they were both thinking Mason would run if he knew a cop was coming to talk to him.

"You can come over in the morning," Rayna said. "If you come tonight, he might run off while we're asleep. I don't want to be roaming the fields in the dark looking for him."

"And Tara, you come with him," Thomas added. "It'll be less threatening if he sees you as family first."

She nodded. "How about we come for lunch? I'll bring food." She glanced at Jace, who gave a quick nod.

Rayna looked at Thomas as he turned to her.

"You think we can act natural the rest of tonight and tomorrow morning?"

She shrugged. "I guess we'll find out." She nudged him in the side with her elbow. "You should get back, though. I told him you'd be home to eat with him. I left some shredded chicken for you guys."

He rolled his eyes at her, one side of his beautiful mouth quirking up. "Oh, sure. Let me be the one to keep the secret."

She grinned. "I'm sure you'll be fine. Take him to the barn and put him on a horse. He couldn't take his eyes off them while we worked today."

"Yeah?"

"Yep."

He hummed a non-answer before looking at the others, his gaze encompassing not just his sister and her fiancé, but Declan and Macy too. The smile slid from his face as a seriousness took over. "I don't think I need to stress the importance that none of you breathe a word of this to anyone?"

They all shook their heads.

Declan leaned against the counter and crossed his arms. A disturbed frown pulled down his brows. "As much as I hate to admit it, I think you were right to wait to tell anyone. I know from when Macy and I were in the system, there were some corrupt motherfuckers who would do anything to make a buck. It sounds like whoever handled Mason's case was one of those. And I'd say they had help, too, if he's been in that situation for that long."

That's what Rayna was afraid of, too.

~

Thomas walked into the kitchen and set his plate in the sink, done with his dinner, and turned to Mason, who stood next to the stove, eating a cookie for dessert.

"Finish that and go put your shoes on."

A quizzical frown crossed Mason's face, his mouth full.

Thomas smiled. "It's time for your first riding lesson."

The young man's eyes widened, and he chewed faster, stuffing half the remaining cookie in his mouth.

"Don't choke. You won't get to do anything if you pass out."

He slowed a bit, but still finished the treat in record time. When he headed for the back door and his shoes, Thomas went to get their coats.

"I've never been on a horse," Mason said as they walked out the back door and started for the barn near the main house. "I hadn't even seen a horse up close until I got here."

"Really?" Thomas couldn't imagine that. Horses had been part of his life since he was born.

Mason nodded. "I was a city kid until the Smiths came along. Their house was remote, but they didn't have any animals, big or small. I read a lot about them, though, while I was there. They were big on reading. It was all I did in my free time."

"What did you like to read about?"

"Animals, mostly." He ducked his head. "Your job sounds great."

Thomas smiled. "Yeah? Well, maybe you'll have to shadow me and see if it's something you'd like to do. If it is, we can work on getting your vet tech certification. You'll need some experience to get into vet school if that's your ultimate goal."

Mason shrugged. "I haven't really thought about that stuff. It still seems weird that I can. What Rayna does interests me too. She showed me her greenhouse. I think she could grow anything and it would flourish."

"Yeah, she's got some crazy skills. She's a walking plant encyclopedia, too."

"So, did she, like, go to college and learn it all?"

"Not really. She took some online courses after high school, but she was like you and read a lot. And she's been growing things since she was a little kid. It's all she's ever wanted to do. You don't need a fancy education to have a great career. Mine just happens to require the fancy education."

"Is being a vet what you always wanted to do?"

"No. I wanted to be a racecar driver when I was young. Tara and I—well, we were responsible for a lot of the gray hairs Mom and Dad have now. I don't know how they lived through us."

"Why? What did you do?"

Thomas barked a short laugh. "It's more like what we didn't do. Our craziest stunt was probably when we were fourteen. We'd been driving farm trucks since we were probably nine and were tired of the slow, only on the ranch trips. We found an old, broken down truck in one of the barns Dad hadn't had time to fix. Tara and I not only fixed it, we gave the engine a boost. We drove all the way to Pueblo because we wanted Mexican food. The cops pulled us over on the way back, because, of course, Tara and I didn't know all the driving laws. We ended up sitting in a jail cell in Pueblo until Mom and Dad came to pick us up. They were livid. We spent the summer doing the most disgusting, labor intensive chores Dad could think of. They also made us go work for the local mechanic a few hours a week for free."

"Wow."

"We also took the Duvall's prized stallion for a trail ride. I broke my arm on that one. When he was done, he was *done*. Tara broke into the principal's house and stole his underwear as a senior prank. Oh! We also set several cows loose on the football field."

Mason stared at him with wide eyes. "How are you two not in jail?"

Thomas laughed. "Because, underneath it all, we knew right from wrong. Our little pranks were mostly harmless. The truck thing probably went too far, which is why we got in so much trouble. We could have really hurt someone."

"Is driving hard?"

Thomas shrugged, realizing the kid probably never had an opportunity to learn to drive. "Not really. It just takes some practice. Rayna and I will teach you. Once you feel like you're ready, we'll take you to get your license. You're going to need one anyway for identification."

"Don't I need a birth certificate for that?"

"Yes."

Mason's face fell. "I don't have that."

Thomas patted his good shoulder. "That's what state and county records departments are for. You were born in Denver?"

He nodded.

"Then we shouldn't have any trouble finding you. Don't worry. We'll get you sorted."

Tears pooled in Mason's eyes. "Thank you. I don't know what I did to deserve landing here, but I'm grateful I did."

Thomas felt the sting of emotion in his own eyes and blinked a few times before answering. "You lived. You endured and survived. That's enough. And we're just as grateful you're here."

"Why?" Mason frowned over at him. "I mean, I'm grateful to you and Rayna, but why are you grateful for me? I'm just some stranger with a lot of issues who showed up. You should want to be rid of me as fast as you can."

"You don't run away from something just because it's difficult. Vet school sucked out the wazoo, but I still did it because the end was worth it. It's the same with you. Are the next few weeks to months going to suck as we figure all this out? Probably. But you're worth it, Mason. I'm grateful you're here because it means you're out of that situation. And I can't speak for Rayna, but I'm grateful to you for bringing me here. It's made me deal with some stuff I haven't and should have."

"Rayna?"

Thomas cast him a glance, not surprised the kid had seen the undercurrents between him and their lovely hostess.

"Yeah. I've been holding onto some anger for something she didn't even really do, because I was hurt. She was dating someone who turned out to be a really bad guy, and it put Tara in danger, even though Rayna didn't know who he really was. In reality, I was more upset she was with someone else and latched on to any excuse to justify my anger." He took a deep breath, feeling some weight lift off his shoulders at the admission. He'd forgiven her almost immediately, but the anger he'd held onto kept him from realizing that.

"Does she know that?"

Thomas frowned. "No. We haven't talked about what happened."

"You should."

"Yeah, well, that's easier said than done."

"Just say you're sorry."

"Words don't mean much unless you back them up. I'm afraid she won't believe me after I've destroyed her trust in me twice now. Once, when we broke up years ago and then again when all the shit went down with Tara."

Mason shrugged and reached for the barn door as they reached the large white building. "You won't know unless you do it." He pulled open the door, letting Thomas go first. "And she might surprise you."

Thomas doubted that. Her opinion of him wasn't stellar, and he couldn't blame her. "Maybe. But that's a worry for another time." He stopped in front of a stall containing a snowy white horse with blue eyes named Bing. The horse hung his head over the door and nudged Thomas, looking for treats. He scratched the animal between his ears.

"This is Rayna's mom's horse, Bing."

Mason edged forward. "Can I pet him?"

"Of course. Hold out your hand near his nose and let him sniff you for a second, then scratch him here." Thomas rubbed the horse's soft muzzle.

The young man took a couple steps forward and held out his hand. Bing's nostrils flared as he got a whiff of the new person. The big animal snorted and tipped his head, bumping Mason's hand.

"He likes you," Thomas said.

A wide grin split Mason's face. "Yeah?" He rubbed Bing's face with a gentle hand. "Hi, Bing. I like you too, buddy."

Thomas looked on with pride. The boy was a natural. "How about we take him out to the corral and see about putting a saddle on him?"

"Mrs. Nydert won't mind?"

"No. The other horses have a bit too much spirit for a new rider, but Bing is nice and calm." He pointed to the wall to the right. "Grab that rope hanging there and snap it to the ring on the side of his halter."

Once Mason did as directed, Thomas unlatched the stall door and led the horse out.

"Are you going to ride?"

Thomas shook his head. "Not tonight. This is about getting you comfortable in the saddle. If you're going to stay around here, you need to learn to ride. Horses are used for work on a ranch. My brother, Brady, runs our family's ranch with my dad, and they ride every day. Rayna and her dad use them too, though you see Rayna in her UTV a lot now. But they still use them to ride fence lines and to check on the herd."

He led them out to the corral and looped Bing's lead rope to the fence. "Let's go get his tack and I'll show you how to get him ready."

For the next twenty minutes, Thomas instructed Mason on how to brush and saddle a horse. The boy absorbed every word like a sponge, showing he had an aptitude for learning.

That sense of pride he felt earlier was back, along with the feeling that if they could find his abductors and stop the trafficking ring he'd fled, Mason had a bright future.

EIGHT

Rayna's heart fluttered at the sound of a car pulling up. She turned to see Jace's bright, cherry red truck come to a halt outside the market building. She glanced at Mason, who stopped working to look warily at the vehicle, a hint of fear in his eyes.

She held out a hand. "It's okay. They're family. It's Thomas's twin, Tara, and her fiancé, Jace. They came for lunch and to help me get the market ready."

He nodded, but the frown stayed between his brows.

"Come on. I'll introduce you." She motioned him forward as she took a step toward the door. The breath stalled in her chest as he debated her words. When he moved her direction, she let out a quick sigh of relief.

"Hey, guys," she said as she stepped outside.

"Hi," Tara chirped. "Where's my derelict brother?"

"Knox called. One of his mares was having trouble foaling."

"Yikes. I hope everything's okay."

"Me too." She glanced at Jace. "It's Pike and Elbert's mom."

His eyes widened. "You mean there are going to be more of them?"

Rayna grinned. "Potentially."

"Awesome." He returned her smile, rubbing his hands together.

Mason shifted next to her, and she looked over at him. "Mason, this is Jace and Tara. Guys, this is Mason Lund."

Jace walked forward, hand extended. "Nice to meet you, young man. Rayna and Thomas tell me you had quite a time before you arrived here."

Eyes downcast, Mason shook Jace's hand and nodded. "Yes, sir."

Rayna shared a look with Jace, who had the same stunned expression on his face she and Thomas had the other day as he took in the bruises around Mason's eye and the burns just visible beneath his rolled-up shirtsleeves—and he'd done a lot of healing since he arrived.

Tara, sensing Mason's anxiety, stepped forward, a covered dish in her hands. "Hi, Mason. It's very nice to meet you. You sure know how to pick a refuge. Rayna's is the best you'll ever find. Although, her decision to involve Thomas leaves something to be desired. He's a pill."

Mason frowned at her in question, some of the stress leaving his face.

She stepped closer, smiling brightly. "He's a terrible tease. And a wise-ass."

A ghost of a smile lit the young man's face. "He's cracked a couple jokes, but he's been nothing but nice."

Tara gave a quick nod. "Good." She looked up at Jace. "Grab the basket from the truck. I'm starving."

He and Rayna laughed at her abrupt statement.

"You're always starving anymore," he said, turning back to the truck.

"It's your fault."

He shook a finger at her as he opened the back passenger door. "Don't blame this on me. You liked to eat *before* you got pregnant."

She huffed, making Rayna giggle. Tara looked at her and frowned with mock annoyance. "He's supposed to just say, 'yes, dear.'" She shook her head, then laughed.

Laughing at her friend, Rayna stepped forward and looped an arm through Mason's. "Come on. Let's have some lunch and appease her."

He stiffened for a moment at her touch, then relaxed and smiled at her. "I guess I could eat."

Tara scoffed and rolled her eyes as she spun toward the house. "Listen to him. Mr. I-could-fit-in-my-skinny-jeans guesses he could eat. And here I am, knowing that even after I'm no longer pregnant, I still won't fit back in those pants."

Jace chuckled as he joined her. "You're still beautiful no matter what size you are." He leaned in and pressed a kiss to her cheek.

"Is she always so hyper?" Mason whispered as they followed.

Rayna nodded. "Normally, yes. The last few years she's been kinda subdued. Her husband died, and she miscarried their baby shortly afterward. She just kinda went through the motions of life until Jace came to town over the summer. He's really brought her back to life."

He looked down at her with wide eyes. "They've only been together a few months?"

"Yep. Crazy, huh? But, I guess when love finds you, it doesn't matter how long you've known someone. He's a good man. With his own tragic past. It's what bonded them together so quickly. He lost his wife and daughter to a boating accident."

"Wow."

She smiled up at him. "Kinda gives you hope things will be okay, doesn't it?"

He cast a glance down at her. "I'm supposed to find a life lesson here, aren't I?"

Her smile widened. "Maybe."

"Okay, *Mom*."

Rayna's breath caught. Even though she knew he was joking, it still tugged her heart strings to hear him call her that. She'd pretty much given up on ever having children of her own. With several failed relationships, every year, it seemed less and less like a possibility.

She gave his arm a squeeze. "Just take heart that things change. Life isn't always bad. And I'd say you're due for some good."

"We'll see. In my experience, the good things are few and far between."

Tears threatened, and she forced a smile to keep them at bay. "We're going to change that." She quickened her step to catch up with Tara and Jace. "But first, we're going to eat the delicious lunch Tara brought. If she doesn't eat it all first."

They stepped over the threshold into the kitchen. Tara was pulling containers out of the basket and lining them up on the counter.

"What did you make?" Rayna stepped over to the plate cabinet and pulled several down, handing them to Mason. He took them and went to the silverware drawer to get out utensils.

"Brisket, coleslaw, and mac and cheese." She looked up from uncovering the meat. "And I used the last of the summer fruits you gave me to make a trifle." She pointed to the dish on the stove.

Rayna's mouth watered. "Did you use London's sponge cake recipe?"

"Is there any other?"

"No," she giggled.

The front door opened, and she turned to see Thomas walk inside.

"It's about time you showed up," Tara said, smiling at her twin.

Thomas came to a stop in the kitchen doorway, leaning on the half wall. "Baby horses wait for no one."

"Did everything go okay?" Rayna asked.

He nodded. "Mama and her little girl are doing fine."

"So, Pike and Elbert have a sister now?" Jace said.

Thomas smiled. "Yep. She looks just like them. Spunky, too. She was already trying to stand when I left."

Tara shook a finger at her fiancé. "I know what you're thinking. We do not need another horse."

"*We* don't, but our children will need their own."

She rolled her eyes. "It will be several years before these two will be old enough to ride."

"Good. Gives us plenty of time to train her. And to find another for his or her sibling."

Tara rolled her eyes, exasperation all over her face. "Someone remind me to call Knox later and tell him not to accept any of Jace's calls."

He pouted. "That's cruel."

She patted his cheek. "Poor baby." Reaching over, she took a plate off the stack Mason set on the counter and shoved it in Jace's hands. "Fill the void with food. You'll be fine."

"I can still drive over there, you know," he said, piling brisket on his plate.

Tara snatched the plate from his hands and held it out to Mason.

"Hey!"

Her saccharine smile dripped mischief. "Now you get to go last."

Mason stared at them with wide eyes.

Thomas stepped forward and took the plate, handing it back to Jace. "Cool it, T. You're scaring the kid."

Her eyes went to Mason's, and her mouth rounded in surprise. "Sorry. I was only teasing him. I'm not really angry. And we probably will end up with that horse. You hang around here long enough, you'll realize the joshing is one way we all show affection." She picked up an empty plate and held it out to him, motioning toward the food. "Sometimes, I can forget not everyone understands our humor."

He took the plate, his face relaxing. "It's okay. I'm just not used to good-natured teasing."

Thomas rested a hand on Mason's shoulder. "Like she said, you hang around and you'll get used to it."

Rayna picked up a plate of her own. "And we definitely want you to hang around. Can we eat now? It's been a long time since breakfast." She changed the subject, hoping to put Mason at ease again. Tara could be—overwhelming.

They filled their plates and sat down around the table to eat, conversation scarce while they assuaged their hunger. Once their plates were clean, Tara dished out the dessert.

Rayna spied Jace eyeing Mason and knew he was getting anxious to ask the boy questions. She wanted answers too. For those other kids' sakes. She scooped up another spoonful of the trifle and brought it up to her lips. "So, how's being acting sheriff going, Jace?" She slid the spoon between her lips, maintaining her nonchalance even as her heartbeat sped up.

Jace barely missed a beat at her question, catching on to her ploy. He ate another bite of his dessert and shrugged. "Makes me glad I'm only the chief deputy. There's too much politics involved in Seb's job. And the city mayor and the D.A. are both assholes."

Mason set his spoon down on his plate, his movements slow and deliberate.

"Well, I'm sure Seb will be glad to know his job is safe,"

Rayna remarked.

"Yep. I'll stick to locking up the bad guys. He can worry about the funding for the department."

"Other than the jerks in office, how do you like your job?"

He ate another bite of his dessert before answering. "It's good. I have a lot more autonomy than I did in Nebraska. A little more responsibility, but it's mostly the same job since there's no official detective for the department."

Mason's head popped up at that. "So, you're completely new around here, then?"

Hope surged in Rayna's chest. If they could get him to trust Jace, they could really make some headway.

Jace nodded. "I've only been in Colorado since the end of June. Look, Mason. I know you don't trust cops. I understand why, but I need you to trust me. We need to find where you were kept and put a stop to the people who did this to you."

Mason chewed on his bottom lip as he regarded the man across from him. "I don't know what I can tell you. It was dark when I ran away. I know I went south because the sun always set on my right. I changed elevation a couple times too, because I remember cresting a couple rises before I found myself in the field here."

"How long did you walk?"

"I ran through the night the first night and stopped for a few hours near daylight to rest. I kept moving the rest of the day and only stopped when I couldn't see very well and almost fell in a ravine. Once the moon came out, I started moving again and kept going until Rayna found me in her field."

"You did all that with a dislocated shoulder and only one eye open?"

The boy nodded.

Jace stabbed the air with his fork. "Don't ever let anyone tell you that you can't do something, because a lot of people would have just curled up and let the elements take them."

Mason's cheeks reddened, but he stayed silent.

"If I took you out on horseback, do you think you'd be able to retrace your steps?"

His eyes widened, and he stiffened.

Rayna reached out and grabbed his hand. "Thomas and I would go with you. You won't have to face the Smiths alone. If at all."

"Absolutely," Thomas said.

"But how will you be able to get away?" Mason said to Rayna. "You have your opening day next weekend. It'll take us a couple days to ride that far and back."

"You let us worry about that," Tara said. "The Archers band together when we're needed. Rayna may not be blood, but she's family. We'll make sure the market's ready."

"If Tara says it's handled, you can believe her," Jace said. "So, what do you say, kid?"

Rayna found herself holding her breath again. Mason glanced around the table, his eyes pausing on Thomas, then finally her. She held his gaze, doing her best to telegraph that she stood behind him no matter what.

"Okay." He turned to Jace. "Let's do it."

Thomas's boots thudded softly in the grass as he crossed the yard to the market building. After lunch, he'd been called back out for several other farm calls. Jace and Tara stayed to help Rayna and Mason, but they must have left. Jace's truck was gone.

As he got closer to the building, he could see Rayna moving around inside. She'd lowered the plywood flaps that served as a checkout counter to let in some air while they worked.

"Hey. You about ready to knock off for the evening?" he

asked, stepping up to the window. "I brought pizza so you don't have to cook."

She smiled, her pretty eyes lighting up. "Pizza sounds great." She turned. "Mason?"

The boy rose from behind a stack of boxes.

"Thomas brought pizza. Are you ready to eat?"

He nodded.

"Go on in and wash up, then dig in," Thomas said. "We'll be there in a minute."

Mason loped past them.

"Don't eat it all!" Thomas called after him.

The young man looked back at them, a light grin on his face, before he continued to the house.

Thomas turned his attention to the tired woman still stacking things. He walked around the side of the building and went inside. He took the jars from her hands and set them on the shelf, then pulled her away from it.

"Thomas."

"Putting out the jellies can wait until tomorrow."

She blew out a breath, the hair that had come loose from her ponytail flying up, only to settle right back where it'd been. "I know, but I don't want to leave anymore than necessary for the others to do. I'd like to have everything in here set up for the most part. Then, all they need to do is pick pumpkins and squash and make signs."

"You still have all day tomorrow. We don't leave until Monday." They'd decided to wait until Seb returned, so they could give him a full rundown before they set out. They were still hoping he would know who the Smiths were.

"I know. But I feel like we didn't even make much of a dent today, and there were four of us working."

Thomas looked around. There was still a lot to do, but it looked better in here than it had this morning. "You got a lot done. There's always a lot of cleaning involved when you first start, and that sucked up most of your time today. You're past that now, so I don't think it'll take you long. You fret about this market every year, but it always turns out great."

She sighed. "I know. I added to it this year, though. The greenhouse is doing much better than I expected, so there's going to be a lot more than just pumpkins and squash. I have to retrofit one whole side of the building with bins for all that produce." She pointed to the stack of wood on the floor against the far wall.

"I'll help put that together tomorrow." He took her hand. "Come on. Let's go eat."

She sighed again, but didn't argue. He helped her close the plywood flaps over the windows and they left the shed.

"Thank you, by the way," she said as they walked across the yard.

"For what?"

"For backing me up earlier when I told Mason we'd go with him. I didn't ask you beforehand, and you didn't hesitate to say yes."

It hadn't even crossed his mind to say no. The only thought he'd had was how quickly he could rearrange his schedule and find another vet to cover for him.

"Mason needs us. I'm not going to sit by and do nothing when I can do *something*." His jaw worked. "What he's been through—I just don't understand how anyone can be so cruel to another human being. Especially a child."

"Part of me wants us to find the Smiths when we're out and for them to put up a fight. I'd like nothing more than to give them even an ounce of the pain they caused Mason and the other kids. If that makes me a terrible person, so be it."

He took her hand again and squeezed it. "It doesn't. It makes you caring. I'd very much like to do the same thing."

"I want to offer him a place here on the ranch. I really

could use the help, and it'll give him a chance to figure out what he wants to do."

"Maybe once it's safe for him to be out in the community, I'll take him with me on calls. Give him some experience with animals. He did really great with Bing yesterday, but I don't think he's really spent much time around them. It sounds like he was kept indoors most of the time. There's also an old Airstream at home. I'll clean it up and tow it over. Give him some space of his own."

She frowned up at him. "Are you sure he's ready for that? And that it's safe?"

"He's eighteen, Ray. Every kid that age needs their own space. He'll still be close, though, in case he needs us—you," he quickly amended. Once the threat was past, Thomas would go back to the Broken Bow. That shouldn't be a depressing thought, but it was.

He bumped her shoulder with his. "We'll park it right outside the back door. He'll be okay."

They reached the house, and he opened the door for her. One pizza box sat on the counter, three-quarters of it missing. They could see Mason sitting in the living room, eyes glued to the laptop. He'd been spending a lot of time learning about the world he'd missed.

"I hope he left some in the other box," Thomas muttered.

Rayna giggled. "I'm sure he did. Even a teenager can't eat that much that fast."

He arched a brow as she moved toward the boxes. "Do you remember me and my brothers when we were younger?" He gestured to the pizzas. "The three of us could eat at least a pizza each."

"Oh, I'm sure he'll get there. Once he gets used to eating bigger meals, I'm sure I'll be restocking the cabinets a few times a week."

She reached into the cabinet and pulled out some clean

plates, handing him one.

"Can you take on a teenager's food bill? I can chip in if you need me to."

Rayna took the last two slices from the open box and grabbed a napkin, giggling. "We sound like a couple of divorced parents discussing school clothes or something."

He grinned. They did. Oddly enough, when he thought about Mason, he felt like a parent. There was something about the young man that brought out those feelings. "You dragged me into this. I'm just seeing it through."

She smiled. "I appreciate it. But I can afford him. I won't argue if you want to buy him things; just don't go overboard, please."

He flipped open the other box and piled pizza on his plate, a mock pout on his face. "Ruin all my fun, why don't you?"

She waggled her eyebrows and spun away, headed for the living room, leaving Thomas to trail after her. They sat in the chairs flanking the couch where Mason rested and dug into their food. The boy barely glanced at them as they joined him.

"What has you so enthralled?" Thomas asked.

Mason glanced up, then back down at the screen. "I found an article about that serial killer—Ryan Marsters? There's a picture of him here. I met him."

The pizza settled like lead in Thomas's stomach and he set down the slice in his hand. "You did? When?"

He looked up from the computer. "He came to the house. There was a girl there he liked. Gilly. She disappeared over the spring."

His food rolled in his belly. He saw Rayna's face turn white, her hands shaking as she lowered the slice of pizza she held back onto her plate. She looked at him, eyes full of sadness.

"I'll call Jace," he said, rising, no longer interested in his pizza.

NINE

"Seb's going to hate us, you know that, right?" Jace said as they walked up the front steps to London's B&B, The Lilac Inn.

Yes, he was, Thomas couldn't help but think. "He kinda signed up for this when he ran for sheriff." He pushed open the front door and motioned Rayna and Mason in ahead of him.

After they'd talked to Jace yesterday about Mason's revelation, they'd agreed to give the newlyweds a couple hours to themselves after they returned from their honeymoon before they burst their happy bubble.

Thomas's mom, Jenny, came out of the kitchen. She'd been minding the inn along with London's niece, Abigail, while Seb and London were away.

"Hey, Mom."

"Hi. What are you guys doing here? And who's this?" She gestured to Mason.

"We'll explain it all in a bit, Jenny," Jace said. "Are Seb and London still upstairs? I called to tell Seb I was on my way over to talk to him."

"They're out back on the patio."

They walked toward her to go out the back door in the kitchen.

"Thanks." Thomas leaned in and kissed her on the cheek as they filed past.

"You're welcome?"

She was going to corner him later and grill him, but they needed to talk to Seb before they told anyone else what was going on.

Outside, they found Seb and London cuddled together on the wicker loveseat. Seb took one look at their faces—and the bruised face of the young man with them—and cursed.

"I go away for a week and all hell breaks loose."

Seb rose from his seat, and Mason took a step back, his eyes widening as he took in Seb's imposing figure.

Thomas put a hand on the boy's good shoulder. "It's okay. He's one of the good guys, I promise."

"Good guys?" Seb frowned. "What's going on? Who is this?" He speared Thomas and Jace with a glare, skimming his eyes over Rayna with a quick quirk of his brows.

London stood next to her husband. "I'm going to go make us all some coffee and find some cookies."

Seb nodded and watched her go before motioning them all to the long metal table. "Let's have a seat. Then you can tell me why I won't be seeing my brand-new wife much for the foreseeable future."

They sat down, Thomas and Rayna flanking Mason for support. Seb sat across from them, next to Jace.

"Speak." Seb stared at Thomas, but it was Rayna who replied.

"This is Mason Lund. I found him, injured, in one of my fields six days ago. He says he ran away from a couple who'd held him captive and trafficked him for the last seven years."

Seb's eyes widened, and his mouth worked silently for

several moments before he slammed it shut and cleared his throat.

"Hell."

He looked over at Jace. "What have you done so far?"

"Not much. They didn't tell me about all this until Friday."

"Mason didn't want to go to the authorities. They've turned him back over to his captors in the past. They're masquerading as his foster parents," Thomas added.

"Foster parents? How old are you?"

"I'm eighteen now."

Seb studied Mason like a bug under a microscope, but the young man stared right back. Thomas felt a surge of pride for the strength he showed.

"And they aren't your foster parents?"

"No, sir. I ran away from my foster home just after I turned eleven. These other people found me on the street a few months later and offered to help me. They seemed nice. It wasn't until they got me back to their house that I realized what a mistake I'd made. I've been captive ever since. They rent me out to their customers. One of them got lazy, and I got away."

"And you didn't go to the cops right away because you were afraid they would turn you back over to these people?"

Mason nodded.

"Even though you're an adult?"

Mason nodded again. "I wasn't sure how old I was—the days all blended together. And I know they've got forged documents of some kind, so I wasn't sure they wouldn't change them to show that I was only seventeen still."

"You're sure they have forged papers?"

"Yes. I got really sick a few years ago—more than what the doctor they have come out to tend to us could manage. I had to have surgery for appendicitis. I tried to tell the hospital staff

I needed help, but no one would listen. They convinced the doctor and the social worker I was high on painkillers. I wasn't." He swallowed hard and continued. "When I was thirteen, I broke my arm. Their doctor couldn't come out, so they took me to the emergency room. The doctor there called social services, because it wasn't the only injury I had, but nothing ever came of it. I never saw the social worker again."

"You said 'us.' You mean you and the couple who held you?"

Mason shook his head. "No. There are five other kids there. There have been others. I don't know what happened to them."

"He saw a picture of Ryan Marsters online and said he used to come out to this place to visit one of the girls there. She's been missing since the spring," Jace said.

Seb sat back and stared at them all again.

"Fuck." He leaned his elbows on the table and put his head in his hands a moment before running his fingers through his hair and looking up. "Okay." He took out his phone and opened a notepad app. "Jace, I need you to get a hold of Marsters' phone records again. Match all his calls from this year up until he died to a name. Then, get a subpoena for Mason's medical records. See if we can run down the social worker." He glanced up at Mason. "Where is this place?"

"I don't know. Anytime they took me anywhere, they blindfolded me."

"We have a plan to find it," Jace said, drawing Seb's attention. "Tomorrow, Mason, Thomas, Rayna, and I are going to set out on horseback and try to retrace the route he took before he ended up on the Double Moon. He walked a couple of days before he landed there."

Seb looked back at the boy. "You walked days before you found another house?"

Mason nodded.

"Hmm..."

"You have an idea of who it is, don't you?" Thomas said, leaning forward. "That's another reason Jace hasn't done much. If the abuse the doctor noted got swept under the rug, someone in a position of power is involved. We didn't want to tip our hand."

Seb drew in a deep breath. "Not a name, but I've heard rumors about a place deep in the mountains that deals in drugs. I haven't heard anything about people, though. That's a first." He turned to Jace. "Have you checked missing person's reports for him yet?"

Jace shook his head. "We wanted to talk to you first. If there's a cop involved, it could set off some alarm bells for that person, and we could lose the other kids."

"There have been several changes at the department since I took over and since his last run-in with law enforcement. It's possible whoever it was isn't there anymore. Give it to Wilder. She'll keep it quiet. You start the inquiry on Marsters' phone records and Mason's medical records, then hand both off to her, too, so you can head up that search tomorrow. Tell her she can pull Gentry in on it if she wants, but no one else. We limit this to a select few we trust. If anyone asks where you went, I'll just say you needed a few days off after being me for a week."

Jace chuckled. "That's not really a lie. I'm very happy to hand the title of sheriff back to you."

"What, politics don't suit you? Never would have guessed." He laughed before looking around the table again just as London came out the back door with a tray in her hands. He stood up to take it from her, then they both settled at the table.

"Mason, if I sit you down with a sketch artist, could you describe the Smiths?"

Mason nodded.

"Good. I'll set that up for later this week, after you get

back from the scouting trip. We *will* get to the bottom of this," he told Mason. "You have my word on that. I don't know what other cops have said to you in the past, but I am one of the good ones. I think you trust my brother and our friend or you wouldn't be here. I'm hoping you'll trust me too."

Mason looked around the table, his gaze lingering on Rayna, then Thomas. They both offered him encouraging smiles. He looked back at Seb, expression serious, but hopeful. "I'm trying."

Thomas smiled brighter, feeling slightly more hopeful about the situation as well, knowing it was in Seb's capable hands. It was a start.

Weariness weighed down Rayna's muscles as she stuffed the last of the camping goods into the pack she was taking tomorrow. After they left the inn, it had been a whirlwind of shopping and packing to make sure they had what they needed for several days. They figured it would take them about two on horseback to reach the area where Mason fled, but there was no guarantee they would find the place easily.

Thomas's bag landed next to hers with a clink as the metal buckles on the straps hit the floor.

"Did you get all of Mason's things?" he asked.

She nodded. "Yeah. He wanted to help pack, but he was starting to look more than a little worn down, so I took it all and made him go to bed."

"Good. He's still healing from his injuries and needs the extra sleep."

"That's what I told him. He still argued with me, but when he yawned so hard his jaw popped, he gave in."

Thomas grinned, and Rayna looked back down at her

stuff, praying he would go to bed too. She was tired and couldn't handle his sexiness right now. That impish smile of his always did something to her insides. Had since they were teenagers.

She zipped the bag closed and looked up. "I'm ready to go to sleep too."

"Same here," he said, stifling a yawn and stretching his arms over his head.

Rayna spun toward the kitchen, but not before she got a glimpse of rock hard abs and a line of dark hair above his waistband as his t-shirt rode up his torso. Huffing at herself and her wayward hormones, she stomped through the dining room and into the kitchen, where she opened the fridge and pulled out an open bottle of wine. She was going to take a page out of Tara's book and sink into her bathtub with a glass of wine and pray she could get her mind to relax enough to let her sleep.

"Hey, are you okay?"

She jerked and spun back around to see him standing in the doorway. A crease split his brow as he stared at her.

"I'm fine. I'm going to go soak in the tub, then go to bed." *Move!* He stood in her path to freedom.

When he started toward her, her stomach twisted. That wasn't what she'd meant with her silent plea.

She stiffened her spine and met his gaze, determined not to show how much he affected her.

"Why are you so tense? You can't be that worried about this trip. It's more of a scouting expedition than anything."

Rayna shrugged. She was sure he didn't want to know the real reason for the tension making her shoulders stiff.

His dark eyes took on a heat, and his nostrils flared as he continued to stand there and stare at her.

Or maybe he did.

"I'm tired of fighting this," he said, his voice a rough whisper.

"Me too."

He took the wine from her and set it on the counter behind her, then grasped her face in his hands and pressed his mouth to hers.

Fireworks went off behind Rayna's eyelids, and the breath left her lungs on a gasp. He took full advantage and deepened their kiss. Her head spun, and she held on for dear life. She couldn't believe she was kissing Thomas Archer again after all these years. She'd given up hope of ever feeling his mouth on hers again.

But what the hell were they doing? And what happened to the anger he carried toward her?

She pushed back and spread her hands over his chest to create some distance, trying not to notice the firm muscles beneath her palms.

"What was that?"

"Me finally admitting I've been a jackass."

Surprise had her dropping her hands and taking a step back.

He sighed and ran a hand through his hair. "I'm sorry I've been so standoffish and rude. I was upset, not just that your relationship put Tara in danger, but because you—seemed happy with Thorpe or Fetter or whatever you want to call him."

Her brows drew down as she processed what he said. "Wait. This whole time, you were pissed at me because I was happy with another man?"

He nodded.

Incredulity sent them winging the other way. "Seriously? And now, since you're tired of fighting your feelings for me, you think you can kiss me and magically make everything better? After months of me torturing myself over my part in the whole mess, thinking I had disappointed you, you tell me you weren't really mad over that, but because I dared to be *happy*?" She snatched the bottle of wine off the counter. "You have lost your damn mind." Pushing past him, anger growing, she headed for her bedroom. She doubted the bath and wine were going to help her sleep now, but it would at least get her away from him.

"Rayna—"

She held up her free hand and flipped him the bird, not bothering to look back. "Goodnight, Thomas."

TEN

Thomas led his black mare, Raven, into the barn the next morning behind Jace and the silver gelding he was using for the trip, Pike. He spotted Rayna standing with her chestnut-colored mare, Poppy, outside Poppy's stall. A huge yawn broke over her face as she double-checked her saddlebags. Guilt hit him hard as he realized he was likely the cause of her fatigue. She'd still been angry this morning. He'd only gotten a handful of words from her before he left to fetch Jace, Raven, and Pike.

The thud of their cowboy boots and the clack of a horses' hooves on the barn floor drew her attention. She looked up from her task and frowned, her eyes on Jace's horse. "Where's Elbert?"

Jace's frown matched hers. "Thomas didn't tell you? Damn fool horse sprained his fetlock. I can't take him on a ride like this without risking further damage. Seb let me borrow Pike."

She looked past him to Thomas, concern on her face. "Is he going to be okay?"

Thomas nodded, looping Raven's reins over the bars of an

empty stall. "He'll be fine with some rest. Brady's keeping him confined to his stall and a smaller corral so he can't build up any speed. Pike might be a better choice for a ride like this, anyway. He's not so eager to run and listens better."

Jace looked back, a teasing smile on his face. "You just don't want me to leave you in the dust like I did when we raced."

A sardonic tilt lifted Thomas's mouth. "You still will on him. He's just less likely to make that decision on his own."

"True," Jace said with a laugh. "So, are we about ready to go?" He looked around the barn. "Where's the kid?"

"He's out in the corral with Bing. I saddled him up first and told him to take his horse for some warm-up laps. He needed the distraction. He was up bright and early this morning, chomping at the bit to go. I came out to find he'd already started breakfast. He's a quick study. He had bacon frying and scrambled eggs cooking, and he's never even used a stove before."

"It was good, too," Thomas said, stepping around them to get his saddlebags.

"It was." She tied the last string on her bags, then swung up onto Poppy's back. "I'm going to go out there with him."

Jace nodded. "We won't be long."

She gave them a curt nod and spun Poppy around, walking her out of the barn.

"Okay, what the hell did you do?" Jace asked as soon as she was out of earshot.

Thomas looked up from adjusting the saddlebags over Raven's back to see Jace glaring at him, his blue eyes flinty.

"What makes you think I did anything?"

Jace rolled his eyes. "Um, maybe because she didn't crack a single smile, and the only time she wasn't glaring at you was when she was concerned about Elbert?"

Thomas sighed. Having a cop for a brother-in-law was not

useful in this case. He noticed too much and wasn't afraid to ask personal questions. "I kissed her last night."

A corner of Jace's mouth ticked up in the start of a smile.

"It didn't end the way I thought it would—or even hoped it would. She asked me why I kissed her, and we got into a conversation about why I've been angry the last few months, and—well, let's just say she's right to be ticked at me."

Jace tied on the second of his saddlebags and shook his head. "If that's the case, you better start thinking of a way to make her not mad at you." He put his foot in the stirrup and mounted his horse. "From everything I've learned about that woman the last few months, she's the best thing to have ever happened to you, and you're a fool if you let her get away again." He gave Pike a nudge, and they followed Rayna out of the barn.

Thomas leaned his forehead against Raven's hip, silently cursing himself, knowing Jace was right. He really had made a mess of things and had no one to blame but himself. He needed to figure out how to fix it.

Pushing back, he finished his preparations with quick, angry movements before hoisting himself into the saddle and exiting the barn. His gaze landed on Rayna, her midnight hair gleaming deep purple and blue in the rising sun. What was it about the woman that turned him into an imbecile? Why couldn't he get things right with her?

"Are we ready?" Jace asked.

The three of them nodded. Thomas shifted in his seat and forced his mind off his relationship problems.

"Okay. Mason, you lead the way," Jace continued. "Start with where Rayna found you and go from there."

The young man nodded. Rayna rode up next to him, and they started toward the fields.

"That was the row you were in," Rayna said after several minutes of riding.

"I walked through the rows from that way." Mason pointed ahead of them to their left. "I only stopped because I heard you and didn't want to get caught."

Rayna offered him a soft smile. "We can ride around the perimeter of this field and pick up where you came out on the other side. The horses won't fit through some of the rows because of the bean trellises." She gave Poppy a squeeze and nudged her into a quick walk around the field. Mason pointed to where he'd cut through the trees in the valley as he'd come down the mountain, and they followed his lead.

Leaves rustled overhead, and the temperature dropped as they ducked beneath the tree canopy. The horses picked their way over the forest floor, the creak of leather and the jingle of bridle the only accompaniment to the chatter of the birds out looking for their morning meals. Thomas wished the peace around them wasn't in direct juxtaposition to the reason for this trip. It almost felt wrong to enjoy the ride when what waited for them at the other end was so sinister.

He studied Mason as they rode, amazed at the change in him in just a few days. The kid was still wary, but the terrified boy was gone, replaced by a young man with fledgling self-confidence born from the hope that the world wasn't *all* bad. Thomas was going to do whatever he could to nurture that growing confidence. Mason brought out a paternal instinct Thomas didn't think he had. Maybe it was his appearance when he first saw him, all bruised and scared and downtrodden. The injustice of the kid's situation wasn't lost on him, and it made him furious that someone could commit such a heinous act against a child. He wanted to right that wrong, even though he hadn't been the one to hurt the boy.

Regardless of why he wanted to help Mason, the young man's arrival had changed Thomas's life forever. Just how much remained to be seen.

~

Crickets chirped, and the fire crackled in the chilly night air. Rayna stuffed her gloved hands in her pockets and huddled closer to the flames. She wanted to climb inside her sleeping bag, but her growling stomach came first. They'd brought MREs for their meals, and Thomas offered to prepare them. Mason, being curious about what they were and how they worked, had immediately abandoned her to help. Jace was off using a satellite phone to give Seb an update and check on Tara. It gave Rayna a few minutes alone with her thoughts she did not want. With no distractions, they turned to the man currently preparing her dinner. She still seethed with anger over his revelations from last night.

She was also angry at herself for letting what he thought of her matter so much. It had her all twisted up inside. She shouldn't care what he thought—they'd been over for a long time—but even with all her protestations that she was over *him*, she wasn't. It was just a lie she'd been trying to convince herself of for more than a decade. Even now, angrier than angry with him, she still wanted him to kiss her again. Why couldn't her body get the message her mind kept telling it?

Mason walked up to her, two MRE pouches in his hand. He held one out to her along with a plastic spoon.

"Thanks." She took the MRE from him and patted the log she sat on, asking him to join her.

He lowered himself with a wince.

"Your legs hurt?" She stirred her food, blowing over a spoonful of the chili to cool it down.

"Yes. I know you warned me, but I really didn't think it would be that bad. All I'm doing is sitting. At least my butt doesn't hurt too. It's just numb."

She chuckled. "Well, you're not alone. I can guarantee that even us seasoned riders have some aches after a ride like this. I haven't spent this much time in the saddle since I helped on cattle drives when I was a teenager."

He stuffed a bite of his food into his mouth and chewed, a thoughtful look on his face. "Do you really think we'll find the Smiths' place?" His voice was quiet.

Rayna shrugged. "It doesn't hurt to try."

"What if I can't remember the way? I mean, it was dark for a lot of it."

"You've already done great. From what you said, you actually walked almost forty-eight hours in total. We found the ravine you nearly stumbled into, so we've already backtracked about half that. By sundown tomorrow, we should be in the vicinity of the Smiths' house. You did the right thing by keeping the sun to your right. It gives us a direction to follow. We know we need to head north, thanks to your smart thinking." She patted his knee. "We'll find them."

He spooned another bite into his mouth, his expression still thoughtful. Rayna dug back into her food, appeasing her grumbling tummy, and prayed she was right. She couldn't stand the thought he might have to leave them so he wouldn't have to look over his shoulder for the rest of his life.

The wild, frightened whinny of one of the horses pulled Thomas from a deep sleep. He sat up and scrambled out of his sleeping bag, reaching for the tab on his one-man tent. He hurried out in just his stocking feet, dragging his jacket with him. Jace emerged at the same time. Rayna and Mason both poked their heads from their tents.

Another terrified scream came from the horses, this time followed by the loud growl of a mountain lion.

"Get the rifles," Thomas said. "Rayna, you stay here with Mason." He didn't wait for her to respond. He dove back inside his tent to grab his rifle and a flashlight. As he stuffed his feet into his boots, the big cat screeched again, and the horses shrieked. He exited the tent at the same time as Jace, and they raced toward the horses, flashlights bobbing. The beam bounced off the glowing eyes of a large but skinny cougar. It hissed at them from its position on the other side of the horses.

"Why would one dare attack a group of horses?" Jace asked.

"It looks like it might be sick, or it could have had an injury that kept it from hunting. It's really thin. A tied up horse, even in a group, is easy pickings."

The cat paced, watching them.

"It's not leaving," Jace muttered, rifle trained on it now.

"He's trying to decide if the easy meal is worth taking us on." He shined his light over the ground, looking for some decent-size rocks, seeing a few closer to the animals. "Walk forward a bit. We need to get to those rocks."

"Why can't I just shoot it?"

"Because it hasn't actually attacked us. I'm hoping we can scare it away."

They moved forward at a steady pace until they reached the stones. Thomas looped the rifle strap over his body and moved behind Jace to crouch down and pick up several rocks. Stepping out from behind the bigger man, he moved to his left until he was beyond the horses, but could see the cat. It watched him as it paced.

He palmed a rock and pulled his arm back. Aiming for the ground in front of the cougar, he let it fly. It landed at the animal's feet, making it hiss again as it moved away. Thomas threw another one at it, still aiming for the ground. The cat took two paces back and let out a loud growl, advancing.

So much for scaring it. He really hadn't wanted to hurt the cat, but it wasn't leaving him much choice. Pulling his arm back with the last rock, he hurled it at the cat's side as hard as he could. It hit the animal in the shoulder with a solid thud, making it let out a surprised snarl. It loped away several yards.

Thomas brought his rifle up and aimed at a tree to the side of the cougar, hoping the noise of the gun and the impact on the wood would be enough to finish the job and make it leave. He took a breath to steady his aim and fired. The horses all neighed and pulled at their ropes at the loud retort. The mountain lion took off running and disappeared into the trees.

Jace jogged over. "Do you think it left?"

Thomas kept his light and his eyes trained on the forest. "I'm not sure. Come on."

They moved past the horses and deeper into the woods.

"Keep an eye to the side. Mountain lions like to ambush."

Jace gave him a quick nod, his eyes moving from side to side as they walked. After about fifty yards, Thomas paused to listen.

"I think it left." He lowered his rifle. "We should probably move on, though. There are only a couple hours until daylight, and the moon is bright. I don't think any of us will get much sleep now."

"I know I won't."

Thomas wouldn't either. He was riding an adrenaline high that left him wide awake.

The two men turned around and walked back to camp. As they broke through the trees, Thomas scanned the site for Rayna, but didn't see her.

"Rayna? It's safe. The cougar ran off."

The rasp of the zipper on her tent flap met his words, and she climbed out, Mason following.

"You didn't shoot it?" she asked.

He shook his head. "I hit it with a rock, then shot a tree

next to it, and it ran away. I'm not sure it'll stay away, though, so we need to break camp."

"Why did it come so close?" she asked as she turned back to her tent to get her sleeping bag. "They don't normally mess with horses."

Thomas walked to the tent next to her, while Mason and Jace headed for theirs. "It was really thin. I think it was just looking for an easy meal."

"I hope it doesn't follow us."

"Me too."

They made quick work of breaking camp and were soon back in the saddle and headed north once more. As they rode, Thomas kept an eye on the woods, hoping that cat was the biggest danger they faced on this trip.

ELEVEN

Rayna could tell when they got close to the Smiths' property. Mason's back stiffened more with every minute they rode, and the corners of his mouth turned down. He might not be sure they were there, but his subconscious knew. She dropped back to talk to Jace.

"I think we're close."

He nodded. "I noticed the difference in him too. Does he recognize anything?"

She shook her head. "Not really. He said it looks a bit familiar, but he can't say for certain."

"Okay. Keep your eyes open. I'll tell Thomas."

She nodded again, then rode back up to Mason's side while Jace dropped back. Before she could say a word to the boy, a shot rang out and a searing pain ripped through her side, knocking her from her horse.

She hit the ground with a grunt, struggling to catch her breath, both from the shot and the hard fall. Rolling to her back, she had enough wherewithal to keep rolling when she saw Poppy rear above her. The horse's hooves came down where her head had been a split second before.

"Rayna!"

Thomas's voice cut through the cacophony of squealing horses and the sound of their riders trying to calm them.

Another shot rang out, hitting the dirt behind Mason and Bing.

"Everyone take cover!" Jace yelled.

Rayna winced and rolled again, moving behind a tree. The others finally managed to spin their horses around and find cover. Poppy followed Rayna and stopped several yards past her. Ears twitching, she let out soft whickers and snorts as she stomped her feet.

Holding her side, Rayna scooted backward and put her back to the tree, stretching her feet out in front of her. She pulled her hand away from her side to see blood covering it. Tears formed in her eyes, and she closed them tight, resting her head against the rough bark.

The rustle of someone moving through the forest to her left jumpstarted her heart. Her eyes snapped open, and she turned her head. Thomas emerged from the foliage and she breathed a little easier.

"Ray!" He hurried toward her, skidding to a stop on his knees by her side. His face turned ashen as he took in the blood on her shirt. "Fuck!"

She agreed. "Where's Mason?"

"Tucked against a tree about twenty yards back. Jace is circling toward the shooter. Let me see your wound." He knocked her hand away and pulled up her shirt.

She hissed as the material grazed the wound. "How bad is it?"

"It looks like it just grazed you, but I need to stop the bleeding. Hang tight."

She rolled her eyes as he hurried back the way he came. "Sure." Her head fell back against the tree. "I'll just wait here."

Rayna took a few deep breaths to calm herself. Her

thoughts were in a blender and she needed to be able to think straight. Another shot rang out, making her flinch. She gritted her teeth and looked behind her, past the tree. Nothing moved. Turning back, she blew out a breath. They must have tripped some motion sensor or something. They hadn't seen evidence of anyone as they rode through.

The brush rustled again and Thomas reemerged, a small canvas pack in his hands that contained the first aid supplies he carried.

~

Thomas kneeled next to Rayna, willing his hands not to shake as he took in the growing bloodstain on her shirt. He'd come very close to losing her. A few more inches to the left and he would have. He didn't want to think about that or why it mattered so much.

He unrolled the canvas pack and started removing the items he needed. "Open your shirt."

Her unsteady fingers worked the buttons free of their holes as he pulled on gloves and opened bandages. He picked up the small bottle of peroxide and flipped open the lid. His dark eyes met her violet ones, and he held her gaze for a moment. "I need to clean it. This isn't going to feel pleasant."

"Just do it." She bunched her hands around the edges of her open shirt as he raised the bottle over the wound.

With one last glance at her face, he poured the liquid on the injury. She gasped, and he winced.

"Sorry."

She made a low sound in her throat and closed her eyes.

He removed a large gauze pad from the kit and dabbed the wound once the peroxide stopped bubbling, wiping away some of the blood so he could see if he needed to stitch it closed. The bullet had torn a half-inch wide gash, three inches long, across her right flank down to the fat layer. It continued to ooze blood.

"You need some stitches." He looked down at the kit, doing his damnedest to focus on what he was doing and not on who he was treating. If he didn't, his hands would start shaking again, and he'd be worthless to her.

She moaned. "There's no lidocaine in there, is there?"

Thomas rooted through the kit and found a foil packet with two numbing swabs inside. "I have these." He showed them to her. "It won't do the job completely, but it'll be better than nothing." He ripped them open and quickly wiped them over her skin around the gash.

More shots rang out, making them both jump.

"One of those sounded different," she said.

"Yeah. I think that was Jace." He prayed it wasn't just wishful thinking.

"Why did they shoot at us? They couldn't know who we are."

"Maybe they recognized Mason even with his dyed hair. Or even Jace. He's been around long enough for people to know him and know he's a cop. Or maybe they just shoot at anyone who rides through their land." He took out a suture kit and tore it open, removing the threaded needle with a pair of forceps he doused in alcohol.

"Ready?"

She nodded. "Do it."

"Scoot down and lie on your good side."

She did as he asked, and he moved behind her.

"Okay, here we go," he mumbled, more to himself than to her. He took a deep, steadying breath and pushed the needle through her skin.

Rayna hissed, but stayed still.

"I'm sorry, honey. I'll be quick." He fought not to rush,

knowing if he did, he could make things worse. Thankfully, she only needed a handful of stitches.

Within a couple minutes, he tied off the last suture and cut the thread. "I just need to put a bandage on it now."

Noise behind him had him reaching for the rifle.

"It's me!" Jace said, emerging from the thick brush.

Thomas's shoulders fell in relief, and he set the rifle down, reaching for the bandages again.

"She okay?" He kneeled next to Thomas.

"It was just a deep graze. It's going to hurt like crazy for a few days, but she's good to go." *Thank God.*

"What happened?" Rayna asked, looking over her shoulder at Jace. "Did you find the shooter?"

He nodded. "Yep. He's dead, but I don't know that there aren't more coming."

More rustling in front of them had both men bringing their guns up. Mason came into view and they lowered them again.

"I told you to stay put," Thomas said, tearing off a piece of tape.

"Yeah, well, I got tired of waiting." He crouched in front of Rayna and took her hand. "Are you okay?"

"I'm fine. It just nicked me."

Thomas grunted at the characterization of her wound and smoothed another piece of tape over the bandage. "What's the plan, Jace?"

"We still need a location on that house. I'm going to push forward and see if I can find it. Hopefully, it'll be before they can scoot with the kids."

"You can't go alone. Let me finish cleaning Rayna up, and I'll go with you."

"No," Mason said.

Thomas looked up at Mason in surprise at the hard note in his voice.

"This is my fight. I'll go. She needs you in case she starts bleeding again. Get her out of here."

"Mason, I'm fine. You don't need to go. It's too dangerous." She looked back at Thomas, her eyes imploring him to agree with her.

As much as he wanted to stay with Rayna, she was right. They couldn't send the boy back to that house.

"She's right. You should stay here."

Mason rose. "No. I'm going." His firm tone told them there would be no dissuading him.

Thomas shared another look with Rayna. The kid was determined to go.

"We're wasting time," Jace said. "And he knows the property better than any of us. Go get the rifle from the scabbard on Poppy, kid."

Mason took off for the chestnut horse still milling in the trees a few yards away.

"Jace, no," Rayna pleaded.

"I'll take good care of him. You two get to safety and call for help. Maybe we'll get lucky and this will all be over in a couple hours."

Mason returned, holding Rayna's Winchester and a box of bullets.

"You know how to use that?" Jace asked.

"Sort of. Thomas gave me a quick lesson yesterday."

Jace stood. "Good enough. Let's go." He laid a hand on Thomas's shoulder. "Be careful. And stay in touch."

Thomas nodded. "Don't die, or my sister will kill you."

"She's going to kill me for this hair-brained idea, anyway. But I'll watch my six. Come on, kid."

The two of them ran off toward their horses, leaving Thomas and Rayna alone. He finished bandaging her wound and helped her sit up.

"Do you think you can ride?" he asked, handing her some

pain medicine, which she dry-swallowed. There was morphine in the kit, but if he gave her that, she'd fall off her horse.

"Yeah." She struggled to her feet, swaying as she stood.

Thomas wrapped an arm around her. "Are you sure?"

He felt her legs gain some starch, and she nodded. "I'm okay."

He made sure she was steady before he let go to clean up his mess and pick up his rifle. She wandered over to Poppy and pulled a clean shirt from her saddlebags, shrugging into it and buttoning it up while he stowed the med kit. She donned her jacket again and stuck a foot in the stirrup to mount her horse.

"Whoa. Let me help you so you don't tear out your stitches." He walked around Poppy and wrapped his hands around her waist, lifting as she pressed up.

"You good?"

She nodded, breathing hard.

He pulled a bottle of water from one of her bags and handed it to her. "Drink. You need the fluids."

She downed half the bottle, then handed it back to him. He stowed it back in the saddlebag, and took Poppy's reins, leading her to where he left Raven tied up. He quickly sheathed his rifle, then pulled out the GPS locator and his sat phone. They each had one for this trip in case they were separated.

Thomas turned it on and punched in the number to Seb's cell. It rang twice before his brother picked up.

"Jace?"

"It's Thomas. We've had some trouble. Rayna's been shot —just a flesh wound. The shooter's dead somewhere up here. Jace went after him while I tended her injury. You need to send the cavalry. Jace and Mason went off to find the house. Do you have a pen? I'll give you our current coordinates. We're not at the Smiths' yet, but we're close."

Sebastian let out a string of curses and Thomas heard the

rustle of papers as he looked for a pen. "Okay. Read them to me."

Thomas rattled off the location on the GPS device.

"I'll pull it up on a satellite map and see what's near there. You need to watch your back. There might be others. I ran a search for missing teenagers matching Ryan Marsters' victimology and got several hits. The girl Mason remembers may not be the only one Marsters visited. We could be looking at quite an extensive operation."

A fierce frown marred Thomas's face. He was afraid of that. "Okay. We'll be careful. We're heading out of the area because of Rayna's injuries, but I'll call you once we find a road. And don't tell Tara Jace went off alone. She'll be the first one up here if you do."

"No shit. Okay, see you soon."

Seb hung up, and Thomas put both items back in his saddlebag, then mounted his horse.

Rayna turned her horse back the way they'd just come.

"Where are you going?"

"To help Jace and Mason."

"What?" Was she crazy? "No. We need to get you home. You probably need antibiotics, and you definitely need to rest." She hadn't lost a lot of blood, but it was enough that she was going to be a bit tired for a couple days. The ride down the mountain wasn't going to help that, either.

"I'm fine. Do you want to explain to Tara why you left her fiancé up here with an eighteen-year-old kid who barely knows how to use a rifle as his only back up?"

He frowned and turned Raven around. "No. But you're in no shape to be of much use."

She looked back over her shoulder at him. "I'm *fine*. You can go find that road if you want, but I'm going that way." She pointed ahead of her.

Thomas growled. Damn stubborn woman. He gave Raven

a squeeze, sending her after Poppy and quickly catching up. "At least let me take the lead, since I have the gun," he said, coming alongside her.

Rayna pulled her horse to a halt, and he rode ahead.

"You tell me if you need a break," he said, looking back over his shoulder.

She nodded, but the look in her eyes told him she would do no such thing. He let out a frustrated sigh and turned around. She was injured just enough to make him worry, but not enough to slow her down to the point she'd listen to him. "Tara isn't the only one you have to worry about pissing off," he growled.

"She's scarier than you."

Despite his irritation, one corner of his mouth lifted in a smile. She wasn't wrong.

Thomas pushed the horses as fast as he dared through the forest. He had no idea what waited for them the closer they got to the Smiths'. There could be any number of booby traps closer to the house. Getting his horse caught in some snare, or having them all blown up by a landmine, was not on his agenda for the day.

He glanced back at Rayna, who tried to sit relaxed in her saddle, but her shoulders hunched ever so slightly and there was a pinch to her face that told him the movement was not helping her pain level.

Biting back the desire to make her turn back or rest for a while, he focused on their movement through the trees, hoping they were following Jace and Mason's path.

After ten minutes with nothing but more trees in sight, Thomas started to get discouraged. Just as he decided to stop and rethink their route, he caught a glimpse of a building through a break in the trees. He pulled up on the reins, slowing Raven to a walk. Rayna rode up beside him.

He pointed toward the house. "See that?"

She nodded.

"We should probably go on foot the rest of the way." He glanced over at her. "Can you handle that?"

She frowned at him and climbed off Poppy without a word.

Thomas muttered under his breath again. He didn't remember her being so stubborn before this.

He followed her down and pulled the rifle from its sheath and took his sat phone from his bags, stuffing it into his front pocket. "Watch your step," he murmured, coming up beside her. "And keep your head on a swivel."

"Don't worry, I will." She laid a hand over her side.

They tied up the horses and took off through the forest, pausing at the tree line to scan the clearing. A large, gray, two-story farmhouse sat in front of them. Several outbuildings were scattered around it. He didn't see any sign of Jace and Mason—or anyone else, for that matter.

"Where is everyone?" Rayna asked, echoing his thoughts.

"Not sure. Let's circle around and come up behind that garage. It'll give us more cover." Not waiting for an answer, he backed away from the tree and slipped into the woods, hurrying around the perimeter of the clearing until they were behind the detached garage.

He glanced back at Rayna. "Ready?"

She nodded.

Thomas stepped out from the trees, rifle at the ready. They ran toward the back of the garage and leaned against the wall. He glanced down at her, gauging her pain level.

"You okay?"

Her face was pinched, and her breathing rough, but she nodded. "I'll be fine. Let's get to the house."

He nodded. "Stay close."

"Like glue." She hooked her hand into his belt at the back of his waist. "You have the gun."

Heart thumping, Thomas pushed away from the garage and eased around the edge of the building to look at the house. Still, nothing moved. With his gaze swinging back and forth, he jogged toward the back door. Grasping the knob, he gave it a turn. To his surprise, it spun beneath his hand, and the door creaked open.

Nerves made his hands shake. *Fuck*. This was why he left the police stuff to Seb. He wasn't cut out for this shit.

Raising the rifle, he pushed the door open and stepped through the back door into a mudroom. He could feel Rayna's hand locked around his belt as he moved forward.

They walked into the kitchen. Half-eaten plates sat on the small table pushed against one wall, and dirty dishes littered the stove and sink. Someone left in a hurry.

Thomas walked further into the house, entering a large living room. It, too, was empty. He headed for the entrance to a hallway on the far side of the room.

"Do you think they're all gone?" Rayna whispered as they entered the darkened corridor.

"Maybe." He gestured to a room at the end of the hall with a light shining under the door. "Maybe not."

Cursing their boots, which made their approach less than quiet, they walked toward the door. Thomas tucked the rifle into his shoulder and reached out with his other hand. Grasping the knob, he turned it and pushed in the same motion, tucking them against the doorjamb to make them as small a target as possible as they stepped into what looked like an office.

Movement near the window behind a chair caught his attention. Jace rose, his own rifle pointed squarely at Thomas.

"Goddammit!" Jace lowered his gun. "What the hell are you two doing here?"

Thomas put the safety on his rifle and lowered it. "Ask

Rayna." He glanced back at her to see her scowl at him. He turned back to Jace. "Where is everyone? Where's Mason?"

The closet door opened. "I'm right here," Mason said, stepping out.

Rayna scurried around Thomas to hug the young man. He looked at Thomas, stunned, before wrapping his arms around Rayna to pat her back.

"I was so worried," she said, pulling away. "Are you okay? What happened? Why is this place empty?"

Mason cleared his throat and swallowed hard. "Um, it was empty when we got here."

"I think they bailed just before we arrived," Jace said. "I saw a couple cameras in the woods on our way in. It's likely they saw me kill their scout, then head for the house. I'm guessing they packed up the important stuff and the kids and ran."

"Did you call it into Seb yet?" Thomas asked.

Jace shook his head. "We've only been here about ten minutes. I wanted to make sure there wasn't anyone here, so we didn't get ambushed again. Did you see anyone on your way in?"

Thomas and Rayna both shook their heads.

"Have you checked the outbuildings?" Rayna asked.

"First place we looked. Mason said they hid them in the cellar a lot, which is connected to the tool shed via a tunnel. Both were empty."

Mason's face was carefully blank as Jace discussed what they'd seen. Thomas could only imagine what he was thinking and feeling right now. He clenched his jaw, fighting the urge to punch something.

"Where do you still need to search?" he asked instead.

"We haven't been upstairs yet."

"Okay." He dug his sat phone from his pocket and handed it to Rayna. "You two stay here and call Seb, then see if you can find something with their real names on it. This looks like an office, so you might get lucky." He looked at Jace. "Let's finish searching."

Jace arched a brow as Thomas barked orders, but Thomas didn't care. They stood a chance of catching the bastards if Seb could get a perimeter set up on the roads leading out of here.

"Tell Seb that if he puts a chopper or a drone in the air to look for a larger vehicle or two smaller ones traveling together. With five kids in tow, they're going to need space," Jace said, joining Thomas by the door.

She nodded. "Be careful."

Thomas gave her and Mason one last long look and walked out of the office.

TWELVE

The tailgate on her brother, Brady's, truck dipped as Tara sat down next to her. Following the cadre of law enforcement that arrived after her call to Seb, Brady and Tara had pulled in, towing a trailer for the horses.

"How are you doing?" Tara asked.

Rayna looked at her friend and offered her a tired smile. "Sore. Tired. It's been a long fucking day."

Tara laughed. "Watch yourself. You're starting to sound like me and Macy with that mouth."

Rayna grinned. "It's the truth, though. Even when London was missing and we were waiting on word about you and Jace, I didn't feel this drained."

"Well, you did get shot."

"It's not just that, though it hasn't helped. It's just been one thing after another the last few days."

Tara looped an arm around her shoulders and leaned her head against Rayna's. "It'll get better. You guys found the bad guys' hideout, which is huge!"

"Yeah. I just wish we'd found the kids too. Mason didn't say anything, but he's devastated. I hope Seb and Jace find something to tell us where they might have taken them. Have you heard anything about the drone they put up?"

She shook her head. "No."

Rayna bit her lip to hold back the tears. Those poor kids could be anywhere. She sniffed and looked around the compound. "Where are Mason and Thomas?"

"Thomas went with Jace, Seb, and Dr. Randall. I'm not sure where Mason went, actually."

Alarmed, Rayna stood, wincing as her stitches pulled. "He was with Thomas last I saw him. Did he go with them too."

Tara shook her head. "I didn't see him with the group."

Rayna walked up to the house and the deputy standing at the door. "Can you radio the sheriff and ask if Mason is with them, please?"

The deputy did as she asked. Seb's negative response was not what she wanted to hear. She looked back at the deputy. "Do you know if he's inside?"

The man shook his head. "Last time I saw him, he was near the tool shed."

"Thank you." Rayna spun around and headed toward the outbuilding, Tara following. Worry bit into her, making her break into a quick jog. They'd left him alone, assuming he was safe since the property was abandoned. But what if someone snuck back and saw him? They could have grabbed him amid the commotion.

"Mason?" She reached the door and yanked it open. The shed was empty. Worry turned to fear and burned hot in her belly. "Where is he?" She backed out of the shed. "Mason!" Tears formed in her eyes as her voice took on a frantic note.

"Rayna, calm down," Tara said, grabbing her arm. "We'll find him."

They had to. She couldn't let those monsters get their hands on him again.

A noise in the shed registered a moment before the door opened and Mason appeared.

"Rayna?"

"Mason!" Heedless of her injury, she rushed forward to wrap him in another hug. Pulling back, she shook his shoulders. "Don't ever disappear like that again. I thought someone grabbed you in all the chaos. Where were you?"

He frowned down at her. "I'm sorry. I was just looking at the old tunnel. They didn't like us talking unsupervised, so we devised a way to get messages to each other by hiding them in the tunnel. When they put us out here, they locked the door to the house, but not the trapdoor in the shed because it only locked from the shed side."

"Messages? Did you find any?"

He grinned and held up a piece of paper. "Nina dropped her list for us to find."

Rayna stared at the paper between his fingers. "List?"

"She was the bravest of us all. She'd sneak a peek at the wallets of the guys she was with and write down their names."

"Are you serious?" Tara stepped forward. She took the list from him and opened it, quickly glancing through it. "Holy shit." She looked up, her eyes going from Rayna to Mason and back again. "We need to get this to Seb."

"There's a deputy back at the—"

Tara cut her off with a wave of her hand. "No. This needs to go directly to him. I don't trust it to not 'get lost' before he sees it."

Rayna frowned. "Why? Who's on it?"

Tara turned it around, and Rayna couldn't hold back the gasp as she read it. *No. Way.*

～

The low growl of a mountain lion reached Thomas's ears as they neared the spot where Jace left the man he killed earlier. The others paused.

"Dammit." Thomas shared a look with Jace and kept walking, both men lifting their rifles.

"Thomas! Jace!" Seb hissed. "There's a cougar up there. We need a plan."

"If it's the one I think it is, it's not going to go quietly," Thomas said, not stopping. "We had an emaciated mountain lion try to take out Bing early this morning." *Jesus. Had it been less than a day still?* "We scared it off, but it must have followed us. That was a warning growl. He's going to put up a fight over our evidence."

Seb groaned and motioned to the two deputies with them. "Stay with Dr. Randall and his team."

The three of them advanced, spotting the animal after another fifteen yards. The cat let out a loud yowl, warning them further to back off.

"Are we going to shoot it this time?" Jace asked.

"Depends. How much of our dead guy did he eat?"

"Can't tell yet. We aren't close enough."

"Well, let's get closer. I wish I had a tranquilizer gun. I really don't want to kill it."

"What about my taser?" Seb asked. "Cougars weigh about as much as a man."

Thomas lowered his rifle. "That could work. But we still need to be able to restrain it once it's down."

"What about one of the tents?" Jace suggested. "We could wrap it up in it while it's stunned and tie its feet with the ropes."

"That's not a bad idea," Seb said.

"I'll go get it," Thomas said. "Don't shoot it unless you have too." He wasn't normally a bleeding heart, but when it came to animals, he would do anything he could to preserve their lives. Lowering his weapon the rest of the way, he backed away until he was out of sight of the big cat, then turned and ran toward the horses, which were tied up a few yards back so they wouldn't contaminate the scene.

Pike was closest, so he untied the tent from the back of the saddle and jogged back to his brother and Jace, doing his best to avoid crashing through the woods. He didn't want to scare the cougar off this time.

"I got it." He stopped beside Seb and unfurled the nylon tent. "I sure hope that taser of yours packs a punch, or he's going to slice through this tent like it's paper and then whoever's trying to restrain him."

"We work as a team," Jace said. "Seb, you tase him. I'll wrap him in the tent, and Thomas, you tie him up."

Thomas picked up the rope and coiled it. "We have to be quick. And we're going to have to be close when Seb tases him."

"Yep. Are we ready?"

Seb and Thomas nodded.

"Let's go."

In unison, they moved steadily toward the mountain lion and his dinner. As they cleared the trees and the scene came better into view, Thomas could see the cougar had already done a number on their dead guy. His abdomen was split open, spilling its contents onto the ground. It looked like the hungry animal had gone for the nutrient-dense liver first.

The cougar growled low in its throat and straightened from its crouch over the dead man.

"Slow and steady," Thomas whispered. He hoped Jace and Seb heard him. He could barely hear himself over the blood rushing through his ears.

With measured footsteps, they spread around the mountain lion, with Thomas in the middle, Jace on his right and Seb on the left. At fifteen feet away, the cat let out an ear-piercing roar. His muscles coiled, and Thomas knew it was now or never.

"Now, Seb!"

The taser made a pop as Seb fired it, sending the probes flying toward the mountain lion's side. The animal let out a screech and dropped as electricity crackled down the wires, paralyzing its muscles. Jace ran forward and wrapped the cat in the tent, rolling him until he was covered. Thomas took the rope and tied a quick slipknot around the animal's front feet. The whole thing only took a few seconds.

"Let up!" he yelled to his brother. The cat's spasms stopped, and it laid stunned. With Jace's help, he wrapped the rope around the cat's body and its back feet, securing it inside the thin nylon tent. As he finished, the cougar regained its faculties and began to struggle.

"Is that going to hold?" Jace asked.

"Long enough," Thomas replied, breathing hard. "We need to wrap him in a second tent and tie him a little more securely. There's some morphine in the first aid kit I can give him to calm him a bit."

"Let's do it, then. I don't relish trying to catch him again," Seb said, removing the taser cartridge from his gun and holstering the weapon.

Thomas ran back to his horse to get the first aid kit and his tent. He took a moment at Raven's side to catch his breath, glad their plan worked.

Twigs snapped behind him, and he pushed away from Raven, turning around to see Dr. Randall and Katie Mitchum striding toward him.

"Is everything okay?" The M.E. asked.

He nodded. "It's fine. We caught the cougar. I just came for reinforcements." He held up the tent and first aid kit.

Dr. Randall's eyes paused on the med kit. "Did someone get hurt?"

"No. It's for the mountain lion. I need to sedate him so he doesn't hurt himself."

"Oh. Is it safe for us to come up now?"

Thomas nodded. "Follow me." He led Randall and his crew through the trees. As the scene came into view, he could see the big cat bucking inside his nylon prison, yowling his rage.

He hurried forward and opened the first aid kit, pulling out the morphine vial and a syringe. He took a guess on the cat's weight and did some quick calculations in his head for the correct dosage and drew it up.

"Can someone hold him down?"

"You want us to touch him?" Jace said.

Thomas cast a glance at him as he put the morphine vial away. "Just lay your weight over him. He's all wrapped up; you'll be fine."

"Says the man who just gets to stick him," Jace muttered.

"I'll help," Dr. Randall said. "Where do you want me?"

"One of you hold his back feet and the other put your weight over his shoulders from behind. I'm going to stick this in his hip."

Jace and the M.E. moved around the animal and did their best to hold him still. Even skinny, he was a beast. Thomas leaned down and poked the needle through the tent fabric into the cat's rump, depressing the plunger to administer the medication. The cougar yowled at him.

"Okay, let him go," he said, straightening and backing away.

The others got up, and the animal started his struggles once more.

"How long will that take?" Seb asked.

"Not too long. Five or ten minutes."

"Can we get to work in the meantime?" Dr. Randall asked.

Thomas shrugged. "So long as your team doesn't mind working around an irate mountain lion."

Katie stepped forward. "I've been around worse things. My ex, for one. Let's get busy. They were calling for snow later up here, and I'd rather not have to set up a tent over all this. It's bad enough we're going to need lights." She looked at the sky where the sun was descending as the day waned. Sighing, she moved up near the dead man's head and set down her case, opening it.

Dr. Randall rolled his eyes and let out an exasperated sigh. "That woman is going to be the death of me," he muttered.

Seb's lips twitched. "What's the matter, Alex? Don't like sharing your space?" Katie and the rest of the county's forensic science unit had moved into the pathology lab in the hospital after Jared Fetter and Tim Jacobsen blew up their lab, trying to destroy evidence.

"No. And there isn't much sharing with her around. She's taken over my whole damn lab. How long's it going to be before the new criminology building is ready?"

Seb laughed. "A while, my friend. They just finished clearing the debris."

The M.E. gave a low grunt. "It can't happen fast enough."

"You talking about me again, Doc?"

They looked over at Katie, who crouched next to her open case, removing the items she needed to collect evidence. She glanced up at Dr. Randall over the rim of her clear pink glasses, lifting one dark brow, a reproachful look on her pretty face.

He rolled his eyes again and walked away, going to fetch his own equipment.

Thomas bit back a smile. It sounded like they'd had too much togetherness of late. He stepped back and let them get to work, going to stand next to his brother.

"Can you radio down the mountain and have them bring

up a handheld stretcher? We need a way to carry the cougar down."

Seb nodded and put in the request.

"What are we going to do with him when we get him down there?"

Thomas's lips flattened to a thin line. "I've been thinking about that. I have those pens in the barn at my clinic meant for birds. With some reinforcing, one of them should work. I was thinking we could put him in the horse trailer while he's doped up and transport him there. We need to monitor his fecal output for a day or so and collect it for evidence. In the meantime, I'll make some calls to find him a new home."

"Works for me."

Commotion in the trees drew Thomas's attention, and he turned to see Rayna, Mason, and Tara emerge from the forest. All three of them paused at the grisly sight of the dead man. Katie quickly pulled a cover over his head and upper body when she saw them, but Tara's face still turned white and she swayed.

"Babe, what are you doing up here?" Jace asked, running forward to steady her.

Thomas's eyes landed on Rayna as he walked over to them. She turned to keep the body out of her line of vision. Dark circles rimmed her violet eyes and fatigue pulled at the corners of her mouth. She really should be on her way home to rest.

"Mason went exploring," she said. "Freaked me out because he disappeared. But he found something." She nudged the young man. "Show them."

Mason held out a folded sheet of paper to Thomas. "It was in the tunnel."

Thomas took the paper and opened it.

"What is it?" Seb asked. He and Jace flanked Thomas to read over his shoulder.

"It's a list of some of the men the Smiths trafficked one of the girls to. Nina," Mason said. "She hid it in a little hole we dug out of the tunnel to pass notes through."

"How'd she get the names?" Jace asked.

"She'd peek in the wallets of the ones who were too stupid not to leave that stuff in their cars."

Thomas's eyes widened as he read the names. One in particular stood out. "Sebastian. Do you see what I see?" He pointed at a name and looked up at his brother, who frowned down at the list.

"Yep. I knew he was slime, but I didn't think he was this bad."

"Who are you—?" Jace started, then stopped as he read the name. "Brian Stillwater. The *mayor*?"

"Yep." Seb rubbed his forehead. "This is a mess. Now, I'm wondering who else might be involved." He looked at Mason. "It's no wonder you weren't believed and sent back. Stillwater has a lot of pull around here."

Mason's shoulders slumped. "So, nothing gets done. Just like before."

"The hell it doesn't," Seb retorted. "I don't like the mayor. He's a pompous, micromanaging jackass. He's also not my boss. And I have evidence he was here." He pointed at the paper in Thomas's hands.

"That's not going to hold up in court, Seb," Jace said. "It wasn't logged as evidence before it was removed."

Mason's face brightened. "Actually, it was. That's a copy I made in case something happened to the original."

"Seriously?" Seb said.

The young man nodded. "I told the forensic tech who was working the shed about the tunnel and that I wanted to see if there was anything in the hole. He asked me to show him what I was talking about. The guy took pictures and put one of those evidence markers down. I took a sheet of paper from his notepad and wrote the names down. He has the original."

"That's fantastic. Okay, Jace, go get that note and go back to town. Pick up Stillwater for questioning. I don't want it to leave your possession until we have him in custody. I don't know who we can trust."

Jace gave a curt nod. "On it." He gave Tara a quick peck on her cheek, then took off at a run toward his horse.

"How far does this go, Seb?" Rayna asked, her voice quiet. Creases marred her forehead as she frowned.

Seb rubbed his neck. "I don't know, but I'm damn sure going to find out. I can't believe something like this operated under my nose for the two years I've been here, and I had no idea." He looked to Mason. "I'm genuinely sorry. If I'd had any clue this was going on, I'd have been all over it. You can bet, though, I'm going to track down every last person who had any hand in this."

Mason stared back, studying the sheriff. "I just hope we can find the others."

Thomas laid a hand on his shoulder. "Seb will do everything he can to find them. The mayor isn't the only one around here with pull. And Seb's extends past the county."

"That's right," Seb said. "I was a fed. Our illustrious mayor is about to get his life turned upside down and inside out in any way I can think of."

Puffing up his thin chest, Mason stood straight. "I'm trusting you, and so are my friends. Please don't let me down."

"I won't."

Thomas hoped that was a promise Seb could keep.

Thirteen

With a wince, Rayna climbed from her truck. Her side burned, sharp pain lancing through her every time she twisted a certain way. Driving probably hadn't been the best idea, but she'd be damned if she was going to go back to her house and sit there, waiting. Mason was still up at the Smiths' helping Sebastian comb through the property, pointing things out the investigators would have overlooked. Those kids had several hidey-holes. She was impressed with their ingenuity and tenacity.

There was also the genuine possibility her mother would pop over, seeing she was back, and then she'd have to explain why she moved like there was a board stuck down the back of her shirt. That was a conversation she wanted to put off as long as possible.

So, here she was at Thomas's clinic. Once he and several of the deputies carried the cougar down the mountain, Brady drove it back here in the horse trailer. Rayna had stayed behind to make sure Mason was okay, then started to feel a bit like she was hovering, so she'd left. She had to remind herself that Mason was an adult, and he was in good company with Seb.

After a quick trip to the local urgent care for a wound check and some antibiotics, she'd been at a loss, so she'd driven here.

Closing the truck door, she walked up to the front of the clinic and tried the double glass doors, finding them locked. Knowing he was probably in an exam room or surgical suite, which were in the back of the building, she walked around the side and knocked on the back door. It took several moments, but soon, Thomas's veterinary assistant, Lorraine, answered her knock.

"Rayna, hi. Come in." The older woman stepped back and motioned her inside. "Thomas has been filling me in on what happened while we work on the mountain lion. Are you doing okay?"

Rayna nodded. "I'm fine. Pretty sore, but okay. Can I help with the cat?"

She shrugged and closed the door, brushing her salt and pepper bangs out of her face. "Not sure there's much you can do, but you can come on back and watch." She turned and led her down a long hallway. "We gave him some proper sedation to examine him. He's really thin. The x-rays we took showed he had a healed fracture in his left front leg. It's amazing he survived at all after an injury like that, so it's no wonder he's so skinny. Thomas thinks with some proper care, he could regain his strength and hopefully be released into the wild again."

"That's great. I'm glad he—"

"Lorraine? Who was at the door?" Thomas poked his head out of a room at the end of the hall. "Oh. Hey." He stepped into the corridor. "What are you doing here? You should be at home resting."

"I'm fine, Thomas."

"No, you're not. You got shot." His dark eyes spit fire.

Rayna's back straightened, and she narrowed her eyes.

"I'll just go keep an eye on our new patient." Lorraine slid past Thomas into the room.

He stepped forward and wrapped a hand around her bicep, leading her away.

"Where are we going? I wanted to help with the cougar."

He turned down the hallway that intersected the one they were in. "My office so you can rest."

"Thomas, I'm *fine*." Honestly, if he didn't stop trying to baby her, she was going to snap. "I went to urgent care. The doctor said your stitches looked good. He gave me a prescription for an antibiotic and sent me on my way."

His expression fierce, he twisted the knob on his office door and pushed it open, pulling her inside. "You're not fine, Rayna. You almost *died*." The stern set to his face broke then, and Rayna realized just how scared he'd been.

Her anger faded, and she stepped closer. Lifting her hands, she cradled his face. "But I didn't. I really am okay."

He covered her hands with his, shuffling his feet closer. Turning his head, he pressed a kiss to her palm, then moved his hand to the back of her neck, his fingers sliding through her silky black hair. "I almost lost you," he whispered. "I can't lose you."

Her heart flip-flopped at his soft words. Stretching up, she pressed a gentle kiss to his lips. Pulling back, she looked into his eyes, getting lost in their chocolate depths. "We have a lot to talk about."

He nodded.

"But you have a mountain lion to look after first."

"I know." He sighed. "Will you at least sit and drink some water?"

She rolled her eyes. A smile tugged at her eyes, and she stepped back. "Fine, but it has to be in the room with you and the cat. I want to watch, and not just sit here staring at your office walls."

"Deal." He took her hand and led her out of the office to the break room, where he took a water bottle from the fridge and shoved it in her hands. "Do you want something to eat too?"

"I wouldn't mind something to nibble on." Lunch felt like eons ago, and it was well past suppertime now.

He found a snack-size bag of pretzels, then took her hand again, leading her back to the room with Lorraine and the mountain lion.

The older woman looked up as they entered, running her assessing gaze over them before she smiled. Thomas led Rayna to a stool tucked into the corner.

"Sit."

"Yes, boss."

"Don't get smart. You agreed to rest."

She stuck her tongue out at him and snatched the pretzel bag from his hand. "Go." She made a shooing motion, the pretzel bag crinkling as it waved. "Attend to your patient."

Lorraine giggled, and Thomas shot them both an annoyed look before spinning toward the animal. "Has anything changed?" he asked his assistant.

She shook her head. "Nope. His breathing is steady and his heart rate is good. We get the rest of this bag of fluids in him, we can probably wake him up."

"He needs a name," Rayna remarked.

Thomas glanced at her. "We're not adopting a mountain lion as a pet. Stick to your plants."

She gave him a withering look. "I know that. But even animals in temporary shelters have names. What about Max? Like Mad Max? He certainly did everything he could to survive."

"Oh, I like that," Lorraine said.

Thomas looked down at the sleeping cat. "I guess you're Max now, bud." He turned to Lorraine. "Help me carry him out to the barn. We'll put him in the pen we use for wild birds.

I'll probably have to reinforce the wire, but he'll be sleepy for a bit yet."

She unhooked the saline bag from the pole while he grabbed a couple of syringes and a medicine vial, stuffing them into his pocket.

Rayna finished her pretzels and tossed the bag in the trash on her way to the door. She held it open as Thomas and Lorraine carried the cougar through, then skirted around them to get the back door.

Once in the barn, they laid the mountain lion on the straw covering the floor in the bird pen. Thomas removed the IV from its leg, then loaded up a syringe with the sedative reversal. He injected it into the cat's shoulder, then he and Lorraine left the cage.

"There's a roll of chain link behind the barn left over from the new kennels we just finished. I'm going to go get it so we can reinforce this wire. Rayna, can you go get the nails, a hammer, and the wire cutters from the supply room while Lorraine keeps an eye on our friend?"

She nodded and spun away, hurrying through the barn to the small room where Thomas kept tools and other miscellaneous items. Rummaging through the drawers in the workbench, she found a tub of nails and a hammer. The heavy-duty wire clippers were hanging on the pegboard on the wall. She grabbed them and headed back to the cougar's cage just as Thomas walked back into the barn carrying a roll of chain link.

Her mouth went dry as she watched him approach. The bundle wasn't light, and his muscles bulged as he held its weight, reminding her that Thomas was much more than just a vet.

He set the bundle on the ground, then went to retrieve a ladder, which he leaned against the frame of the cage.

"I'm really glad this thing is against two outside walls," he remarked. "I don't think I'd have enough fencing to do three sides. Two's going to be pushing it." He studied the fencing before taking the hammer from her and several nails from the bucket.

Climbing the ladder, he hammered the nails in a line across the top board, then came back down to unroll the edge of the chain link.

"This is going to be a bitch." He stared up the ladder at the nails holding the fencing.

"Can we cut off a section first?" Rayna asked.

"We're going to have to. It's too heavy and awkward for me to hold with one hand and climb." He laid the end on the ground in the middle of the aisle. "Stand on that."

Rayna did as he asked, and he unrolled the fencing, eyeballing the length and cutting off a piece. He climbed the ladder again with the chain link and hung it over the nails.

"I need the hammer."

Rayna passed it up to him, and he bent the nails over the fencing to hold it in place, then added more nails to the cage framework, securing it in place. They repeated the process three more times to cover the walls of the ten-by-ten cage. By the time they were done, the cougar was fully awake and pacing, making low noises in his throat as he watched them work.

Thomas cut the links around the door, so they could open the cage, securing it to the door itself.

"You think that'll hold him?" Lorraine asked.

"I hope so. The frame is bolted to the barn itself, and I put nails everywhere to hold the fencing on. We'll just have to be careful feeding him, so he doesn't push through the door. I'm going to run and get some hinge locks to add some strength to it. Can you stay here with him?"

She nodded. "Of course. Max and I are buddies now."

He smiled at her. "Thanks, Lorraine."

She waved a hand. "Sure thing, Doc."

"Have you called the cougar rescue yet?" Rayna asked.

He shook his head. "Haven't had a chance."

"Why don't you do that, and I'll go get the locks."

He narrowed his eyes. "You should be resting."

She glared right back. "Don't start that crap again. I'll rest tonight."

"Fine," he huffed.

She grinned in victory and started toward the clinic.

FOURTEEN

Thomas walked into the sheriff's department on his way home from the clinic later. He smiled at the young deputy behind the front desk. The young man straightened.

"You're one of the sheriff's brothers, aren't you?"

Thomas glanced at the deputy's name tag.

"I'm Thomas. It's nice to meet you, Deputy Reeves. Can you buzz me in so I can go talk to him?"

Reeves hesitated. "He's in interrogation right now."

Now Thomas *really* wanted to go talk to him. He had a few words for the mayor.

"I can wait in his office or one of the conference rooms."

The young deputy hesitated another moment. Thomas arched a brow, silently asking to be let in.

Reeves sighed and pressed a button. He pushed a visitor's badge through the slot in the plexiglass. Thomas pinned it to his shirt as the door to his right buzzed.

"You know where his office is?"

Thomas nodded and pushed the door open. "Yep. Thanks." He had no intention of sitting in Seb's office.

He wandered down the hall, crossing the bullpen, heading

in the general direction of his brother's office. Once he was sure the deputy couldn't see him, he veered away and headed for interrogation, ducking in the door to the viewing room of the only interrogation room in use.

Seb looked up as he walked in, and Thomas gave him a sheepish grin.

"I thought you'd be on the other side of the glass." He stepped in and shut the door.

"I was." Seb arched a brow. "What are you doing here?"

"I wanted to hear what the asshole had to say for himself." He motioned to the glass, where the mayor fidgeted at the table opposite Jace.

Seb sighed. "You shouldn't be here, Thomas."

He frowned at his older brother. "Humor me. I'd like to be able to tell Mason something when I go home."

"Home?" Seb arched a brow.

Thomas flushed, realizing he'd called Rayna's house home. It wasn't far from the truth, though. He felt more "at home" there than he did in his own house. Everything that made a house a home was at her place.

He cleared his throat. "You know what I meant. What has he said so far?" he asked, changing the subject.

"Not much. He tried to tell us we had nothing, but then we showed him the list Nina wrote, and he turned white. Clammed up and asked for a lawyer. Jace is in there just to make him uncomfortable while we wait on his attorney."

"Any idea who he hired?"

"Steven Amherst."

"Is that good or bad?"

"Bad if we can't build an airtight case. He's good."

The door to the other room opened, and a man in his mid-fifties wearing a dark blue suit and gray tie stepped in, carrying a briefcase.

"That's Amherst," Seb said.

Thomas stepped closer to the window to watch. Seb turned up the volume on the speaker as Jace rose to greet the lawyer.

"Deputy Travers. It's nice to meet you. I hope you haven't been questioning my client without me present," Amherst said, taking a seat next to Stillwater.

Jace returned to his own seat and shook his head. "No. I've just been keeping him company while we wait on you."

A corner of Amherst's mouth quirked in a knowing smile. "I see. That's very nice of you." He looked at the mayor. "Is that what he's been doing?"

Stillwater nodded. "He hasn't said a word other than to ask me if I wanted a drink after I asked for you."

Amherst gave a short nod. "Good. Let's get started so you can go home, shall we?"

Jace snorted. "Okay. Yeah, sure."

"So, it seems you think my client is part of some child trafficking ring."

"We have evidence linking him, yes." He slid the note across the table for the attorney to see.

The lawyer perused the note and slid it back. "You have his name on a piece of paper."

"That we found at a property where the trafficked children were held."

"It still proves nothing. Not without the child's testimony. Do you have her?"

Thomas frowned. So did Seb and Jace.

"How do you know it's a girl who wrote the note?" Jace asked, picking up on his pronoun choice.

Amherst's eyes widened slightly for a split second. "It looks like a young girl's handwriting."

Seb inhaled a sharp breath. "Sonofabitch! He's in on it too."

"You're sure?" Thomas looked at his brother, then back at the lawyer.

"I'd bet my badge. Fuck! We're legally bound to share all evidence with Stillwater's attorney. This case just got a lot more difficult."

Thomas's heart leaped into his throat. "Mason. He's going to be listed on the witness statements."

"Yep."

He pulled out his cell. "Rayna was supposed to pick him up from the ranch and go home."

"Call her and tell her to stay on the Broken Bow. I think I'm glad you moved in with her now."

"I'd still feel better if you posted a deputy." He thumbed through his contacts until he got to Rayna. Touching the phone icon, he called her.

"Don't have a reason to without concrete evidence. My gut feeling won't cut it. But I might be able to work up a volunteer rotation like we did when Marsters targeted London."

He nodded as the phone call connected.

"Hey, where are you?" he said in lieu of greeting.

"Getting ready to head home. We just got in the truck."

"Go back inside and stay there until a deputy or I show up."

"What? Why?"

"I'll explain everything later; just please, listen to me. Mason's safety depends on it."

There was a moment of silence as she digested what he said. "Okay. Do you think it'll be long? We're both ready to eat and go to bed."

He cast a glance at Seb, who stared through the window, listening to Jace's conversation with Amherst. "Not sure. Hopefully not."

"All right."

"Tell Brady and Dad to lock the doors and keep an eye out."

"Jesus, Thomas. What's going on?"

"It's just a precaution. I need to go. I'll see you soon."

She let out a tired sigh. "Fine."

They said goodbye, and he pocketed his phone, tuning back into the conversation happening in the interrogation room.

"Look, at the most, you have my client on suspicion of solicitation."

"Of a minor. Which is a felony."

"Prove it." Amherst's smile told them he knew they were grasping at straws without more evidence.

Jace returned Amherst's empty smile. "Oh, I will. In the meantime, I have enough to hold your client for twenty-four hours."

Stillwater blanched.

"Fine." Amherst pushed his chair back. "Unless there's anything further, I think we're done. Brian, I will be by in the morning. I'm sure with a few phone calls, we can get this mess cleared up."

"You're leaving me in here?"

"Unfortunately, yes. Deputy Travers is correct. And with the late hour, I'm afraid you're stuck." He patted Stillwater on the shoulder. "But don't worry. I'm sure we can get this straightened out and clear your name."

Thomas didn't miss the undercurrent of a threat that ran through Amherst's words and the look he aimed at the mayor.

Stillwater swallowed hard and nodded.

Amherst rose and held out a hand to Jace, who also stood.

"Deputy, again, nice to meet you. I'll be in touch."

"I'm sure." Jace glanced back at Stillwater. "Sit tight. I'll have someone come take you to a cell." He punched in a code on the wall and motioned Amherst from the room, following behind.

Seb shut off the speaker in disgust, turning to the door. Jace walked in a moment later, his mouth set in a grim line. He nodded to Thomas in greeting.

"Anyone else think that attorney's as dirty as my boots after I walk through the pasture?"

"Yep," Seb said. "Our number one priority right now is to keep Mason safe. Then we need to find the rest of those kids."

"If they're even still alive."

Thomas closed his eyes at that thought. He didn't want to think it was possible, but having seen Mason's injuries, he wouldn't discount the possibility.

"I'm heading out to the ranch. Let me know when you put together that rotation," he said to Seb.

His brother nodded. "Watch yourselves."

"We will."

He stepped from the room, determined to do what he could to protect his family. Let Stillwater's buddies come try something. They'd find out being a rancher's son left him with plenty of skills to protect those he loved.

FIFTEEN

Rayna's side burned. She stacked the last empty crate in the wagon attached to her UTV and climbed into the passenger seat. Mason sat in the driver's seat and started the engine. She'd been teaching him to drive the last couple days as they finished the prep work for her fall market. All the available produce was out and ready for tomorrow's customers. They opened bright and early at eight a.m.

"Can we have pizza?" he asked as he drove them to the greenhouse to offload the wagon.

She closed her eyes and rested her head against the seat. "I texted Thomas a little while ago to bring something home with him. I'm not sure what it'll be."

He pulled up behind the large plexiglass building she'd added a couple years ago and climbed out to unhitch the wagon. Too tired to help, she stayed in the UTV and waited.

The utility vehicle rocked as he got back in.

"You going to fall asleep?"

She smiled, her eyes still closed. "Maybe." Despite telling Thomas she'd take it easy, she'd done very little resting the last couple days. After that first night, she hit the ground running. The time leading up to the fall market was always one of her busiest. Even with Mason's help, they worked sunup to sundown the last two days. She was just glad she finished harvesting her other crops before all the trouble started.

"You should go to bed after you eat. Your body could probably use the extra rest."

She scoffed and opened her eyes to look at him. "You're one to talk. I saw you flexing that shoulder earlier. Thomas will have your head if you throw it out of place again."

He rolled his eyes. "It's fine"

"Mmm-hmm." She smiled and closed her eyes again. "Be sure to tell him that when he puts it back into place."

Mason laughed. It was a sound Rayna loved to hear. Even with all the uncertainty in his life at the moment, he was finding joy. They hadn't had any trouble at the ranch, but the threat hung over their heads. Everyone in the county knew what the police found at that house and that the mayor was involved. He was out of jail, pending formal charges, and keeping a low profile so far.

The UTV came to a halt, and Rayna opened her eyes with a sigh. She didn't want to move. But she did want to eat. Thomas's truck was parked next to hers, so she knew her supper awaited.

Mason jogged ahead of her, holding the door open. She crossed the threshold and smiled at Thomas, who was in the process of spreading food onto three plates.

"No pizza?" Mason pouted.

Thomas grinned. "Not this time. I stopped at Boone's and got cheeseburgers and fries all around." He held out a plate to the young man.

Mason took it with an answering grin. "I suppose that works just as well. Thanks." He walked out of the kitchen to sit at the table, leaving Rayna alone with Thomas. They'd yet to talk about their relationship. With Mason sitting only feet away, she didn't see it happening now, either.

She was still confused, anyway. And angry. But getting shot and seeing how upset he was helped temper that somewhat. He never had been very good at expressing how he felt.

Taking the plate he offered, she joined Mason at the table, eating her dinner to quiet conversation. She learned that the mountain lion sanctuary had come today to pick up Max and take him to his new temporary home. She was sad she hadn't gotten the chance to say goodbye, but glad he was being properly looked after. The cat was a survivor. Her eyes slid to the boy to her right. Just like Mason.

They finished eating, and Rayna excused herself. Her side was on fire, and she just wanted to go to bed.

In the bathroom, she took a quick shower. Toweling off, she stood in front of the mirror, looking at the angry red slash across her ribs. The skin puckered where the stitches held it together. Her hands shook as she donned her underwear and nightgown, remembering the blood that seeped through her fingers as she held pressure on the wound. The injury could have been much more serious if Thomas hadn't been there to stop the bleeding.

She shut off the bathroom light and walked into her bedroom, pulling back the covers and climbing into bed, moaning as her head hit the pillow. Morning would come way too soon for her liking.

After several minutes of trying to find a comfortable position, she got up and went back to the bathroom, downing more pain meds. Getting back into bed, she laid on her back, propped against several pillows, and closed her eyes, waiting for the medicine to kick in.

Half an hour later, her side feeling better, she still couldn't shut her mind off and fall asleep. She'd heard Mason go to bed and Thomas retreat to the bathroom to shower. Figuring now was a good time to get a cup of tea and get back to bed without talking to him, she got up, tiptoeing to the kitchen.

She took a mug from the cabinet and heated some water, steeping an herbal tea bag while listening to the water run through the pipes as Thomas showered.

An image of his naked chest, slick with water, popped into her mind. She gripped the counter and shook her head to dispel the idea. Thinking about him like that would not help her sleep. It would just make her lie there wide awake for an entirely different reason.

She heard the shower shut off as she took the milk from the fridge and stirred some into her tea. Realizing she needed to hurry if she wanted to make it back to her room before he emerged, she put the milk away and set her spoon in the sink. She picked up the mug and retreated down the hallway. Her heart thumped. Another ten steps and she was home free.

The bathroom door opened.

Noooo! I was so close!

Rayna shut her eyes as Thomas stepped into the hall, desperate to block out the sight of those damn gray sweats riding low on his hips. His naked chest, still damp from the shower, glowed softly in the hallway lit by a single nightlight. His dark hair fell in slick waves around his head, and fine black hair dusted his chest and abs. She clenched her hands around her tea mug to stop herself from touching.

"Can't sleep again?"

She opened her eyes to see him gesture to the tea clenched in her hands, oblivious to the effect he had on her. Sucking a quick breath through her nose, she nodded.

He cocked his head, studying her for a moment. "Why don't we go sit outside for a bit? We haven't had much of a chance to talk the last couple days."

No. Absolutely not. Not with him fresh out of the shower, looking like Poseidon as he rose from the sea. She cleared her throat. "Um, I'm pretty tired. I just needed this to help shut my mind off."

Those dark eyes watched her, glittering like black diamonds in the low light. She felt her resolve wavering.

He smashed it to bits when he stepped closer and wrapped his hand around one of hers, pulling it away from the cup she carried.

"Come on. I'm not ready to fall asleep yet either." He took a couple steps toward the living room, and Rayna felt her feet follow. *Dammit.*

Thomas grinned and walked faster. Rayna sighed internally. Why did she do this to herself?

With her hand tucked into his, he led her into the living room, where he shrugged into his coat, foregoing a shirt and fueling all her sexy rancher fantasies. He just needed to stick his cowboy hat on—and swap those sweats for some tight jeans. But she wasn't complaining about the pants. They were just as hot in their own way.

Like a lemming following the leader to its doom, she followed him outside to the porch. The chilly air against her bare legs helped to chase away the spell he put on her. She set her tea on the table while he removed a blanket from the chest. When he offered it to her, she took it, wrapping it around herself.

"Are you warm enough, or do you want to go back inside?"

Oh, how she wanted to go back in. And straight to bed. With him. No, it was much better to stay out here where the cold kept her from stripping them both of what little clothing they wore.

"I'm fine." She snaked one hand out of the blanket to pick up her tea and take a drink.

Thomas pulled the lapels of his coat together, tucking the jacket closer to his body.

Not trusting herself to speak, she sat there and sipped her tea, waiting for him to say whatever was on his mind.

He rested his head in his hand, his elbow propped on the armrest, and stared out over the yard. The bright moon overhead allowed her to make out the muscles ticking in his jaw as he thought.

"I've been an idiot." His quiet voice broke the silence. Rayna looked at him over the top of her tea mug. She wouldn't argue with him there.

"And for a lot longer than the last few months." He sighed and leaned forward, resting his elbows on his knees and clasping his hands.

"I don't regret telling you I wasn't ready for a family. I wasn't, and me pretending otherwise would have been disastrous. I was young and immature. Children would have forced me to grow up, but I'm not sure I wouldn't have been a little resentful—toward you, not them—for taking away what I viewed then as a time for fun. I needed those years to grow up on my own." He looked over at her. "What I regret is not having a talk with you like this and laying out how I felt instead of just telling you I wasn't ready and letting things end. By the time I realized that, it was too late. You moved on, and any chance I had of mending our relationship was gone. I destroyed that, and I'm sorry."

Rayna sipped her tea and digested what he just said. He wasn't entirely at fault for the way things ended all those years ago. She knew he was a bit immature, but truthfully, she had been too. She'd been so in love and didn't have the experience to see reality through those rosy glasses. In hindsight, telling him she wanted to get married and potentially have kids soon when he was just starting vet school hadn't been the best idea.

"We both destroyed it. You by running away and me by pushing the issue of marriage in the first place. I was so scared of losing you because you were leaving, I lost you anyway for an entirely different reason. Neither of us were ready for what I wanted. But you're right that it didn't have to end. We just didn't have the maturity to figure out how to make it work."

"What about now? Can we make it work now?"

Her breath caught at what he proposed. Did she want to go down that road with him again? Being around him was like being pulled into the sun. She didn't want to get burned. Their break-up had nearly crushed her. She wasn't sure she wanted to put herself in a place where he could do that to her again. But she wasn't sure it would matter. She did her best not to think about him with other women, but if he ever got serious enough about someone to marry her, she had a feeling it would hurt just as much as their break-up.

She swallowed a sip of her tea and looked away in thought. "I'm not sure. We're different people now. And I'm still pissed at you for the way you've acted lately. That really hurt, Thomas. And it colored the way I thought everyone else viewed my actions too. I'm just now starting to not feel so guilty when I'm around your sister."

He winced and sat back. "I'm sorry. The anger came from a place of jealousy and fear. Seeing you with another man—I didn't handle it well. Then, when we found out who he was, fear for what could have been—for both you and my sister— made me lash out, and I blamed you, even though I knew you had no clue what Fetter was up to." He held up a hand. "I'm not making excuses for my behavior. I'm just trying to explain why I reacted the way I did. I let my emotions get the better of me instead of thinking things through."

She stared at him through the darkness, weighing his words. He reached over and took her hand.

"I'm just asking for another chance, Ray. I know we're different people than we used to be, but we've become friends through the years. That has to count for something. We can take things slow."

She pursed her lips. He made a good argument. Though she wasn't sure how long the slow part would last. Not with the way her body reacted to his. Even now, through the seriousness of their conversation, she was aware of him.

"So, what do you say? Will you go on a date with me?"

Staring into his dark eyes, the feelings she had for the young man he used to be surfaced. Yearning, desire, and love all battled for a place inside her. But how much of what she felt now was for the man she remembered, and not the one she knew now? Didn't she owe it to both of them to figure that out?

Praying she wasn't making another mistake in the romance department, she turned her hand over in his to lace their fingers together. "Okay. Yes, I'll go on a date with you."

Arms full of produce crates to restock the bins in the market, Thomas rounded the corner from the storage building. At this rate, Rayna would be out of produce by the time the weekend ended.

"Oh!"

His muscles flexed as he fought to keep the crates from toppling as he stopped short to avoid running over Adelaide Martin. Peppers tipped out of the top crate and bounced over the grass.

"I'm so sorry," she said.

Thomas set his load down with a sigh, eyeing her warily. Glancing around, he noted there weren't any people close enough for him to wave down as a chaperone. Where was Mrs. Chisholm and her well-timed entrance when he needed her?

He looked back at Adelaide. "It's okay. I wasn't watching where I was going. What are you doing here?" He hadn't seen much of her in the last few months, which was fine with him.

He hadn't missed her pursuit of him one bit, even if the reason for her absence was terrible. It was good she was getting the help she needed to get over what Ryan Marsters had done to her. It was even better that she stayed away from him in the process.

"I brought some brochures by from other local businesses. Rayna was going to display them for the customers to take." She picked up a pepper that had rolled near her feet.

He'd forgotten that Tara told him Adelaide was creating a cooperative marketing program for the local businesses. "So, why are you over here and not up at the market building?"

"I saw how busy things were and offered to help. She asked me to get a crate of tomatoes." She smiled at him, her eyes a little sad. "Don't worry. I didn't come to corner you."

Surprise made him straighten and stare at her as she read his thoughts.

She laughed. "I'm well-aware of how I used to be, Thomas. I'm not that woman anymore. Marsters and my therapist have made sure of that."

"How *are* you doing?" he asked, genuinely interested and feeling a bit of shame for his earlier thoughts.

"Better than many people thought I would—me included. It hasn't been easy, but I decided to use the experience positively. I didn't like myself before Ryan abducted me. Didn't like the bitchy tramp I'd become. I'm sorry I ever made you uncomfortable. You were the kind of man I always wanted, but I knew I didn't deserve you. I'm hoping to change that."

His eyes widened.

"No!" She laughed again. "I didn't mean you. You were always Rayna's. But someone like you is what I'd like to find someday. I need to finish fixing myself first, though."

"I have to say, I'm impressed. The girls have been telling me you're different, but I didn't believe them. But you really are. I'm sorry it took what happened to you to make you want to change, but I'm glad you're using it to better yourself. If there's anything I can do, let me know."

She gave him a sly look, and he immediately wondered what kind of trap he'd just walked into.

"How about giving me your marketing business?"

He laughed. "Is that all? I don't have much need for marketing. I already have all the business I can handle and then some. But yes, if I find myself in need of advertising, I will call you first."

She grinned back at him. "I do websites too. I noticed yours kinda sucked." She sauntered past him toward the storage shed. "Call me."

Shaking his head, he picked up the rest of the peppers while she got the tomato crate. He picked up the three crates Rayna sent him for as she walked back out of the building.

"I met your new friend. Mason," she remarked, falling into step beside him.

"Yeah?"

"Yep. He seems nice. London told me about him."

He looked at her sharply. Up until a couple days ago, Mason's existence was supposed to be a secret. They still weren't making it well-known who he was. To the casual observer, he was just a worker on the Double Moon.

"It wasn't idle gossip. She wanted to know if I thought my therapist could help him. From what I can tell, he's dealing with it pretty well on his own, but something like that—he definitely needs to talk to someone."

"Yeah. Actually, I'm glad she thought of you. Rayna and I talked about finding him some help, but neither of us really knew where to start. So, do you think your therapist could help?"

She nodded. "Definitely. I'd be happy to talk to him too if he needs someone who gets it."

"Really? That's great, Adelaide. Thank you." They reached the market shed, which still teemed with people.

"You're welcome. Just let me know."

"We will."

"We will what?" Rayna asked, coming up to them and taking the top crate off his stack.

"Call Adelaide if Mason needs someone to talk to outside of us and a therapist."

Rayna paused a moment to give the other woman an assessing stare before nodding and walking toward the produce bins on the side wall. "Yes. If anyone around here would understand, it would be you."

Thomas and Adelaide followed and set their crates on the floor to unload them into the bins.

"Where is he, anyway?" Thomas asked.

Her lips twitched. "Driving the hay wagon."

Thomas's eyes widened. "You let him drive the tractor? He's only had a handful of driving lessons."

"Relax. He's a smart kid and has picked it up quick. I'm going to stop in town on Monday and pick up a driver's license packet for him so he can study for the test."

"That reminds me," he said, stacking peppers. "I need to file the paperwork to get his birth certificate. Now that his secret's out, we can start getting all that in order."

Adelaide laughed, and they both turned to look at her, frowning.

"What?" Thomas asked.

She waved a hand at them. "You two sound like parents. I think having you guys around is the real secret why Mason's doing so well. You love him, and he's picked up on that."

He glanced at Rayna to see a contemplative look on her face as she considered what Adelaide said. Thomas hadn't given exactly how he felt about Mason all that much thought.

He just knew the boy had become important to him, and he would do anything to make sure he was safe.

Commotion outside drew their attention. At the sound of raised voices, Thomas hurried out of the building to see April Stillwater standing next to the tractor, yelling in Mason's face.

Thomas broke into a run, reaching them in seconds.

"Mrs. Stillwater, what are you doing?"

She turned glassy eyes on him. "You stay out of this. This is between me and this... this *whore*."

Fury ignited in Thomas's chest. He clenched his fists and sucked in a breath, ready to give her a piece of his mind.

Rayna beat him to it. She pushed between them, fury making her violet eyes spark. "If you ever call him that again, you'll say your next words without your teeth. Mason's done nothing wrong."

April swayed on her feet, and Thomas realized she was drunk off her ass. Adelaide, who was watching the exchange, stepped closer, ready to catch the woman if she fell.

"If it wasn't for this—*boy*, my husband would never have been arrested."

"Your husband is in trouble because he gets his jollies raping children," Rayna retorted. "Stop taking your anger out on others and put it where it belongs. Go yell at him."

The woman's face turned bright red. She shook a finger in Rayna's face. "You're as complicit as that kid you're protecting. Neither of you are safe. Brian will *ruin* you. He has friends!"

That caught Thomas's attention. He wrapped a hand around Rayna's wrist and pulled her back so he could talk to the irate woman.

"Tell me about these friends, Mrs. Stillwater."

"They're powerful and will avenge my husband. You won't get away with any of this!"

"Uh-huh," he placated. "Who should I be on the lookout for?"

She opened her mouth to reply, but some part of her brain was still working through the alcohol, and she snapped it shut. Narrowing her eyes, she backed up. "They'll find you, and you'll all pay." She turned around, getting her feet crossed and stumbling several steps.

Adelaide reached out and grabbed the woman's elbow to steady her. "Mrs. Stillwater, you can't drive. Let's go over here and have a seat. I'll call you a cab."

She yanked her arm away. "I'm fine!" Her eyes traveled past Adelaide toward the crowd she'd drawn with her outburst, and she burst into tears.

Rayna brushed past him to go to the woman and help Adelaide get her inside. Thomas looked back at Mason, who stood next to the tractor, that carefully blank look on his face as he watched them walk away.

"Mason."

The boy looked at him, muscles working in his jaw. "She's right," he whispered. "I am a whore."

"No, you're not." Thomas's gut clenched. He glanced around at the people still milling about, watching for more drama. "Come with me." He placed a hand on Mason's arm and steered him toward the house. They stopped near the large oak in the backyard.

Reaching out, Thomas put a hand on each of the young man's shoulders and looked him in the eye. "Listen to me. You are not a whore. What was done to you—it didn't make you anything but a victim. You didn't choose to do those things."

"Sometimes I did," he said, voice thick. His eyes met Thomas's for a moment before he looked away in shame. "When I was tired of fighting back, I just did it."

Thomas inhaled a sharp breath. "It was still never your choice. Without the Smiths, you would never put yourself in a position to sell your body. It wouldn't even cross your mind. And you *never* have to do it again. You. Are. Not. A. Whore. Mrs. Stillwater is mad because everyone now knows how much of a slimeball her husband is. And from what she said, they're about to find out she's pretty slimy herself. The dominoes are crumbling and the players are lashing out." He moved his head to catch Mason's gaze. "No matter what anyone says, this is *not* your fault, okay?"

Mason nodded, and Thomas tugged him into his chest for a hug, heart thumping as he held the boy. His anger at April Stillwater surged as Mason wrapped trembling arms around him and hot tears splashed onto Thomas's shoulder. Someone needed to pay—and pay dearly—for what they'd done to this kid.

A cool breeze blew through the market building as Rayna closed up for the night much later than she intended. Once they calmed April Stillwater down, they'd called Seb. He'd taken her back to the station to find out what she knew about her husband's "friends." Word about what happened spread through town, and soon she had twice the customers. Locking the register, she moved it to a shelf to the left of the flip down counters, then lifted the counter and locked it into place to shutter the window.

The door opened, and Thomas shouldered his way in carrying another stack of crates to replenish the produce bins.

"This was everything left in the storage building." He set the crates near the bins.

She came over and helped him unload it all, groaning as she straightened. "My whole body hurts. Can we get pizza?"

He laughed. "How about some of my mom's home cooking instead? Jace called while I was in the other building.

He has an update for us and said everyone's gathering at Mom and Dad's."

Rayna giggled. "I'm not so sure about that. She *did* try to put relish on barbacoa."

He grinned. "The fancy stuff is more Tara's thing. I'm sure it'll be something much more traditional. Like meatloaf. Or fried chicken."

She sighed and headed for the door. "So long as it's comfort food, I don't care." They exited the building, locking the door.

As they crossed the yard to the house, Thomas called to Mason, who was restacking hay in the wagon. He looked up, and they motioned him over. The boy jumped from the wagon and jogged over.

"You up for a family dinner?" Thomas asked.

Mason straightened, surprise crossing his face, along with a healthy dose of apprehension. "What do you mean?"

"My parents invited us over for supper. Jace has some information on the case, and Mom decided she wanted to cook for us all. It's just family. My parents, Jace, Tara, Seb, his wife and her niece, and my other siblings —family."

Mason took a deep breath, then nodded. "Sure."

"Good. Let's go get cleaned up. I'm starving."

"Me too," Rayna echoed.

The three of them hurried inside and changed, then piled into Thomas's truck, making the short journey to the Broken Bow.

Noise greeted them when they walked inside Lee and Jenny's house, most of it coming from the kitchen. Thomas led the way, the sound growing louder as they reached the room.

Jenny looked up as they entered, a smile spreading over her pretty face. "Good, you're here. We can eat."

"It's about damn time," Tara said. "I was about to dig in whether Mom let me or not."

Jenny thrust a bowl of potatoes at Tara. "Take that in the dining room and leave your brother alone."

Tara took the bowl, sticking her tongue out at Thomas as she passed. Rayna covered her mouth to hide the grin. She didn't want to start a war at dinner.

"Can I help, Mom?" Thomas asked.

She waved a hand. "Grab the salad bowl."

Thomas picked it up while Rayna grabbed the basket of dinner rolls. Jace snagged a platter of fried chicken from the counter, and Lee picked up the other one. They filed into the dining room where Tara sat, already piling potatoes onto her plate. She lifted a brow at them, then looked at Jace and pointed at the table in front of her. "You can set that right there."

With a flourish, he set it in front of her. The murderous look she gave him only made him laugh. He sat next to her and draped an arm over the back of her chair.

Jenny sat on Tara's other side. "You just couldn't wait, could you?"

Tara turned. "Excuse me, I'm eating for three, thank you, and I didn't have a snack this afternoon."

Jenny patted her hand. "I'm just teasing. I remember how hungry I was all the time when I was pregnant with you and Thomas. I never felt full." She picked up her fork and speared a piece of chicken. "It was a struggle not to gain a hundred pounds."

Tara groaned and put down the third piece of chicken she just picked up. She patted her belly. "Sorry, babies. You'll have to share."

Jace took the piece of chicken she put back. "I'll eat it for you, babe."

She rolled her eyes, making Rayna grin. It was nice to see

Tara being herself again.

The group made quick work of filling their plates and digging in. Conversation was sparse as they appeased their hunger.

Rayna cast a glance at Mason beside her. When Tara first glared at them all, she'd seen some fear on his face, but he'd relaxed since then, no doubt lulled by the amazing food.

"So, how are you liking it here?" Jenny asked Mason, shattering his relaxed mood by putting him in the spotlight. The young man stiffened next to her and he set his fork down, clearing his throat.

"It's nice. Rayna and Thomas have been great."

Jenny smiled sweetly at the two of them. "Yes, I imagine they'd make wonderful parents, don't you think?"

One corner of Mason's mouth ticked up. "I guess so."

"Hmm." She eyed the two of them, and Rayna felt her face flush. Now that she'd decided to go out with Thomas, all the things she hadn't dared to let herself dream were resurfacing. The number one item on that list was children of her own.

"Mom..." Thomas narrowed his eyes at her.

Jenny held up her hands. "What? I want grandchildren."

"Tara's having twins! And Seb just got married. Why don't you work on him and London first?"

She grinned. "A woman can never have enough grandbabies. And with five children all over thirty except for one, I should have oodles by now." She scooped up a bite of potatoes. "Get busy." She slid the fork between her lips as Rayna's face turned twelve shades of red and Thomas choked on the sip of water he just took. Lee laughed at his wife and their children.

"That means you too, Brady," Jenny said, pointing at him with the utensil.

"I don't even have a girlfriend."

"I know someone willing to fill that bill," Tara said with a wicked smile.

Rayna laughed, glad the heat was off her and Thomas. While she might be dreaming of children again, it didn't mean she was ready for them.

"Who?" Brady asked, bewildered.

Tara hummed a non-answer and took a bite of her chicken.

He looked at Rayna, squinting. "Who is she talking about?"

She reined in her smile and shrugged, taking a drink. She was not about to tell him Macy fancied him. Being banned from Peppy Brewster was not on her to-do list.

He glared at them both. "This conversation has grown tiresome." He looked at Seb. "Update us on Mason's case."

The mood around the table altered as everyone turned their attention to Seb. Rayna shifted forward on her seat, eager to hear what progress Seb and Jace had made on finding the Smiths and the other children.

"There isn't too much to tell. We pulled the mayor's phone records. There were a few calls made from his cell to some burner phones. We're also looking at people he knows in positions of power because of what his wife said earlier. But that's quite an extensive list since he's the mayor. Mrs. Stillwater clammed up at the station, then Amherst showed up and we had to let her go."

Rayna frowned. The people April ranted about could be anyone from a lowly police officer to the governor or even a state representative.

"The drone we sent up for aerial surveillance didn't find any sight of a van or two vehicles driving close together, which makes me think they have another site nearby where they're hiding out." He looked at Mason. "Did you ever overhear them talking about another property or a friend's house?"

Mason frowned down at his food. "I'm not sure. I'll think about it, but nothing is coming to mind right away."

Seb nodded. "Even if it seems inconsequential, tell me or Jace."

"I will."

"What about the guy Jace shot?" Thomas said. "Do we know who he is?"

"Actually, that was interesting," Jace said. "Katie got a DNA match. Turns out he was kidnapped when he was two. The Smiths must have raised him as their own."

"Wait," Mason said. "Are you talking about Adam? *That's* who you shot? I didn't get a good look at him the other day."

"Who's Adam?" Rayna asked.

"I thought he was the Smiths' son. He called them Mom and Dad. They used him like a guard. When they weren't around, he kept an eye on us."

Seb took out his phone and pulled up a picture, showing it to Mason. "Is this him?"

Mason nodded.

"Were there any others like him?"

"No."

"Well, that's good," Jace said to Seb. "At least we know we're only dealing with the Smiths now." He looked back at Mason. "And you're sure you can't think of any place they'd go?"

Mason pursed his lips as he thought. "No, sorry."

"So, what now?" Thomas asked.

"Now, we tear the mayor's life apart," Seb said. "See what shakes out."

They couldn't do that soon enough, as far as Rayna was concerned. Every minute they spent looking for the Smiths was another minute those kids weren't safe. She looked at Mason. She wanted nothing more than for Mason and his friends to be safe.

Sixteen

Rayna fidgeted with the hem of her dress as Thomas drove them onto the Broken Bow. They were going on their date. He hadn't wasted any time setting it up, either. It was Sunday, not even two full days since he asked her out.

She glanced over the truck seat at Mason. "Are you sure you'll be all right while we're gone?"

He rolled his eyes. "I'll be fine. Despite his profession, I like Jace. I'm more scared of Tara. She's kinda intense."

Thomas laughed from the driver's seat. "I'd tell you it's because she's pregnant and moody, but she's intense all the time."

Rayna giggled. "Her trigger's just a little quicker now."

"That's the truth. Poor Jace." He pulled into Tara's driveway and turned off the engine. "He'll be fine, Ray." He unbuckled his seatbelt. "Come on."

They climbed out of the truck and made their way to the front door. It opened before they reached the porch. Tara beamed at them from the entryway.

"You two look nice," she said, stepping back so they could enter.

Rayna fought the urge to adjust the skirt of her dress. She knew she should have worn pants. They were only going to a winery. It didn't require her to wear a dress.

But she'd wanted to look nice for her first date with Thomas in twelve years. His face when she walked out of her bedroom had been worth the thirty minutes she stood in front of her closet, agonizing over what to wear.

"Thanks."

Jace walked up behind Tara, putting his hands on her shoulders. "So, where are you guys going?"

"That winery near Gunnison," Thomas replied.

"Nice," Tara said. "I carry some of their wine at the restaurant. You'll like that place."

"Good." Thomas said, putting a hand on Rayna's shoulder. Tingles raced outward to spread up her neck and prick her scalp. She suddenly wanted him to run his fingers through her hair.

"We should get going," she said. Turning to Mason, Thomas's hand slipped away, giving her back her ability to think straight. "If you need anything, we'll both have our phones on."

He nodded. "I'll be fine. You guys go have fun."

"We'll keep him safe," Jace said.

She rolled her lips in and nodded, but didn't move toward the door. Logically, she knew Mason would be fine with Jace and Tara—probably safer than with her and Thomas—but it didn't change the fact she would worry about him while they were away.

Thomas took her hand and led her to the door. "Call us if you need us."

"We will," Tara said. She waggled her eyebrows. "You kids have fun now."

Tara's levity broke through Rayna's worry, making her grin. "And don't do anything you wouldn't, right?"

"Of course."

Thomas snorted. "That isn't a very long list, T."

She smiled sweetly at him. "I know. Now, shoo." She walked toward them, herding them through the doorway. "Goodnight."

As soon as Rayna's feet cleared the threshold, the door shut behind them. With it, came the reality that she was actually going on a date with Thomas. They were alone. *Really* alone.

She glanced at him as they walked back to his truck. He wasn't the only one who liked the way the other was dressed. The dark jeans he wore hugged his legs and emphasized their long length, while his charcoal dress shirt and black leather jacket showed off his muscular torso and broad shoulders. He looked yummy enough to eat.

Heaven help her.

Thomas held the door as Rayna stepped from the truck, doing his best not to stare. She looked beautiful in the deep purple sweater dress, tall black boots, and denim vest. Her inky hair was pulled back into a sleek ponytail, showing off her face and long, graceful neck. A neck he desperately wanted to kiss.

He looked away and focused on the winery. The main building was a tall, rambling, single-story stone lodge. At the entrance, the roof peaked and windows ran floor to ceiling. The surrounding grounds were lush, their fall colors in full bloom, but he could imagine it in the summer when all the plants were green and flowers blossomed. It would be spectacular.

He pulled open the glass door and ushered her into the lodge, stopping to give his name to the hostess. When he made the reservation, he booked them on a tour of the facility and orchard before dinner, so she led them through the bar area to the back. A man in a crisp polo and khakis greeted them.

"Hello. I'm Marcus, and I'll be showing you around."

Thomas held out a hand. "Thomas. This is Rayna."

Rayna waved. "Hello."

Marcus motioned to a golf cart a few feet away. "Shall we?"

They all got into the cart, and Marcus drove them around the winery, explaining the types of grapes they grew and the challenges of growing them in Colorado's climate. Thomas barely listened, though. He was too distracted by Rayna's scent and the feel of her pressed against his side as they sat on the small golf cart seat. Oh, how he wished they didn't have a tour guide at the moment.

Once they toured the vineyard, Marcus drove them back to the lodge and led them into the distillery, showing them the giant tanks where the wine fermented until it was ready to be bottled. They sampled several types before he took them back to the dining room and seated them at a table. A server followed him and they soon ordered.

Thomas eyed the clock throughout their meal. It felt like they'd been there for hours, but it had nothing to do with boring conversation. Staring at her across the table while they ate, after sitting next to her in that damn golf cart, had him riding a razor thin edge of arousal, which he could do nothing about in the crowded winery. It didn't help matters that he kept catching her staring at him like he was dessert. He felt like a randy teenager on his first date all over again.

When the check finally came, he snatched it up and handed the server his credit card before the guy could walk away. Rayna excused herself to use the restroom while he waited on the man to come back with the slip for him to sign and the wine they bought during the tour. He left their server a healthy tip on the bill, then went to wait for her.

The ladies' room door swished quietly as she pushed through, and Thomas's heart stuttered when she emerged.

"Ready to go?"

She nodded, and he took her hand, leading her outside to his truck. Buckling in, he pulled out of the parking lot and headed for home. In the darkness of the vehicle's interior, he could just make out her face. A small frown marred her brow.

"Everything okay?" he asked.

She looked at him. "You tell me. I was just about to ask you the same thing."

It was his turn to frown. "What?"

"You took me to a romantic restaurant, we toured a winery, but you didn't do more than hold my hand all evening."

He sighed. "It wasn't because I wasn't having a good time. Now that we've agreed to give us a go again, I'm having a hard time remembering that despite our history, we need to treat this like a new relationship."

Her frown turned quizzical. "Wait. You're saying you kept a polite distance all evening because you didn't want to keep your distance?"

He nodded. "Exactly."

"Hmm." She folded her arms over her chest, her expression turning thoughtful.

"I know we agreed to take things slow, and I'm not pushing you for more. I'm just explaining my behavior so you don't get mad. Keeping my hands to myself is a little harder than I thought it would be."

She poked her tongue into her cheek and smiled. "Maybe I don't want you to keep your hands to yourself."

Christ almighty. Was she trying to kill him? He moaned quietly and closed his eyes for a quick moment. "That's not a great idea."

She unfolded her arms and leaned toward him, her hand

snaking over the center console to curl over his thigh. Thomas shifted as blood rushed south to tighten his pants.

"Rayna."

Her hand inched higher. Thomas saw a sign for a scenic overlook coming up and pulled into it. He slammed the truck into park and unlatched his seatbelt as he turned. He punched the button on her belt and hauled her across the console, latching onto her mouth. She speared her fingers into his hair while his hands roamed over her back and down, bunching the fabric of her dress so he could reach her skin beneath.

"What happened to slow?" he asked, coming up for air.

"Screw slow." She kissed him again, moaning in frustration as the console bit into her hip. "This isn't working."

"Agreed." He pushed her back into her own seat. "We aren't that far from home. Buckle up." He clicked his belt into place, then put the truck in gear as she fastened hers.

"Are we crazy?" she asked, breaking the heavy silence. "I mean, we were barely speaking just a couple weeks ago." She chewed on her lip, and Thomas could tell she was having second thoughts.

He sighed. "Look, I know you don't trust me not to break your heart again. I don't blame you. But I'm not the same man anymore, Rayna. Even from what I was last week."

She raised an eyebrow, and he laughed.

"I know I sound nuts, but it's true. Mason has made me realize some things that were long overdue. I never stopped loving you." She gasped, but he didn't give her a chance to speak. "I just buried it and refused to think about it. Having him around has made me realize I've been a dumbass for refusing to deal with my feelings for you and about having kids. We could have gotten to this point a long time ago if I had. Fetter wouldn't ever have been in the picture if I had."

"What are you saying?"

"That I—"

Her ringing cell phone cut him off. He bit back a frustrated growl as she fished in her purse for the device.

"It's my mom." She frowned and touched the talk button. "Hello?"

Thomas looked on as Rayna's face morphed into horror as she listened. "Rayna?"

She held up a finger. "We're on our way." Taking the phone away from her ear, she disconnected the call and looked at him with tears in her eyes.

"Babe, what's going on? Is Mason okay?"

"He's fine. My greenhouse is on fire."

Seventeen

"Oh my God," Rayna breathed as Thomas pulled into the drive. The flashing lights of the firetrucks shone through the smoke to bounce off the trees and buildings, lending an eerie feel to the scene surrounding the blackened frame of her greenhouse.

"Jesus," Thomas whispered. He drove as close as he could, parking about ten yards from the emergency vehicles.

She slid from the truck as he turned off the engine, covering her mouth as she took in the scene. There was nothing left.

"Rayna!"

She turned at the sound of her mother's voice. Izzy and John hurried toward her. She met them halfway, falling into her mom's embrace.

"Oh, baby. I'm so sorry."

Rayna swallowed hard around the lump of tears in her throat and pulled back. "What happened?"

"We're not sure," her dad answered. "I went to the kitchen during a commercial break to get a snack and saw the flames out the window. The fire department just put it out not too long ago."

"There's Declan," Thomas said, pointing to one of the trucks.

The four of them walked over to the fire lieutenant. As they reached him, Thomas's phone rang. He took it from his pocket, frowning at it as he saw the number.

"Who is it?" Rayna asked.

"The alarm company at my clinic." He answered the call. "This is Dr. Archer."

Rayna shared an alarmed look with Declan. "You don't have a report of a fire there too, do you?"

He shook his head. "Not that I've heard."

She looked back at Thomas as he swiped a hand over his face. "Thank you for calling. I'll head over there."

"What?" Rayna asked, dread filling her.

"The alarm went off at my clinic on the front door. The alarm company called the police, but I need to go meet them." He looked over her head at the remnants of her greenhouse, indecision on his face.

"Go," she said. "I'll be fine here."

He looked down at her. "Are you sure? I can call Lorraine and see if she can go."

"No. It's your business. Just like this is mine. Go. See what happened. We'll meet back at Jace and Tara's later."

Thomas drew in a breath through his nose, then sighed. "Okay. But stick close to your parents, please. It's really chaotic here and we don't know what's going on."

She nodded. "I will." She had no desire to be alone right now.

He bent and pressed a quick kiss to her lips. "I'll see you at the ranch."

"Watch yourself," she told him. "You don't have an army of people around like I do."

"I will. I'm going to call Seb and have him meet me there if he isn't already on his way."

"Okay."

He offered her a reassuring smile and turned, jogging to his truck. She turned back to Declan as he climbed inside and drove away.

"What happened?"

Declan frowned. "Someone torched it."

Rayna's head spun at his blunt words. "What? Are you sure?"

"Yeah. We found traces of accelerant. I'm guessing gasoline from the burn pattern."

"Why would someone want to burn down Rayna's greenhouse?" John demanded.

"As a warning," she told her dad. "We've scared someone by finding where Mason was held captive. There are some powerful people involved in this."

"And they think terrorizing you will stop the investigation?" Izzy said.

She shrugged. "Maybe. Whoever it is doesn't know me or the Archers very well, if that's the case. Mason's safety and that of those other kids is more important than my greenhouse."

"Agreed, but what if the next time you're in the building, they decide to burn down?"

Rayna frowned. "It still doesn't change anything. Even if we had the power to make Seb stop investigating, we wouldn't change anything."

"Well, I'm sure with what we've found, Seb's going to offer you guys some protection," Declan said.

Rayna looked at her parents. "Maybe you guys should take a vacation."

Izzy crossed her arms and stared at her, while John gave her a look she remembered from her youth when she'd done something rather stupid and they all knew it.

"Please?" She really didn't want her parents caught up in this mess.

They both shook their heads.

"Even if we wanted to, we can't just pick up and leave," John said. "I have a ranch to run."

She stared at him for a moment before her shoulders slumped and she relented. "Fine. But just promise me you'll be careful? I don't know that whoever did this won't target the two of you."

"Eyes in the back of our heads, dear," Izzy said.

"Good." She turned to Declan. "Can I see what's left?"

He nodded. "Yeah. It's not much, I'm afraid. Come on, I'll take you over."

Rayna gave her mother's hand a squeeze and followed Declan to the ruins of her greenhouse. She covered her mouth as she got a close-up look. Tears sprang up in her eyes, but she dashed them away. It was just a building. She had insurance. But she'd poured her blood and sweat into it and the crops inside. It would take her a long time to rebuild. She prayed Thomas's clinic fared better than her greenhouse. He provided a much-needed service to their community. Losing his clinic would be significant.

"What happens now?" she asked Declan.

"I'll have the state fire marshal come confirm what I suspect. In the meantime, you can call your insurance company and get your claim started."

She sighed. At least they'd spared her market and storage buildings.

Thomas pulled into the parking lot at his clinic. Seb was already there. As he parked beside him, he glanced around for his brother and noted the broken glass littering the ground. The front doors were shattered.

"Shit." He climbed from his truck. "Seb?"

His brother poked his head out from inside the clinic. "You can come in, just watch your step. There's glass everywhere."

He wasn't kidding. It crunched under his boots as he walked toward the door. He stepped through the empty doorframe, taking in the destruction. Both sets of glass doors were gone.

"Is this all they did?"

"Not hardly. Come on, I'll show you."

Thomas followed Seb toward the back of the clinic, a sinking feeling settling in his gut as they neared the supply room—where he kept all his medications. Seb stopped in the doorway and motioned to the room.

"They rifled through some of the exam rooms and operating suites, but this room took the brunt of things."

Steeling himself, Thomas stepped up next to his brother and looked inside. He took a sharp breath as he surveyed the chaos. All the glass from all the medicine cabinets was shattered. The lock on the fridge hung by a single screw, the door open and the shelves inside empty.

"Oh, this is bad," Thomas said. "There were a lot of vials of a lot of controlled substances in here." His eyes ran over the empty shelves. "It looks like they took it all." He scrubbed his hands over his face, then looked at Seb. "The street value on those drugs is thousands of dollars."

"Yeah. I'll put out a notice to local law enforcement to keep an ear to the ground for anyone selling it."

"If it was the Smiths who did this, I fear they're going to use it for other purposes."

Seb pressed his lips into a tight line. "Maybe. I'm pretty sure they sold drugs in addition to kids. They left in a real hurry the other day. We found drug paraphernalia in the cellar. Enough to indicate they were dealing. Stealing your supply kills two birds with one stone. It sends you a message and gives them an influx of cash so they can set up somewhere else."

"Then we need to find them before that happens. If they leave the area with those kids, we may never find them."

"I'm hoping we get a lead off the break-in here. Your security system is state-of-the-art, and as far as I can tell, they didn't disable the cameras."

"Let's check." Thomas whirled and headed for his office.

He sat down at his desk and woke up his computer, typing in his password. When the desktop appeared, he clicked on the alarm system icon, then went to the section for video footage.

"Here," he pushed back and stood. "You do it. Other than someone smashing my front door, I don't know what I'm looking for."

Seb took his seat and opened the footage for the lobby. He slid the play bar back until he got to the point the doors shattered and noted the time stamp before switching to the camera outside. A man stood in front of the doors, but his head was down and covered by a hat, so they couldn't see his face.

Thomas tilted his head and studied the figure. He pointed at the screen. "What's in his hand?"

Seb leaned closer and squinted. "It looks like a weapon." He backed the footage up several seconds and the man stood a little further away, pointing a handgun at the doors.

"Play it."

Seb clicked play, and they watched the man fire four shots at the building. The glass in the doors splintered, then fell to the ground like a curtain of icy rain. The man walked forward, pausing a moment as someone joined him, then they ran into the clinic.

"That wasn't a woman," Thomas said as Seb switched screens.

"Nope. The Smiths have friends." He hit play on the lobby video. The two men ran through toward the back, and Seb followed them on the cameras. In the pharmacy, the men cleaned out his supplies, filling a duffel the second man carried. Seb flipped back to the cameras in the hallways as the men went from room to room before running back out the front.

"There!"

"Yes!" Seb froze the camera on an image of the rear of an older model tan Ford Explorer. The license plate was visible. He punched a couple buttons to take a screen capture, then opened Thomas's email and sent it to Katie and himself. "This might be the break we needed. If we can find these two, they might lead us to the Smiths' new hideout." He pushed away from the desk. "I'm going to put a BOLO out on that vehicle. The crime scene unit should be here anytime to process the place."

"They didn't touch the front desk. Can I use the computer there to start calling patients?"

Seb nodded, lifting his phone to his ear. "Call Dad and Brady, too. They can bring over some plywood to cover the doors until you can get them replaced."

Thomas nodded and left him to do his job and went out to the lobby to do his. It was going to be a long night.

Cattle in the pastures lining the drive at the Broken Bow lifted their heads to stare at Rayna's truck as she drove past. She and Thomas both had meetings all morning with their insurance agents and the bank to start the claims process, so they'd dropped Mason off with Brady earlier. She knew they were probably out working somewhere and would be for a while yet, but she needed to talk to Tara. The mess with her greenhouse and Thomas's clinic had her emotions jumbled, and she desperately needed one of her friends to help her sort through them. London had a houseful of guests, and Macy had a coffee shop to run. Tara's restaurant didn't open until later this afternoon, so here she was.

She pulled into Tara's driveway and shut off the truck, climbing out. On the porch, she hesitated a moment before knocking, some of her guilt over Fetter coming back. Tara had told her more than once she didn't blame Rayna, but Thomas's animosity over the whole ordeal still niggled the back of her mind. After weeks of believing he blamed her, she hadn't quite processed he was jealous and not angry. She knew it, but her emotions hadn't quite caught up.

Taking a deep breath, she knocked on the door. It swung open a moment later.

"Hey," Tara said with a smile. "What are you doing here?" She stepped back so Rayna could come in.

"I need to pick up Mason in a little while, but I wanted to talk to you first."

Tara closed the door and frowned. She studied Rayna's face until she felt like a bug under a microscope. "If this is about that jackass, Fetter, I'm going to stop you now. I've told you several times I don't blame you. You need to let it go."

Rayna huffed and sank onto the couch, hugging a throw pillow to her chest. "It is, partly. How do you not feel any resentment toward me? I gave him all kinds of details about your life. I know he had Claybaugh following you, but he knew specific details about your life because of *me*."

Tara sat next to her and waved a hand. "You had no idea who he was. I didn't either because of his scars, and I spent a lot of time with him when we were in the Middle East. Stop beating yourself up." She squinted at her. "Does this have anything to do with my asshat twin?"

Rayna couldn't stop the giggle that broke free. "A little. Though, he admitted he was more jealous than angry."

"So, what's the problem?"

She sighed. "I guess I'm just having trouble forgiving myself for being such an idiot. Looking back, I should have asked more questions. His reluctance to meet you guys was a huge red flag, but I accepted it because I thought he was just shy because of his scars. Knowing who he is now, I'm amazed I got him to meet you at all."

"I'm not. Jared had an ego the size of Alaska. He probably got a huge thrill out of pulling one over on me. And on duping you. He figured out you love helping others and took advantage of that. None of what happened is your fault. Can you believe me now when I say you're forgiven? Because there was nothing to forgive."

Rayna nodded, her heart a little lighter. Tara was right. Jared had seen a woman who tried to find the good in everyone and capitalized on that. She shouldn't be upset with anyone but him. And he was dead, so she just needed to move on.

"Good. Now, let's talk about Thomas." She gave Rayna a naughty smile. "We got distracted by the fire and break-in last night, so I didn't get to ask how your date went."

Rayna groaned and slid down on the couch, resting her head against the cushion. "Weird."

"Weird?"

"Weird. He barely touched me throughout the winery tour and dinner. When we got back in the truck to come home, I called him on it. He told me he was trying to keep his hands to himself because we agreed to take things slow. Having him close but not touching me for several hours made me realize I didn't want slow, and I told him that. He pulled over and things got—well, heated." Her face flushed, and she cleared her throat before continuing. "The front of a truck isn't the best place for all that, so we got back on the road. My misgivings popped up again, and when I said it was all a little crazy, he told me he never stopped loving me."

Tara gasped and covered her mouth. She squealed and grabbed Rayna's hands. "Does this mean you two are really back together?"

Rayna shrugged. "Mom called to tell me about the fire before we could talk any further. I didn't even get to respond to that bombshell."

"Well, do you still love him?"

She took a deep breath, holding it for a moment as she searched her heart. She had no trouble admitting she loved Thomas—as a friend. But did she love him as more than that? Deep down, she was pretty sure she did. No one had ever made her feel what he did. Hadn't even come close. She groaned and covered her face with the pillow before looking at Tara. "Yes? Honestly, I'm just so confused. You know I've never felt for another man what I felt for your brother, but I'm just not sure I trust him to stick around."

"I get that. Thomas can be childish and immature, but Ray, I've never seen him like this before."

Rayna frowned. "What do you mean?"

"He's different." She rested a finger on her chin as she tried to think of the right words. "Not so much that he's more serious, but just—grown up, maybe? Honestly, at dinner, he reminded me of Seb. I really think he's ready to settle down. That kid you found has changed something in him. He doesn't just want to help him. Neither of you do, for that matter. It's more than that. I think Mason's going to be staying around as more than just a ranch hand."

Rayna stared straight ahead as she thought about that. Her feelings for Mason were as complicated as her feelings for Thomas, just in a different way. There was no doubt she cared about the young man. But did she see him as a son? He was a little old for her to feel that way, but it didn't stop her from wanting to be there for him the way her parents were there for her. To teach him all the things he'd missed the last seven years. And she'd seen Thomas with him. The dynamic between the two was that of a father and son.

She groaned again, closing her eyes for a brief moment, then looking up at the ceiling. "Life is complicated."

Tara laughed. "You're preaching to the choir."

Rayna sighed. "Well, you've definitely given me something to think about."

"Good. Now that I've got you all straightened out, let's talk about my wedding." Tara gave her a cheeky grin, making Rayna laugh.

"In other words, I should stay out of my head, right?"

Tara giggled. "Yep."

"Okay, fine," she said, smiling at her friend. "What do you want to discuss?"

"My dress. The one I picked out isn't going to fit by the wedding. I wasn't planning on twins when I bought it."

"Hmm... Go get it and let's see what I can come up with."

She stood, going to get her dress. Rayna ran a hand through her hair and blew out a breath. Maybe Tara was right, and she needed to go with the flow. It wouldn't be the first time she overanalyzed something. Part of the reason she hadn't had many long-term relationships since Thomas was because she picked things apart and found flaws in every man she dated, essentially self-sabotaging. She'd been looking for a perfect man that didn't exist because she didn't want to get hurt again. Maybe she needed to give the new Thomas a chance without looking through the prejudice of the past.

Eighteen

Finished figuring out what to do about Tara's dress to accommodate her rapidly expanding middle, Rayna climbed back into her truck and headed for the main house to see if Jenny knew where Brady and Mason were. As she passed the building the Archers used for maintenance, she noticed Thomas's pickup parked next to an Airstream trailer. She debated for a moment whether to stop. Her earlier thought about starting a clean slate with him filtered through her brain, and she hit the brakes, turning toward the RV.

Parking beside him, she got out and walked up the steel steps and opened the door.

Thomas looked up from his position on his knees in front of the oven. "Hey."

She smiled and leaned against the doorframe. "Hi. What are you doing here? Why aren't you at work?"

He stood. "The clinic's closed because of the break-in. I handled all the business I needed to this morning for the insurance claim. I had a couple farm calls, then nothing, so I decided to start cleaning this place up. What are you doing out here? I didn't think Mason would be done until later."

"He's probably not yet. I've been over at Tara's. I was on my way to your parents' to see if your mom knew anything when I saw your truck."

He stepped toward her, and her heart sped up.

"So, you just decided to stop?" His voice dropped as he stared down at her.

She swallowed hard. "Yep."

He shuffled just a bit closer. "Well, since you're here, why don't we do something fun?" That devilish smile she loved so much spread over his handsome face.

Lord have mercy! She took a deep breath through her nose. "Like what?"

He leaned in, his mouth inches from hers. "Like—" He straightened and held his cleaning rag in her face. "Help me clean."

Rayna blinked twice, then laughed. She took the rag and pushed him back. "Scoundrel. Okay, I'll help you."

He grinned and stepped over to the counter and picked up another rag. "Good. I didn't realize how much of a mess this place was. I've been in here a couple hours already and haven't made it past the kitchen."

She looked around, noting the dated appearance of the trailer. Dust clung to surfaces, and stains marred the fabric on the cushions. "We need to take down the curtains and remove the covers from the cushions and wash them."

He nodded. "Yeah. I was planning on bringing them home tonight so we could."

A thrill went through her as she realized he thought of her house as home. Once upon a time, she'd imagined a home with Thomas, but that felt like a lifetime ago.

"Do you want to finish the oven while I go start on the bathroom?" he asked.

"Sure." She'd much rather clean an oven than an RV

restroom. Especially as she considered his dad had probably used the Airstream for hunting trips.

Thomas picked up a bottle of cleaner while she kneeled down to start on the oven. He'd already done quite a bit, so it didn't take her long to finish the job. Glancing around, she grabbed a clean rag and started dusting. There was a layer of grime on everything, even the walls.

Once she was done, she climbed up on the sofa bed, intending to take down the curtains, but the cushion slid beneath her and she lost her balance, slamming into the wall.

"Ow." *Damn, that hurt.* She pressed the heel of her hand to her forehead, just above her eyebrow.

"Ray? You okay?"

"I'm fine. Just bumped my head."

"Let me see." He came up beside her and pulled her hand away.

She scrunched her nose and looked up. "I'm okay. Really."

"Mmm-hmm." His fingers probed the spot, making her wince. It was a little tender, but nothing terrible. In a few minutes, she wouldn't even feel it.

The air around them changed as their gazes collided. It crackled with awareness, making her skin tingle. He skimmed his fingers down the side of her face, sliding them around into her hair to hold the back of her head. Her eyes drifted shut of their own volition as she got lost in the feel of his touch. She felt him lean closer, and his breath whispered over her mouth a moment before his lips touched hers.

Rayna swayed into him, letting her palms rest against his chest. He brought his other hand up to cradle her face and deepened the kiss. She curled her fingers into his shirt, holding on for dear life as her head spun and goosebumps erupted over her skin in a wave spreading out from his hands.

He pulled back to look down at her, heat in his eyes. She

stared back, eager to feel his mouth on hers again. Stretching up, she fused their lips together once more. He let out a soft grunt of surprise, then wrapped his arms around her, hauling her into his chest. Rayna slid her hands up to spear them into his hair.

She'd missed the way he made her feel. The electrifying, body-on-fire high she got every time he kissed her.

She fell back to sit on the cushion, bringing him down with her. Thomas's long body covered hers as she laid back. His mouth left hers to trail over her jaw and get reacquainted with the spot below her ear that always made her eyes roll back into her head. She tugged on the dark strands of his hair as his hands drifted around her ribs to cup her breasts through her long-sleeved t-shirt. Rayna moaned when he flicked his thumbs over the tips.

"I forgot how much you like that," he muttered next to her ear. "Let's see what else I can remember." He nipped at that spot, and her breath caught.

"There's one." He kissed his way around her neck to dip his tongue in the hollow of her throat. Sliding down a bit, he pushed her shirt up, then bent his head to kiss her ribcage beneath her breasts, his nose nuzzling the underside.

She tried to exhale, but her lungs quit working. When he raised his head to look at her, she sucked in a deep breath.

He grinned. "There's two."

Rayna groaned and closed her eyes. Was he really going to go all the way down her body to rediscover all the places that sent her into a tizzy?

Thomas slid further down her legs, his fingers unsnapping the button on her jeans. He pushed the material out of the way to press featherlight kisses on her hipbones, then nip at the skin over them. Her hips rose of their own accord.

"Three."

When his tongue darted out to trace the waistline of her panties, a flood of heat swamped her core.

Okay, that was enough.

She reached out and snagged handfuls of his shirt, pulling him back to her, so she could kiss him again. He pressed her down into the cushion with his delicious weight.

Wanting to feel his skin against hers, she gathered his shirt in her hands, pulling it up. He sat up and pulled it off, revealing all those gorgeous muscles dusted with dark hair to her gaze.

"Your turn."

She sat up and took her shirt off, leaving her bra in place. She remembered how he liked to take it off himself.

He reached out to run a finger along the rim of one cup, leaving a trail of goosebumps in his wake. His finger curled over the edge and he pulled it down, then leaned in to take her nipple in his mouth.

Rayna couldn't hold back the gasp as he toyed with her breast, sending flashes of heat along her nerve endings. He let go with a pop, reaching around to unsnap the garment and pull it off her. His eyes turned to fathomless pools as he drank her in. A flush crept over her, adding heat to the fire already raging.

His hands came to rest on either side of her head as he loomed over her. "You have no idea how much I've missed this. Missed you."

Oh, she had a pretty good idea, if it was anything close to what she felt.

"Stop talking." They could talk later. Right now, she just wanted his body on hers. He'd revved her up, finding all those spots he used to love. She wanted him to finish the job.

Rayna locked her fingers around his neck and tugged him down. That electricity came back with a vengeance as their mouths melded together again. Her hands traced over the lines of muscle and bone on his sides and back, then down, to slide beneath the waist of his jeans. She dug her nails into the flesh of his butt, raising her legs on either side of his hips so he could settle against her.

Thomas broke their kiss and stared down at her. "Ray, are you sure?"

Was she? He'd always been able to light her on fire. That much would never change. But if they went through with this, everything else would. Was she ready to put her heart out there again? Saying she wanted to start over with him and actually doing it were two different things. Could she risk that he wouldn't smash her heart to bits again?

An image of him comforting Mason the other day popped into her head. Then she thought of how he went out of his way to buy him a new wardrobe. And ice cream. Maybe Tara was right, and he had changed. If she said no, and they stopped, would she regret not seeing where this could go?

As she looked up into his dark eyes, she realized the answer to that was yes. She would. Very much. Because Thomas was and would always be the perfect man for *her*.

Raising her head, she captured his mouth with hers. He let out a breathy moan at the contact. Then it was like she flipped a switch. His hands were everywhere at once, creating a hum throughout her body so intense she felt like she was vibrating. When he pushed at her jeans, trying to take them off, she lifted her hips and helped, shimmying them down her legs and kicking them to the floor along with her underwear.

"You're wearing too many clothes," she muttered against his mouth. She snaked her hands between them to unfasten his pants, brushing against his erection.

He groaned and put a hand over hers. "You better let me, or we won't get very far."

She tossed him a naughty smile, but pulled her hands back. He stood long enough to shuck his pants and boxer briefs, giving Rayna an eyeful.

Her mouth watered as well as parts further south as she

looked her fill. She'd never forgotten what he looked like—a man like Thomas was hard to forget—but the memory had dimmed over the years. Now, here he was in all his glory.

That impish smile of his returned as he took a condom from his wallet and climbed over her again. "Like what you see?"

She giggled, wrapping a hand around him. His breath left him in a whoosh.

"Quite possibly, yes."

He growled. "You don't sound too sure. Maybe I should refresh your memory about how good we are together." His voice dipped dangerously low, the rumble of it vibrating through her.

She bit her lip and closed her eyes. "Yes, please."

Rayna heard the crinkle of the condom wrapper, then felt him tease her entrance. She fought to keep from wrapping her legs around him and just impaling herself. As good as it would feel, it would be over for both of them much too soon if she rushed things.

His fingers feathered over her face, and she opened her eyes to see him looking down at her, a tender expression on his handsome face.

"I realize you're putting your faith in me again. I promise not to do anything to undermine that."

She gave him a tremulous smile, framing his head in her hands. "I know."

He kissed her and pushed inside her at the same time. Fireworks went off in her head and she gave herself over to the onslaught of sensation.

～

"Is that everything?" Thomas asked as Rayna dropped the cushion covers in the backseat of her truck.

She nodded and shut the door.

He stowed the last of the cleaning supplies he brought in the bed of his pickup and walked over to her, backing her against her vehicle. "Good." His mouth crashed onto hers. Desire ripped through him. He wanted a repeat of earlier. The passion in her kiss suggested she did too.

But it was getting late, and they had places to be. He pulled back. She huffed and rested her forehead against his collarbone for a moment before looking up at him.

He hummed, agreeing with her silent complaint. The real world beckoned, and he didn't like it either. Letting her go, he stepped back to put some space between them and give his brain a chance to clear the fog she put him in.

"We need to go."

"I know." She frowned. "Doesn't mean it doesn't suck."

He grinned. "Yep." He leaned down, unable to resist one last kiss. "But we'll find time for more later."

She fisted her hands in his shirt and kissed him back.

Thomas groaned and pulled away before she could entice him into shoving her in the truck and taking her all over again. "Brady's going to come looking for us if we don't show up soon."

Rayna giggled. "As much fun as it would be to shock Mr. Sensibility, you're the only Archer I'm interested in seeing me naked."

He growled. "Damn straight." He pressed a final hard kiss to her mouth and stepped away. "Come on. Let's go get the kid and go home." What he said registered, and he paused.

She stared at him, just as surprised. "It does feel like we're a family, doesn't it?"

He inhaled through his nose and nodded. "It does. And I like it."

Her smile was sunny. "Me too." Spinning on her heel, she walked around to the driver's side of her truck to climb inside.

Thomas had to give himself a hard mental shake to keep the sappy grin off his face. He never thought he would get to this point with Rayna after he blew it so badly all those years ago. It still hadn't sunk in they were really going to try to make this work.

Gathering himself, he jogged to his pickup and got in, following her away from the Airstream and toward the main house. They'd lingered longer in the RV than he intended. There were no doubt going to be some questions.

He pulled up behind his parents' house, parking next to Brady's vehicle, and climbed out. Rayna met him in front of the cars and they headed inside. His mother looked up from the stove as they walked in the back door.

"We wondered when you were going to show up. I knew that old Airstream was dirty, but I didn't think it was that bad."

"Yep." Thomas stuffed his hands in his pockets to keep from touching Rayna beside him. He still wanted that connection with her, but he wasn't sure she was ready for the world to know things had changed. "It was a mess."

Jenny started to nod in agreement, but his tone must have given something away because she paused, narrowing her eyes at them. Just as quickly, they widened. "It wasn't that dirty. You had sex in there!" she hissed.

Rayna turned ten shades of red while Thomas groaned and looked at the ceiling. He held up a hand. "Geez, Mom. Really? I'm not discussing this with you. I'm not a teenager, so what Rayna and I do isn't anyone's business but ours."

Her brow furrowed. "It is when anyone could walk in on you. Brady was about to go look for you. And Mason was going to go with him. Do you want that boy seeing that? After everything he's been through?"

He frowned back at her, knowing she was right, but hating to admit it.

"We'll be more careful in the future, Jenny," Rayna said. "Can we please not talk about this?"

Jenny's expression softened as she looked at Rayna. "Of course, dear." She set her spoon down and walked over to the two of them. Placing her hands on Rayna's shoulders, she smiled. "I'm so glad you guys worked things out." She pulled Rayna into her embrace and gave her a hard hug before pulling back. "I hoped you two would come to your senses. Seems that boy showing up changed more than just his own life."

Rayna returned her smile. "He did. And no matter what happens from here, we will always be grateful to him for helping us to see a few things."

Jenny patted Rayna's cheek. "Good." She turned back to the stove. "Are you all staying for dinner?"

Thomas looked over at Rayna. Her eyes telegraphed what he was thinking. They were ready to go home.

"I think we're good, Mom, but thanks."

She waved a hand. "Sure. Mason's in the living room with your father."

"Thanks." He stopped at the stove to give her a peck on the cheek before he followed Rayna from the room and down the hall.

"Wow," Rayna said, stopping in the doorway.

Thomas came up behind her to see what was going on, and his eyes widened. Every picture his parents ever took was spread around the room.

Brady looked up, his expression conveying he didn't know how the situation got away from him. Thomas's mouth twitched at his older brother's look of dismay, but somehow he kept a straight face.

"What's with all the pictures?"

Lee grinned up at him from his position on the couch, then shrugged. "I asked Mason if he wanted to see some pictures of you when you were a boy. It kind of took off from there."

Thomas smiled then. "I can tell." He looked at Mason. "Learn anything interesting?"

One corner of the young man's mouth lifted, and he looked at Thomas askance. "You had some, um, different hairstyles in your teens."

Rayna giggled. He shot her a look of mock annoyance.

"You just had to find those pictures, didn't you, Dad?"

Lee laughed. "Of course. They're some of my favorites."

"Hmm. Yes. My punk rock phase was fun." He'd sported a wildly colored mohawk for a few months. As well as a shaved head. He seemed to recall some weird, spiky hairdo as well—before the mohawk days.

"I liked the leather jacket," Rayna said. "It was sexy."

He waggled his eyebrows at her, making her laugh, before turning back to his dad. "I suppose we should help you pick all these up before we head out."

"Nonsense. I got them all out. Besides, there are some I want to show your mother. You head on home."

"You're sure?"

"Yep."

"Okay. Mason, are you ready to go?"

The young man rose from his chair. "Yeah."

Thomas turned to Brady. "Thanks for hanging out with him today."

"Anytime. It was fun. The kid's got a real aptitude for ranch work. He was great with the horses."

"Yeah?" Thomas looked at Mason, who gave him a shy but proud smile. "Don't be shy, kid. Own it. Did you enjoy your time with Brady?"

Mason squared his shoulders and nodded. "Yes. I really liked working with the animals. Brady's a great teacher."

"Well, it's easy when you have a student who's eager to learn and absorbs information like a sponge."

Mason started to duck his head again, but caught himself and gave Brady a thankful smile instead.

Thomas ruffled his hair. "Come on. Let's go see what we can scrounge up for dinner. Rayna and I worked up an appetite." He glanced at her, a wicked twinkle in his eyes. Hers widened a fraction as she silently told him to keep his mouth shut.

"Doing what?" Mason asked.

"Working on a surprise for you."

"A surprise? For me?"

Rayna hooked an arm through Mason's. "Yes. It's not quite ready yet. Thomas likes to tease people and make them squirm while they wait. Soon, though."

Thomas sighed. "She's got me pegged. Has for years. Let's go." He looked at his dad and brother. "We'll see you guys later."

Lee lifted a hand in goodbye, and Brady tipped his chin at them.

Spinning around, he headed for the kitchen. Warmth flooded his chest, knowing that while he wasn't going to his house, he *was* going home.

Nineteen

Thomas whistled softly while he worked. He was back at it, cleaning the Airstream—by himself this time. Rayna was busy working on wedding things with Tara, and Mason asked to help Brady again. He was on call for farm emergencies, and so far, it had been quiet.

He tossed the wipe he used on the walls in the bathroom into the trash bag, then tied it shut. All he needed to do was stuff the cushions and rehang the curtains Rayna washed the other day.

A car door shut outside and footsteps pounded up the trailer's metal steps a moment before the door opened and Seb popped his head in.

"You are not who I wanted to see come through that door," Thomas said.

Seb grinned and tossed his head, running his fingers through the hair hanging over his forehead. "What? I'm just as pretty as your girlfriend."

Thomas chuckled. "Not even close."

"Whatever. My wife would beg to differ."

"I'm sure she would." He picked up a cushion and started stuffing it inside a clean cover. "Why'd you think I was waiting on Rayna?"

"Who else would you want to see?" Seb picked up the second cushion and cover. "And I also heard knocking is advised when entering."

Thomas paused in his task. "Where'd you hear that?" He couldn't imagine Mom said anything to Seb.

"Mom."

Or maybe she would.

"I stopped at the house to take them some goodies London made. When I mentioned I saw your truck parked over here, and that I was going to come talk to you, she told me to make sure I knocked if Rayna was here too. Then she waggled her eyebrows at me and grinned."

Thomas cleared his throat and zipped the cushion shut, tossing it onto the bench. "It's probably not a bad idea."

"You could always lock the door too." Seb grinned. "But I didn't come to talk about your sex life."

"That's a relief."

Seb's smile grew before he turned serious. "I came to give you an update. Katie gave that picture of the vehicle from the break-in at your clinic to the same friend who enhanced the picture from Claybaugh's house, and he worked his magic again to get us a plate number. I ran it and it came back to a pair of brothers who live up in the northwestern part of the county. Frank and Jeremiah Draper. Jace went up today and scoped out their address. He couldn't get too close because it's got a fence around it, but he could see several vehicles there through the trees."

Excitement made Thomas's heart skip. "That could be where the Smiths are hiding out with the kids."

"My thoughts exactly. And, since we have no evidence

linking the Drapers to the Smiths—only to the break-in on your clinic—I didn't have to share with Stillwater's attorney that I filed for arrest warrants for both men and a search warrant for their property. Jace is putting a team together, and we go at first light."

"Seb, that's great news!"

"Yes, but don't get your hopes up. Or Rayna's and Mason's. We might not find anything there except the drugs they stole from you."

Thomas sighed. "Yeah. Okay. I'll make sure they understand. Do you have anything on the fire at Rayna's?"

"Probably nothing you didn't already know," Seb said, zipping his cushion shut and setting it next to the one Thomas finished. "It was arson, and they used gasoline. Without any cameras or witnesses, we've got nothing."

"I was afraid of that." He reached up to take the curtain rod down.

Seb picked up a curtain lying on the counter. "Hopefully, we'll get some answers tomorrow. It's likely the Drapers were the ones who torched Rayna's greenhouse."

"I know. It just bugs me they're targeting her."

Seb threaded the curtain over the rod. "I know how that feels. But we've got some decent leads, which is a hell of a lot more than I had when Marsters was after London."

Thomas spread the curtain out over the rod. "Yeah." So why couldn't he shake the feeling tomorrow's raid was going to lead to more problems? "Does this feel a little too easy to you?"

Seb frowned. "What do you mean?"

"I mean, these people ran a sophisticated human and drug trafficking organization for years without anyone being the wiser. Then they send two goons—who use their own car—to raid my clinic and probably torch Ray's greenhouse, which leads us straight to their heavily fortified house within range of the Smiths' compound? Come on, man. It can't be that easy."

"I get what you're saying, but there's no guarantee the Smiths are hiding out at the Drapers'. We don't even know for sure that all the crimes are connected."

"That's bullshit, and you know it."

"I do. It's too coincidental. But there isn't any evidence linking everything. I can't charge people for trafficking based on coincidences and my gut feelings."

Frustration churned in Thomas's gut. He yanked the other curtain off the counter and pushed it onto the rod with jerky movements. "Look, all I'm saying is be careful. I know I'm not the cop, but something about this doesn't feel right."

"We will. I rounded up the deputies I trust to help with the raid and swore them all to secrecy. They won't know we're coming."

"Never say never, Seb. A few weeks ago, I didn't think I'd ever get another shot with Rayna and look where I am now."

Seb's mouth quirked, and he raised a brow. "You're equating my drug raid to your relationship?"

Thomas rolled his eyes. "Not exactly. It's the same principle is what I'm getting at. The impossible is possible. Just —*please*—promise me you'll be careful?"

"You know I will."

Thomas climbed onto the bench to hang the curtain. His gut still churned, but it wasn't just frustration that bit into it. Worry took up a healthy chunk. He couldn't shake the feeling that raid wasn't going to turn out the way they wanted.

～

"Mason. Have you—" Rayna broke off as she entered the market building. He sat on an overturned crate, his expression pinched as he stared down at the boxes of jelly and jerky he was supposed to be restocking, seeing neither.

His gaze snapped up to hers, and he sucked in a deep breath, the fog lifting from his eyes. "Hey." He cleared his throat, then looked down and picked up two jars to set them on the shelf. "Sorry, this should only take me a minute to finish."

She frowned and walked over, dragging a crate with her so she could sit beside him. "Are you okay?"

He gave her a curt nod and kept filling shelves. She laid a hand over his.

"Mason. What's wrong? And don't tell me nothing. You might not have been here long, but I've learned to read your moods. What's bothering you?"

He dropped the package of jerky in his hand back into the box and turned to look at her. Tears swam in his eyes. "What if they don't find them?"

"Then we'll keep looking. Sebastian's very persistent. The Smiths can't keep running forever, especially not with Seb on their tail."

"Not the Smiths. The other kids. What if they aren't there? I just left them there. I could have—done something!" He broke into sobs, and Rayna pulled him into her arms. She wondered when some of this was going to come out. He'd been very silent on how he felt about the situation.

"You did nothing wrong. You were in no condition to help anyone. Honestly, we're all surprised you survived long enough to get here." She pulled away to take his face in her hands and make him look at her. "If you had stopped to help your friends, the Smiths would have captured you again—or worse. Their best chance was you finding help, which you did. Seb and Jace are doing everything they can to find the others. You have to trust them."

He sniffed, and she let him go. "I'm trying," he said, wiping the tears from his face. "I just wish I'd done more. That I could do more now than just sit here and wait."

"I know. I wish I could do more too. But our job will start when they find those kids. They're going to need a safe place, just like you had, with people who will help them heal."

Mason frowned. "You're going to take all of us in?"

She smiled. "Probably not. My house isn't big enough. But you can be damn sure I'm going to make sure they go to homes that will treat them right. You, though, you're staying right here until you want to leave."

He gave her a watery smile. "I don't know why you and Thomas want a broken kid, but I'm grateful for everything you've done for me. It still feels like a dream. I keep waiting for the bubble to pop."

"No bubble. We want you here. You aren't the only one who's been rescued through this situation. Thomas and I—well, we've had some issues lately. Taking care of you, helping you, has forced us to work together. We've ironed things out and are in a better place than we've been in a very long time. Without you, I don't know as if that would have happened."

"You love him, don't you?"

"Very much. I have since I was sixteen. I wanted everything with him, but he wasn't ready. Looking back, I probably wasn't either. But we are now. Mason, even if Thomas and I never have children of our own, I'm okay with that, because we have you. I don't care that you're an adult and have lived through more crap than most people twice your age, or that I'm barely old enough to be your mother. I want you to think of this place—of me and Thomas—as home."

His tears came back, and one slid free to trail down his cheek. "Really?" His voice came out as a broken whisper.

Rayna sniffed back her own tears and smiled brightly. "Really. You will forever have a home here."

He crushed her in a tight hug, his shoulders shaking silently. "Thank you," he whispered.

She hugged him back. "You're welcome." She pulled away and wiped away his tears. "Come on. Let's finish this up, then go see what my mom's up to. When I stopped over yesterday, they were about out of cookies, so I'm betting there's a fresh batch just waiting to be eaten. Dad loves cookies, so Mom never lets them run out. And she likes to bake in the morning. Says the smell helps set the tone for the entire day."

He took a steadying breath and nodded. "Okay. That sounds good."

Rayna's heart ached, it was so full. Oh, how she loved this kid.

Together, they worked side by side to finish restocking. Within a few minutes, they had the boxes emptied onto the shelves and were headed for her parents' house.

She tugged on the back door and walked inside. Izzy looked up from the stove where she was busy stirring tomatoes. Empty canning jars littered the counter to her right. She smiled at them. "Hi."

"Hi, Mom. We came for cookies."

She rolled her eyes. "Of course you did. You are your father's daughter, after all." She chuckled and motioned toward the counter with a tip of her head. "They're over there."

"Mason, get the milk out of the fridge." Rayna headed for the cupboard to the right of the sink to get them each a glass. "Do you want some, Mom?"

Izzy tapped her spoon against the rim of the pot and set it in the spoon rest on the stove. "I guess I could take a break."

Rayna filled three glasses with milk and handed two cookies to Mason. Izzy held up one finger, so she passed her a single cookie, then took two for herself.

"Where's Dad?"

"The chickens were squawking about something. He went to check it out." She looked at the clock. "Actually, he's been gone a while. He should have been back by now." She set her milk down and took a step toward the door, but Rayna touched her arm.

"I'll go look for him. You watch your tomatoes."

"Oh, okay."

Rayna set her milk and remaining cookie on the counter, then pointed a finger at Mason, narrowing her eyes. "Don't eat my cookie."

He grinned and stuffed what remained of his second one into his mouth.

Izzy laughed. "There are plenty more. Go find your dad."

She rolled her eyes, but smiled. "Fine." Opening the back door, she stepped outside and jogged toward the chicken coop.

"Dad?" She looked around the yard, noting that whatever angered the flock must have moved on. They were all pecking away at the ground with only an occasional cluck.

Walking up the short ramp to the coop, she pushed the door open. "Dad?" She stepped over the threshold. Movement to her left caught her eye, and she gasped. "Dad!" He sat in the corner, tied up with some old rope, a rag stuffed in his mouth.

"Oh my God! What happened?" She crouched in front of him and pulled the cloth from his mouth, then started on the ropes around his wrists, which were bound in front of his bent knees near his ankles.

"I came out to check on the chickens and someone hit me from behind. They dragged me in here while I was dazed and tied me up. They're after the boy. They asked me where he was, and I told them I didn't know. That's when they stuffed that filthy rag in my mouth."

Shit! Her heart started to double-time. "I left him in the kitchen with Mom."

His eyes grew wide. "We need to go. They probably saw you walk out of the house."

She attacked the bonds around his feet, feeling like they weren't getting any looser, until suddenly they fell away.

John kicked the rope off and scrambled to his feet, shoving her toward the door. "Let's go!"

They dashed across the grass, scaring the chickens all over again. He beat her to the house and threw open the door.

Rayna, right on his heels, skidded to a stop as he froze just inside the door. She peered around him to see a man with sandy hair in his late-forties holding a gun on Izzy. Mason stood near the sink, glaring at him.

The man turned mud-colored eyes on her and her dad, offering them a smile that didn't reach his eyes. "Welcome to the party. Come inside and shut the door."

John stood there, his face hard. "Let my wife go."

The man's smile disappeared, and he pressed the gun to Izzy's temple. Izzy sucked in a sharp breath. Rayna dug her fingers into her dad's shirt and pressed her lips together. He vibrated with rage under her hands.

"You're not calling the shots. I said come inside and shut the door."

Rayna gave her dad a nudge. He took two steps forward. Rayna followed and kicked the door shut.

"Happy?" John asked.

"I see where your daughter gets her spunk." He ran an assessing gaze over her. "My clients like that sort of thing. And you're very pretty."

Mason growled and took a step toward the man.

He swung the gun away from Izzy to point it at Mason, halting him. "What's gotten into you, boy? Don't tell me you fell in love with her. Never would have figured you to have a thing for older women."

Anger flared to life in Rayna's chest, burning hot. She stepped around her dad. "Leave him alone."

The man glanced at her, then did a double-take as he studied her face. "Wait." He looked back and forth between her and Mason, then laughed. "Oh, this is great. He's not in love with you. He wants you to be his *mommy*."

John stepped up next to his daughter, cutting off the man's laughter. "What do you want?"

"Oh, that's simple. I want the kid." He turned hard eyes on Mason. "I didn't say he could leave."

"I'm not going with you, Jim."

"Yes, you are. Or," he pointed the gun at Rayna, "mommy dearest here dies. Your choice."

"Don't do it, Mason," Rayna pleaded. "He'll kill us anyway."

"On the contrary, Ms. Nydert. I'm not in the business of leaving a trail of bodies in my wake. If Mason comes peacefully, I will simply leave the three of you tied up. I'm sure Dr. Archer will find you at some point."

"How do you know so much about us?" Rayna asked.

He smiled. "I have little birds everywhere. Now," he looked at Mason, "are you coming? Or do I need to shoot your new friends?"

Mason's face wavered as her vision swam. "No," she whispered.

He stared back at her, some of the fight leaving his shoulders. "I'm sorry," he said before looking at Jim. "Fine. If you won't hurt them, I'll go with you."

Jim's smile was bright. "Good." He turned to Izzy. "Mrs. Nydert, I'm sure a good cook like you has some kitchen twine around here. Where is it?"

Izzy glared at him and said nothing.

He cocked the gun and aimed it at Rayna. "*Where* is it?"

She drew in a breath through her nose. Closing her eyes, she pointed to the drawer next to the stove. Jim moved back a step and pulled it open, finding the ball of twine. He tossed it at Mason.

"Tie them up. Start with Grandpa."

Mason stared at the twine a moment before heaving a deep sigh and walking over to John.

Rayna reached out to touch his arm. "Please, Mason. You don't have to do this," she whispered.

"Yes, I do," he whispered back. "He'll kill you. I can't let that happen."

"But you can't go back there." A tear spilled over to roll down her face.

"I survived once. I will again. But I can't let you die."

"This is all very touching," Jim cut in. "But if you don't hurry up, I'll shoot them all anyway."

"Sorry," Mason muttered. He tied a loop in the twine and slid it around John's wrist.

Izzy, seeing that their captor was distracted, took a shuffle step to her right. Rayna fought to keep her expression clear. There was a block of knives only a foot from her mother's hand. She thought furiously to come up with a way to keep Jim distracted.

"Tell me about Gilly," she said.

His gun lowered a fraction as he stared at her in surprise. "How do you know about Gilly?"

"Doesn't matter. What happened to her? Did Ryan Marsters kill her?"

Jim readjusted the grip on his gun and shifted his feet, looking past her for a moment before settling his gaze back on hers. "So what if he did? He's dead too."

"How many others did he kill? And how could you let a monster like him anywhere near those kids? From what

Mason said, children are 'investments' to you and your wife. Ryan was a killer."

"Yes, but he paid very well for our services. Enough that losing a child here and there didn't affect our bottom line much."

Disgust made bile rise in Rayna's throat. He talked about those kids like they were commodities on the stock market. She swallowed hard and continued. Izzy was only a hand's length away from getting a knife from the block.

"You're a revolting piece of trash. One day, you're going to rot in hell."

Mason finished with John and moved to bind her hands.

Jim shrugged. "Maybe. Or maybe I'll just die."

"Let's find out," Izzy said, coming up behind him.

He turned to look at her, but couldn't get more than his head around before she lunged, plunging a steak knife into his back.

He shrieked and spun away. "You bitch!"

Rayna knocked Mason out of the way and ran at Jim as he turned, raising his gun toward her mother. She snatched the knife from his back and stabbed him again in the arm. He kept hold of his gun, but it lowered, pointing at the floor. She lashed out with the blade again, but he dodged. Izzy grabbed another knife from the block and stabbed at him, but missed as he sidestepped toward the stove behind him. He raised his gun at Rayna and fired. The bullet breezed past her so close she felt the wind rustle the sleeve of her shirt. It imbedded itself in the wall by the door.

Izzy let out a roar and dove at him. "Don't you shoot at my baby!"

In the chaos, Mason untied John, who, now that he had his hands free, entered the melee. He grabbed Jim's wrist to hold the gun away while he leveled a punch across the man's jaw. Jim reeled backward, quickly catching his bearings to raise his gun again, but didn't get the chance to fire it. Izzy picked up her pot of tomatoes and dumped it down his back.

He screeched as the boiling contents spilled over him, finally dropping his weapon. Rayna lunged for it. As her fingers touched it, the back door crashed open, and a gunshot echoed through the room as the newcomer fired into the ceiling.

Rayna looked back from her position on her knees, eyes going wide.

"Judge Brandt?" John said, shock clear in his voice.

Oh my God. What was he doing here? Rayna rose to her feet and faced the newcomer.

The older man stepped into the house. A woman near Jim's age who had to be Anne followed him inside.

"About time you two showed up," Jim said, a bit breathless. "These three are a handful."

"Wait," Rayna said. "Judge, you're in on this? You *knew*? All this time, you knew there were kids being trafficked in this county, and you sided with the bad guys? What the fuck is wrong with you?"

"I didn't side with them, my dear. I'm the one who suggested it to them. Jim was my client about twenty years ago. He had a decent drug operation going and was a shrewd businessman. But the cops who arrested him were sloppy, and he walked on a technicality. Proved very lucrative for me. Ever since then, Jim and Anne have dealt in drugs *and* people. I get a cut of every deal and every sale. Plus, I like the perks."

Bile rose in her throat again. She would never have guessed the mild-mannered judge who she saw around town daily and always brought his grandkids to her harvest market was such an evil, reprehensible human being.

He glanced at Anne. "Tie up Mr. and Mrs. Nydert. Mason, step over there with Rayna and stay put."

Mason, expression closed off, stepped through the mess on

the kitchen floor to reach her side. She looped her arm through his and hung on, determined not to let the boy out of her sight. Anne moved toward Izzy, picking up the ball of twine. She made quick work of tying up her hands, then lashing her to her husband. She shoved them both to the floor, then tied them to the cabinet handles.

Jim grabbed the dish towel off the oven door and swiped at the tomatoes and blood on his backside, wincing. "What now, Judge? They know an awful lot."

"Yep. But that's okay. By the time the cops find them, we'll be long gone. I'm not really in the business of murder. Besides, even if they get free, they won't come after us. Mrs. Nydert's going to be too busy trying to keep her husband from bleeding to death."

Before any of them could react to his statement, he raised his gun and shot John in the abdomen.

Izzy shrieked, jerking her hands against their restraints as she tried to get to the blossoming bloodstain on John's shirt. "John! Oh my God!"

"Dad!" Rayna started toward him, but Brandt stepped in front of her.

"Uh-uh. You're coming with us."

"No!" Izzy shouted.

Brandt glanced at her. "Shut up, or I'll put another bullet in him."

Tears flowed down Rayna's face. "Please. I'll do whatever you want. Just don't hurt them anymore."

"Good girl." He motioned her toward the door. "Let's go."

Rayna took Mason's arm again and glanced over her shoulder as the judge ushered them out of the house to the SUV waiting by the back door. Her mother's tear-stained face bent over her dad was the last thing she saw before she was shoved into the car and Anne threw a hood over her head. Zip ties cinched around her wrists. The only thing keeping her from completely flipping out was the knowledge that Thomas would be home for lunch.

Please, God, let him find them soon before her dad bled to death.

Twenty

Thomas pulled into the police station on his way home for lunch, eager for an update on what Seb found at the Drapers'. He was guessing there were no kids since he hadn't already gotten a call, but he would like to know what else they found. If anything.

Gut churning, Thomas pulled open the door. Alaina Wilder sat behind the front desk.

"Hi, Thomas."

He smiled at the deputy. "Hi, Alaina. Can you buzz me in so I can talk to Seb?"

"Yep." The door buzzed, and she shoved a visitor's badge through the slot in the window. "I'm not sure you're going to like what he has to say, though."

His smile died. "Great. Thanks for the heads up." He took the badge and clipped it to his shirt.

She nodded, and he pulled open the door, speed-walking through the bullpen to his brother's office. He heard him before he saw him. Someone was getting an earful.

Pausing at Seb's office door, he peered through the crack to see him glaring out the window, his phone to his ear.

"I don't care if you think I'm crazy, Dan. Someone leaked details of the raid. That place was spotless. I know it wasn't my people, because I kept this to a select few I trust. It has to have come from your office." He paused as he listened. "Yeah, well, you can take your reelection and shove it up your ass. I'll make sure everyone knows where the leak is and why we still have five missing kids." He slammed the phone down, then rested his head in his hands.

Thomas rapped his knuckles on the door.

"Yeah?" Seb dropped his hands, an annoyed look on his face before he saw who it was. "Oh. Hey. I suppose you heard all that?"

"Yep." He sat down in one of the chairs in front of the desk. "The raid was a bust?"

"Completely. We didn't find a single piece of drug paraphernalia or any signs there were ever any drugs in that house. And everything smelled like bleach."

"So, what now?"

Seb sighed. "There's a BOLO out on the Drapers' car. I'm also bringing in cadaver dogs from the state."

Thomas's posture went rigid. "You think the kids are dead?"

"It's a possibility, yes."

"So, you're searching the Drapers' property?"

"I can't. Not for that. I still don't have any evidence linking them to the kids. Just the drugs."

"Dammit," Thomas muttered. "So, what good are the cadaver dogs going to do? They didn't have enough time to kill and bury the kids when we found their house."

"No, but there might be others buried on the property. Mason said Gilly and others have disappeared over the years. If we can find a body, Dr. Randall might be able to pull some trace evidence that could give us a clue as to whom we're dealing with. In the meantime, there are also APBs out on

Frank and Jeremiah. I sent their picture to every law enforcement agency in the state."

"What if they're not in the state?"

"That's why I also sent it to the neighboring states and my buddies at the FBI. Every agency for hundreds of miles is looking for them. I sent the sketches we got from Mason's descriptions of Jim and Anne Smith to the neighboring states as well."

Thomas ran his hands through his hair. "Man, this was not what I wanted to hear. I don't want to go home for lunch now and have to tell Mason the kids are still out there somewhere."

"I don't envy you. I wish I had better news."

"Yeah, me too." Thomas pushed out of his chair. "If you find out anything more, call me?"

Seb nodded. "I will. Keep an eye on Mason. All indications are that the Smiths have moved on, using what they got from raiding your clinic as capital to start a new life. But I could be wrong, and they're just biding their time."

Thomas sighed. "Okay." He stepped toward the door. "I'll see you later."

Seb waved, and Thomas walked out. He left his visitor badge on the desk with Sergeant Wilder and headed for his truck. The drive to the ranch went much too fast for his liking. He hated disappointing Mason. He was jittery when Thomas left this morning, so he knew those kids were on the boy's mind. That he was worried. It felt a bit like kicking a puppy to have to tell him they had zero leads now on his friends.

Turning into the Double Moon's drive, Thomas pulled around to the backside of Rayna's and climbed out, then jogged to the door and stepped into the kitchen. It was quiet.

"Rayna?" He wandered through the house, but there was no sign of her or Mason. Maybe they were still working.

He left the house and went to the market building. It

didn't look promising. The windows were closed, but he tried the door anyway to find it locked. Frowning, he checked the other buildings nearby. Hurrying from one to the next, he found them all locked.

Perplexed, he looked around. Where the hell were they? Rayna's truck was parked right next to his, so he knew they were here. His gaze landed on her parents' house. It was one of the few places he hadn't looked.

He jogged down the lane between the houses and up the front steps. Knocking on the door, he pushed it open. "Hello?"

"Thomas! Help! We're in the kitchen!"

The panicked note in Izzy's voice sent him running through the house. "Izzy!" He rounded the corner and came to a halt as the chaos registered. She and John sat on the floor, their hands tied to the cabinets. Izzy had her knee pressed to her husband's bloody abdomen. "Oh my God! What happened?" He crouched next to her and John, who was gray, his skin clammy.

"The people who Mason ran from—they were here," she said as he took a knife out of the block and sliced through the twine on her wrists and John's. "They shot John and took Rayna and Mason."

"What? Jesus. Okay." He pulled out his phone, barely able to hold it with his shaking hands, and dialed his brother.

"Sheriff Archer," Seb said, distracted.

"Seb, it's Thomas. I need you to send an ambulance to the Double Moon. John's been shot. The Smiths were here, and they took Rayna and Mason."

"What? God, this case just keeps biting, doesn't it?"

Thomas heard him moving around.

"Wilder! Send EMTs to the Double Moon for a gunshot. Travers, call the state. I need a bird in the air. Sorry, Thomas," he said, lowering his voice. "Do you have any idea where they went?"

"No. But Izzy might." He relayed Seb's question to her.

"I don't know where they went. But Thomas, Judge Brandt was with them."

"What? Why? Hang on." He pulled the phone away from his ear and put it on speaker. "Okay, tell Seb what you just told me."

"Judge Brandt was with the Smiths. He masterminded the whole operation. I don't know where they went, but I saw a dark blue SUV before they closed the door. It looked like a Jeep."

"Holy shit. You're sure it was Brandt?"

"Yes."

John's breathing grew raspy, and she turned her attention to him. "John? Honey, hang on, please!" Her voice wobbled as she pleaded with him to stay alive.

"Seb, I need to go. John's not doing well. I need to see what I can do to stabilize him."

"Okay. I'll talk to you soon." He hung up.

Thomas set his phone down. "Izzy, how long ago was he shot?"

She sniffed. "An hour, maybe? I tried to free us to call for help, but every time I took pressure off his wound, he bled more. I was afraid he'd bleed out if I didn't stay put."

He looked around, grabbing a couple more towels from the drawer and handed them to her. "Use those. They'll help staunch the blood. I need to run back to my truck and get some supplies." He laid a hand over Izzy's. "I'll be right back."

She pressed her lips together and nodded. "Hurry."

Thomas dashed out the back door, running for his truck. Reaching it, he yanked open the driver's door and hopped inside. He stuffed the keys in the ignition and bumped over the grass to the Nyderts. He climbed out and jumped into the truck bed, unlocking the large bed box where he kept veterinary supplies. He pulled out several items and ran into the house, falling to his knees next to Izzy and John.

"Please help him, Thomas. He's getting worse." Tears streamed down Izzy's face as she looked at him.

"I'm hurrying, Izzy, I swear." He yanked on a pair of gloves, then tore open some IV tubing and a bag of saline, thanking his lucky stars he took EMT classes so he knew how to do all this on a human too. He opened the drug kit he brought in and took out vials of potassium and calcium to treat the shock brought on by blood loss, then hesitated. He didn't know the dosages for a human, though.

An idea hit him, and he took out his phone, calling Seb again.

"Go, Thomas."

"I need you to get Dr. Randall on the line. I need a dosage calculation for potassium and calcium."

"Hang on."

Thomas dug a syringe out of his bag while he waited. He heard Seb repeat the question into another phone, then a pause before he came back on the line and told him what Randall said.

"Thanks," Thomas said.

"Yep."

Thomas hung up and pulled the cap off the syringe, drawing up the potassium first. He added it to the IV bag, then opened a second syringe and drew up the calcium, adding it to the bag too. He inverted the bag several times to mix it well, then spiked it with the tubing and primed the line.

Grabbing the IV start kit, he picked up the older man's arm and laid it over his knees.

Jesus, he's gray. He needed to hurry.

Probing the crook of John's elbow, Thomas found the vein and swabbed the skin with an alcohol wipe before sliding the needle into his arm. He prayed the vein hadn't collapsed. John had lost a lot of blood.

A deep red filled the tube, and he let out a sigh of relief. Pulling the needle free, he taped the tube in place and hooked up the IV line, rolling his thumb over the clamp to open it all the way. Standing while holding the bag, he dug in a drawer and found a clip, and attached the bag to a cabinet door.

"Move over, Izzy."

She scooted out of the way so he could get to the wound on John's abdomen. Thomas lifted the towels and pulled John's shirt away, coming face-to-face with his second gunshot wound in a week. Blood leaked from the hole.

"I think the bullet might have hit his liver. We need to slow this bleeding. I think I brought in some clotting gel. Can you find it?"

She moved over to the pile of supplies he dumped on the floor and rooted through them. "This?" She held up a white packet with an applicator inside.

"That's it."

She handed it to him, and he tore it open, snapping the top off the applicator and inserting the tip into John's wound. He moaned, but didn't open his eyes. Thomas squirted the gel inside. "Pass me some gauze."

Izzy handed him several packets of gauze, which he layered over the wound, pressing down. John moaned again, louder.

"I'm sorry, John," Thomas whispered. Where was that ambulance? He glanced at his watch. This far out of town, they had at least another five minutes before it would arrive.

"What now?" Izzy asked.

His eyes met hers. "I've done all I can. He needs a surgeon and blood."

She turned watery eyes on her husband. "Is he going to be okay?"

"Honestly? I'm not sure. He's lost a lot of blood. But he's hung on this long, so that's a really good sign."

More tears coursed down her cheeks. She brushed John's hair back with trembling fingers. "Please don't die."

Thomas took a breath and looked away from them, the pain on Izzy's face almost too much to bear. He took in the mess around him instead, noting the food and blood splattered all over. The Nyderts had put up quite a fight.

"Izzy, did the judge or his companions say anything useful? Leave any clues about where they were going?"

She sniffed hard. "No. He just said they were going to disappear right away. I imagine they're on the move, though we probably slowed them down just a little. Rayna and I both stabbed Jim and dumped a pot of boiling tomatoes on him."

Thomas glanced at the mess by the stove. "So, not all this blood is John's?"

She shook her head.

He grinned and took out his phone again. "Izzy, I could kiss you." He dialed Seb once more.

"You need Randall again?" Seb asked, in lieu of a greeting.

"No. Send the crime scene unit over here now. Izzy and Rayna stabbed Jim before they left. His blood is all over, and the judge said Jim's been charged with drug offenses in the past. Is there a chance his DNA is in the system?"

"Seriously? It depends on how long ago he was charged. The law to collect DNA from individuals charged with felonies has only been on the books about ten years. But there's been one to collect it from those *convicted* for almost thirty."

A frown furrowed Thomas's brow. "Well, then we'll have to hope he has a conviction on record, or that Katie can find some prints. The judge said it was about twenty years ago that they met."

"Hmm... He was an attorney then. I might be able to get a warrant for his client list."

"Just do whatever you have to. He's got Rayna and Mason."

"I know. I'm going to call Katie now. She should be gearing up to come out there anyway, but I'll tell her to step on it."

"I appreciate it."

"Not a problem. Finding them is my number one priority. Keep me posted on John."

Thomas glanced at the man. His breathing was still ragged, but it looked like the bleeding had slowed. "Will do. Thanks, Seb."

"Yep. Talk to you soon." Seb hung up.

Thomas pocketed his phone. "Forensics is on the way." He leaned over John to check the IV and bandages once more, praying fervently Seb found a lead.

Twenty-One

Rayna squinted against the bright light as her hood was removed. She blinked several times as her vision adjusted, and she looked around her. They were in a cabin. A very nice one, by the looks of it. Leather furniture sat around a giant stone fireplace that dominated one wall. The ceilings reached to the second story, where skylights let in an abundance of natural light that competed with what came in through the wall of windows to her right. To her left behind the judge was a state-of-the-art kitchen, and a dining set large enough for Thomas's entire family.

She looked at the judge, doing her best to ignore the gun in his hand that was trained on Mason. "Where are we?"

"Some place safe, for now," he replied. He glanced back at Anne and Jim. Anne was busy attempting to patch up her husband's wounds. From the look of him, he could use a doctor and not just his wife's rudimentary first aid.

"What about my friends?" Mason asked. "Are they here?"

"They're upstairs."

Rayna and Mason both looked up at the balcony that ran along the upper story.

"You two will not be joining them, however. I have a different spot for you to relax until it's time to leave." He motioned them toward a hallway that ran behind the stairs and alongside the kitchen.

Rayna glared at him and kept her feet planted.

He sighed. "Ms. Nydert, you've already caused me quite the headache. I'm not a fan of killing, but you're pushing it." He tipped his gun toward the hallway again and lifted a brow.

She huffed and started walking. If they were going to get out of here, she needed to play this smart. That meant not dying.

They walked a little over halfway down the hall before he called them to a halt.

"Open that door." He pointed to the door to their right.

She reached out and twisted the knob, giving the door a push. It opened into a large bathroom.

Brandt nudged her shoulder with his weapon. "Inside."

Glaring at him over her shoulder, she walked into the bathroom, Mason following. Brandt took hold of the knob and smiled. "If you get thirsty, there's a faucet." He pulled the door closed, and she heard him turn the lock, which had been turned around to face the hallway.

Rayna resisted the urge to kick something. Instead, she brought her zip-tied wrist up and pulled on the piece sticking up, tightening them as much as she could.

"What are you doing?"

"Breaking free." She pulled again to make sure she had it as tight as she could get it. "Thomas and I were still dating when Seb went through FBI training. He taught us all some tricks once. I haven't done this since then, but it's not that difficult to do."

With the plastic tight, she put her hands out in front of her and yanked them toward her stomach, twisting her wrists outward at the same time. They popped apart. She shook them loose and tossed the broken zip tie on the floor.

"Whoa."

She grinned. "Your turn. Put the heels of your hands together, then tighten the zip tie. Pull your arms into your body quickly and twist your wrists out."

He did as she instructed and broke free. "Wish I'd known that a long time ago."

Rayna paused, swallowing hard. She did too.

"So, what now?" he asked, rubbing his wrists.

She turned to the cabinet against the wall, then glanced back at him as she walked over to it. "We try to find a weapon."

"I doubt they left a razor or anything like that in here."

"Not that kind of weapon." She rummaged through the cupboard, letting out a quiet squeal when she came across some small bottles of essential oil.

"What'd you find?" He came up behind her.

She passed him the bottles and turned back to the cabinet. "Thankfully, Brandt doesn't know me very well. If he did, he would have removed everything from this room instead of just the sharp, pointy objects."

"What do you mean?"

Rayna stood on her toes to see into the back of the cabinet. She grabbed a bottle of shampoo and several spray bottles of different sizes. "What I mean," she backed away and turned to face him, "is that I know plants. Which includes the oils they produce." She pointed to the vials he held. "We're going to make some weapons."

Alaina didn't even ask why he was there when Thomas strode into the police station. She slid a visitor's badge through the window slot and buzzed the door open.

"He's in the conference room."

"Thanks." He clipped his badge on and hurried inside. Finding the conference room, he opened the door and walked inside.

Seb looked up from the whiteboard where he was looking at the map taped to it. "How's John?"

"At the hospital. I got the bleeding to stop, but he's not out of the woods yet. The paramedics said he would probably go straight to surgery. Do you have anything new on where they took Rayna and Mason?"

Seb's mouth flattened, and he looked at the map again. "Maybe. Katie just sent me a match for the prints she took off the stove. They belong to a James Paulson. She got another set on the cabinets belonging to his wife, Anne Graves Paulson. He did a couple years as a young adult for drugs. She has a couple misdemeanors."

"Nothing since?"

"Nope. I'm betting Brandt and whoever he had on the payroll here at the sheriff's department had something to do with that."

"You think there was a dirty cop involved?"

"There had to be. I just don't know who it was, or even if he's still on the payroll. Caleb was the only officer who'd been with the department that long other than the previous sheriff," he said, mentioning the deputy Ryan Marsters killed.

"You think Caleb was dirty?"

"I don't want to, but it had to have been him or the sheriff to go back that far. Though, I'm leaning toward Sheriff Thwaite. Caleb just didn't give off the right vibe for a dirty cop. Thwaite was a politician through and through. I can see him blackmailing someone or even having his own skeletons he wanted kept quiet."

"Well, where is he? Go talk to him. And why are you staring at a map?"

Seb looked back at the sharp note in Thomas's voice and cursed. "Jesus, I didn't even think about how you're handling all this." He spun a chair out from the table. "Here, sit down."

"I don't want to sit, Sebastian. Tell me how you're going to find my family." His voice broke on the last word, and he had to blink several times to keep the tears at bay.

"Just take a breath. I know this is hard—believe me, I've been in your shoes. I can't go talk to Thwaite because he moved to the Caribbean when he retired. Said he was tired of winter. But we do have some actionable intel. I was looking at the map because the Paulsons have property in their real names. And I've got someone running down the series of shell corporations that the compound in the mountains is under. Jace is tearing Judge Brandt's life apart right now, there's a chopper in the air looking for a dark blue Jeep, and every air strip within two hundred miles is on alert for private flights carrying children."

Thomas frowned. "You think they're going to fly out of here?"

"I think it's a possibility. Did Izzy tell you anything else about what they said?"

He drew in a deep breath and ran a hand through his hair, trying to remember what she said. "Not really. Just that they were leaving the area right away."

"So, the plane theory might not be far off. Okay. Why don't you—"

Thomas cut him off, holding up a hand. "I swear, Seb, if you tell me to go home and wait, I'm going to punch you."

"I was going to say go keep Izzy company, but I guess I won't."

"Mom can go sit with her. I need something to do."

Seb nodded. "Okay." He motioned him closer. "Come

look at this map."

Thomas walked over and scanned it. "What are we looking for?"

Seb picked up a marker and a sheet of paper, then drew several small X's on the map. "This is the Paulsons' property." He drew another X. "That's the mountain compound." Another X joined the group. "And that's the Drapers'."

"They're all in fairly remote areas."

"Which make them all great places to hide out."

"Sheriff."

They turned toward the door at the interruption, and a deputy walked in.

"Did you find something, Gentry?"

"We'll see. It's mostly just more information. While I was digging into those shell corporations, I found other property under their names." He held out a sheet of paper.

Seb took it and turned to the map, plotting the new addresses.

Thomas stepped closer. "There." He pointed to one about thirty miles from the Double Moon. "All the others are buildings in town or houses with only a small amount of land. But that one is sizeable."

"So?" Seb asked, giving him a quizzical frown.

"I need a topographical map."

Seb looked at Gentry, who nodded and ran out of the room.

"What are you thinking?"

"That maybe they're not taking off from a public air strip."

Seb glanced back at the map. "Shit. If they take off from their own property, they could land anywhere, then board another jet hundreds of miles away."

"Exactly."

Gentry ran back in with a map in his hands. "Here." He

handed the map to Seb, who unfurled it over the table.

They located the property, and Thomas's stomach sank. "It's flat."

Seb pulled the radio off his belt. "Dispatch, this is Archer. Connect me to the state patrol's chopper."

They waited as the dispatcher connected them. In a few moments, the radio crackled to life.

"This is Captain Hilliard. Go ahead, Sheriff."

"I need you to reroute to the following coordinates." Seb went back to the map hanging on the wall and rattled off the GPS location of the property.

"Roger. Changing course."

Seb signed off and changed the channel, sending deputies to the location. He put the radio back on his belt. "Gentry, go take over from Jace and tell him to head northeast. I'll call him with directions."

"Yes, sir."

"Wait!" Thomas said. "I'm going with you."

"Thomas—"

Thomas cut him off again. "I have to, Seb."

His brother sighed, but nodded. "Stay out of the deputies' way and do what Jace tells you. I have to stay here and coordinate."

"I will."

Seb narrowed his eyes. "I mean it, Thomas. Behave."

Thomas rolled his eyes. His brother knew him too well. "I will." He ushered Gentry to the door. "We'll keep you updated." He pushed the deputy through the door before Seb could change his mind. It didn't matter that he wasn't equipped or trained for this kind of thing. He was going to be there to bring the bastards down. If they caught Brandt and the Paulsons, and his family wasn't there, he would get their location out of them one way or another. Seb wasn't the only Archer brother who could be dangerous when pushed.

TWENTY-TWO

"They're coming back!" Mason whispered, ear to the door.

"Okay. Come over here," she whispered back.

He crossed the large bathroom in two long strides. She double-checked his clothing to make sure nothing was showing, thankful for his skinny, but tall build.

The knob jiggled as whoever was on the other side unlocked it. The door swung open, revealing Anne.

She stepped into the doorway and stared at the two of them, a gun in her hands. Her intense look morphed into a frown as she took in their unbound hands.

"How did you get free?"

Rayna gave her a tight smile. "The sheriff is a close, personal friend. And he was a fed. I've learned a few things from him over the years."

Anne shifted her stance and took a breath. "Whatever. It's time to go." She motioned toward the hallway with her weapon, then stepped back so they could precede her down the hall.

Rayna gave Mason a nod, and he started forward. She

followed, and they headed for the living room. Her heart stuttered as they entered the open space. Besides Brandt and the Smiths, there were three girls and two boys of various ages sitting on the floor, their hands bound as hers and Mason's had been.

The kids looked up as they entered. The oldest girl's eyes went wide as she caught sight of Mason, but she quickly masked her expression and averted her eyes.

Brandt frowned and looked at Anne. "Why aren't they bound?"

"They got the zip ties off," she said.

He looked heavenward and sighed. "Ms. Nydert, do you remember what I said to you before?" He picked up the gun sitting on the table next to him and pointed it at her.

She stared at him, defiance shining bright on her face. "You shoot me and there isn't a corner on this earth you'll be able to hide. Thomas will come looking for you. And it won't be to bring you back to the states to stand trial."

Brandt laughed. "A veterinarian is going to hunt me down?"

"A veterinarian with powerful friends and family."

"Ah, yes. The sheriff. I must admit, he's been a problem, especially for our drug operation. But thankfully, his long absence from the area before he took the position worked in our favor. We were able to keep this side of the business much more under his radar."

"I guarantee it's not there now."

"Unfortunately. But, in this line of work, one must plan for problems such as these and have contingencies in place." He lowered the gun and turned to Jim. "Bind their hands again. We've spent enough time here and need to get on the road."

Rayna shifted, brushing against Mason's arm. He gave her a side glance and a minute nod.

Jim stepped in front of Mason, another zip tie in his hands.

"Now!" She whirled, pulling a small spray bottle from her waistband and spraying Anne in the face while Mason pulled out a larger bottle and sprayed Jim. Both of them shrieked and backed away. She spun around again, and she and Mason both aimed for the judge as he brought his gun up. He pulled the trigger, but his shot went wild as a slick mixture of shampoo, baby oil, and a high concentration of essential oils coated his skin. He yelled in surprise and his hands went to his face.

Brandt shouted in rage and raised his weapon again, firing blindly. Rayna ducked, then ran at him, grabbing his gun arm and spinning so her back was to him. She lashed backward with her elbow, connecting with his face, then grabbed his gun, twisting it out of his hand.

He held his nose and squinted at her as she leveled the weapon on him. Glancing over her shoulder, she saw Mason had laid Jim out on the floor with several solid punches. Anne leaned against the wall, tears streaming down her face as she moaned in pain. Her gun laid several feet away, forgotten.

"Is your face on fire?" she asked, turning back to Brandt.

He moaned, swiping at the muck, but having little effect, even using his shirt. "I should have just shot you. What was that?"

"A little of this, a little of that. And a whole lot of essential oil. I might not have lit you on fire, but it's going to feel like it for quite some time."

He moaned again and sank to the floor, the oils penetrating his skin. His eyes were beginning to swell with the irritation.

"Mason, bring the Smiths over here with Brandt. Let's tie them up."

He did as she asked. Rayna found the bag of zip ties in Jim's pocket and tripled the ties, so they couldn't break out.

With their captors now the captured, they found some scissors in the kitchen and cut the kids free from their bonds.

The girl Rayna noted when they entered threw her arms around Mason.

"I thought you were dead," she said.

He pulled back and smiled at her. "No. I stumbled into her field." He pointed at Rayna. "I would have been if she hadn't found me, though. She and her friend Thomas saved my life."

She hugged him again. "I'm so glad you're okay."

"Thanks, Nina." He rested his hands on her shoulders and looked down at her. "How about we get you guys out of here?"

"I think we'd like that very much." She frowned. "But what about the cops?"

"That's a non-issue," Rayna said. "One of my close friends is the new sheriff. And," she glanced at Brandt and the Smiths, "there's evidence all over my parents' kitchen that they kidnapped us. Brandt shot my dad." Tears formed in her eyes, but she sniffed them back. She couldn't breakdown yet. They still needed to get everyone to safety.

"Does anyone know where we are?" she asked.

The kids all shook their heads.

"Great. Let's hope someone can track my phone. Do you see it?" she asked Mason and glanced around, hoping it was in view.

He wandered over to the kitchen, his stride purposeful.

"Did you find it?"

"Yeah. But it's broken." He turned around and held up the device. The screen was shattered.

Brandt laughed through his tears.

She walked over to him. "What?"

"You're stuck here unless you want to hike through the wilderness with all those kids in tow."

"How about I just take your phone? Or better yet, the keys to one of the cars."

He laughed harder. "I don't have my phone. Didn't want to be tracked after we left here. And Jim torched the cars to get rid of any trace evidence."

Rayna looked at the other man who cradled his face in his bound hands, silent in his pain. "That's asinine. He bled all over my parents' kitchen, and he's worried about fiber and prints in a *car*?"

Brandt shrugged. "I didn't see the harm in it. We didn't need them anymore, anyway."

She frowned, confused. "Okay, I know you weren't going to martyr yourselves and blow up the house with all of us in it, so how were we leaving?"

He smiled. "I'll never tell."

Rayna stood and moved back over to Mason. "Either they have other vehicles stashed around here, or there's someone coming to pick us up," she said, keeping her voice low.

"Okay, so what do you want us to do?"

She thought fast, looking at the scared, but now also hopeful faces of the kids. "I'm going to go out and have a look around. Keep an eye on our friends." She picked up Jim's gun and handed it to him. "Feel free to shoot them if you have to. You think you can do that?"

He took the weapon from her, his face harder than she'd ever seen it, some of that life experience he had poking through. "Yes."

"Good. I'll be back soon." Rayna grabbed Anne's gun and left the house.

As she cleared the porch, the smoldering remnants of two SUVs to the right of the house caught her attention. They were little more than hollowed out shells now. Jim must have doused them in some sort of accelerant to get them to burn so fast.

She glanced around the property. If it weren't for the horror show inside, this would be a nice place. It was quite an idyllic setting. They were in a valley, the land flat with mountains rising on either side. Cattle milled in the pastures, and a cool autumn breeze made leaves flutter as they fell from the trees, reflecting their golden colors in the bright sunshine.

A barn past the smoking cars drew her eye, and she ran toward it. Lifting the bar across the double doors, she threw one open and stepped inside, pausing so her eyes could adjust to the dim interior. Her shoulders slumped as she walked deeper inside. The only vehicle inside was a tractor.

Turning around, she ran back out. There was only one other outbuilding, and it was a small shed behind the house— much too small to hold a car. Rayna cursed under her breath and headed back for the house.

As she stepped on the first stair, her ears picked up a droning sound. She turned around and looked out over the valley. That sounded like a plane. Squinting against the bright sunshine, she gazed up at the sky. In the distance, the white fuselage of a small aircraft swooped down over the mountain and into the valley.

"Crap!" she whispered. They had company.

She darted back inside. "Get the kids and take them back to that bathroom," she told Mason.

"What? Why?"

"There's a plane landing. I think it was meant to be our ride out of here."

"You can't face it by yourself."

"There's likely only a pilot on board. Maybe one other person. It looks fairly small. There are ten of us here. It doesn't take an army to keep a group of kids under control. I'll be fine." She started herding the kids toward the hallway. "Go. Keep them safe."

"What do we do about them?" He pointed to Brandt and the Smiths.

Rayna looked around. He was right. They couldn't leave them sitting on the floor. They wouldn't be there for long without someone watching.

She walked over to Brandt and kicked him in the hip. "Get up." She did the same to the Smiths. "You too."

"I can't see!" Anne wailed.

"Don't care." Rayna grabbed the woman by the jacket and shoved her toward the pantry. Mason followed with Jim and the judge.

She pulled the door open, checking that there were no sharp objects, then shoved them inside.

"I need a chair."

One of the kids brought her a dining chair, which she wedged under the knob.

"Okay, you guys go. I'm going to greet the plane."

She turned away, but Mason's hand on her arm stopped her. She looked up at him.

"Be careful."

"I will. Take care of your friends."

He nodded, and she dashed out the door.

The plane was on the ground, taxiing through the pasture. *Dammit*. There was little cover between her and the aircraft. She couldn't just walk out there. The pilot could be armed, and she didn't know if there were other people on board. Sticking close to the house, she ran behind the ruined SUVs to a tree between the house and the barn. If she waited long enough, the pilot would probably come to the house to see what the holdup was.

She leaned against the tree trunk and settled in to wait. After ten minutes, the door on the side of the plane opened, and a man walked down the staircase. He jogged across the pasture, hopping the fence and continuing to the house.

Rayna waited until he was at the door before she ran back, coming up behind him.

"Turn around with your hands in the air."

He jerked at the sound of her voice, then slowly turned.

"Hands up," she said, noting the pistol strapped to his side.

He hesitated, and she raised her weapon from its ready position and pointed it at his chest. "Don't. I've had a really bad day, and I just want to go home. I will not hesitate to shoot you. Take your gun from its holster and toss it into the grass."

"No, you drop it, Rayna."

Rayna stiffened at the female voice behind her. She knew that voice.

April Stillwater walked around to stand beside her, a gun aimed at Rayna's head. "I said, put it down."

One look at the other woman's face, and Rayna knew she wasn't bluffing. She straightened and thumbed the safety on the gun, holding up her hands. The pilot walked forward and took it from her.

"What are you doing, Mrs. Stillwater? I thought you were appalled at your husband's conduct."

"I am. But I will do what I have to to survive. I clawed my way out of a shitty childhood, only to find myself in a shitty marriage. But he provided me with a good lifestyle. I'm not going back to the hell of being poor. Judge Brandt and I have been, well, acquaintances for a few years now. He offered to continue providing that life if I kept my mouth shut."

Rayna scoffed. Was she for real? "You really think a man like Richard Brandt wants to take a middle-aged drunkard like you to some exotic location as a companion? When he has a predilection for young kids? My guess is he's going to traffic you just like them."

"No, he's not!" she spat. "Richard loves me. We just

couldn't be together because he had to keep up appearances. How would it look for a county judge to steal the wife of one of the local mayors?"

"Not to mention, divorce his own wife in the process, right?" Rayna rolled her eyes. She knew she was playing with fire, baiting the woman, but her only chance might be swaying April to see things her way.

"Shut up! Where is he?"

She shrugged. "I escaped, but didn't want to leave without the kids. I don't know where he is," she bluffed.

"Let's go find him."

She gave Rayna a hard shove. One that the pilot wasn't expecting. She crashed into him. Rayna lashed out, kneeing the man in the groin and shoving the heel of her hand into his nose. Blood sprayed as it broke.

A gunshot rang out, the bullet slamming into the wall beside them.

"Enough!"

Rayna lowered her fist and held her hands up.

"I don't want to kill you, but I will." April's voice held a plea.

Rayna turned. "You don't want any of this. Just let us go. Take the pilot and have him fly you somewhere. Start over. You don't need Brandt."

"Yes, I do. I have a few thousand dollars to my name, but that won't take me far. Richard is my ticket out of here." She motioned toward the house. "Go inside."

The pilot grabbed her by the hair and yanked her close. Tears pricked her eyes at the pain, but she refused to give him the satisfaction of hearing her scream.

"I think I might just demand you as my payment instead of my usual fee," he growled in her ear.

"Go for it, buddy," she ground out through her teeth. "I'll break more than just your fucking nose."

The sound of a car coming cut through the air. Rayna glanced at April and the pilot. Each wore a confused look. Rayna grinned.

"Expecting someone?"

They glanced at each other.

"No? I am," she bluffed again, even as she prayed she wasn't. The scene at her parents' was messy. It should have yielded something for Seb to trace.

"This wasn't part of the job," the pilot growled. "I'm just transport."

"Shut up and go inside." April pointed to the door as a sheriff's cruiser came into view.

Yes! Rayna's heart somersaulted.

"Nope. This wasn't supposed to happen." The pilot let go of her hair. "You're on your own." He sprinted off the porch and across the grass to the pasture. The cruiser sped up, coming to a halt out front.

She glanced back at April. The woman watched the pilot.

Rayna exploded into action, knowing now was her chance. She dropped down and swept a leg out, taking April's feet out from under her. The woman crashed to the ground with a shriek, but kept hold of her gun.

Rayna dove behind a planter as the woman sat up and fired. Gunshots came from the yard. She heard April grunt and looked out from her hiding place to see twin blood stains form on her shirt as she fell back onto the porch. Her hands flopped and the weapon fell from her slack fingers.

Rising, Rayna looked out. A familiar figure ran toward her.

"Thomas!"

Twenty-Three

Thomas's heart thundered in his ears as he jumped out of the police cruiser. He started to go after the man running across the grass for an airplane parked in the pasture when he heard a shriek, then gunshots from the porch. He skidded to a stop and turned to see Jace fire back. A dark head popped above a massive planter and his heart stopped altogether before resuming its frantic pace.

Rayna.

He changed direction and ran for the house. "Go get the other guy!" he yelled at Jace as he dashed past. He didn't wait to see if he complied. His only concern was to get to Rayna.

She saw him and shouted his name. He met her in the grass in front of the porch. She crashed into him with a sob, and he held her tight.

"Oh my God! Are you okay? Where's Mason? And the judge?"

She pulled back to look at him. "They're in the house. Mason and I got free and managed to subdue them. He and the kids are hiding in a bathroom. Brandt and the Smiths are tied up in the pantry."

"You two did all that?" He stared down at her, a proud smile lifting his mouth.

She nodded. "Remind me to thank Sebastian for turning me onto jiu-jitsu all those years ago."

Thomas pulled her into another tight hug, laughing. "I'm sure he'll be happy to hear he got to play some role in this take down. Brandt messed with the wrong woman." He tipped her head up to look at her. "I love you."

She stood on her toes, her mouth hovering near his. "I love you too."

He closed the distance between them to give her a searing kiss. Rayna savored the feel of his mouth on hers, knowing how close she'd come to never feeling it again.

The sound of a man cursing broke them apart. They turned to see Jace hauling the handcuffed pilot over the fence. He dragged him over to the cruiser and shoved him in the backseat.

"You're going to need more cars," Rayna called. "Brandt and the Smiths are tied up inside."

Jace sauntered over, shaking his head. "Now I know why you and Tara get along so well."

Rayna grinned and stepped out of Thomas's embrace, but took his hand. "Come on. Let's go tell Mason it's over."

They walked into the house with Jace and were greeted with the sound of banging coming from the pantry.

Jace drew his gun. Rayna stood off to the side while Thomas walked up to the door and removed the chair, taking hold of the knob. At a nod from Jace, he pulled the door open and stepped back. Brandt and the Paulsons stumbled out, looking like bee sting victims. Their faces were all fiery red and their eyes swollen.

"Freeze!" Jace said. "Sheriff's department."

They halted. Anne wilted against the door. "Please, get me something to wash my face," she wailed.

"Jesus, Rayna," Jace said. "What did you do to them?"

"Peppermint essential oil and shampoo," she said. "We sprayed it all over their faces like pepper spray."

Jace glanced at Thomas before reaching for the judge, pulling him forward. "And you had the guts to piss her off?" He gave a low whistle.

Thomas took hold of Jim. "Yeah, well, she had other ways to wound me."

Rayna rolled her eyes. "We're past all that. Are you two good? I'm going to go tell Mason it's safe."

Jace nodded. "You guys go. I have these three." He took his phone from his pocket, calling for assistance.

Thomas ushered her out of the kitchen, eager to see Mason. She led him down the hall and opened a door. Mason stood a few feet inside, aiming a pistol at them.

"Whoa," Thomas said, holding up his hands.

Mason lowered the gun, letting out a harsh breath. Thomas stepped inside and wrapped him in a tight hug. The young man's shoulders shook with silent sobs.

"It's over, Mason."

Mason pulled away to look at him through teary eyes. "Really?"

"Yes. Really." Thomas glanced past him to see five sets of eyes staring at him from around the shower curtain. His eyes widened as he took in the kids. The oldest, a girl, was probably fifteen or sixteen, but the youngest was a ten or eleven-year-old boy.

Rayna stepped inside and turned to the kids. "It's safe now."

Mason motioned them out of the tub enclosure when they hesitated. "It's okay. Everything is going to be okay."

Epilogue

Children's laughter floated on the breeze out back of Lee and Jenny's house. Rayna ladled punch into a cup and stared out over the yard as Mason, dressed as a ghost, ran after the other kids. It had been six weeks since things went down with Brandt, and the children were flourishing. Two of the three had been kidnapped from their parents by the Paulsons and since reunited with their families. The youngest, Justin, and the second oldest girl, Mia, were back where they belonged. Lee and Jenny had petitioned for emergency foster care approval for Nina and the two others, Ellie and Chris. They now lived here on the Broken Bow. Mason had moved into the Airstream, which sat a few yards from Thomas and Rayna's back door on the Double Moon.

The showdown at the property in the valley had put an end to the trafficking ring. They netted Brandt's entire operation from the information he had on a thumb drive. The Stillwaters, Amherst, and several current and former government officials, including Thwaite and a social worker, were now in custody awaiting trial. Seb had also uncovered the graves of six children on the Paulson's mountain property.

"Rayna."

She turned as her mother poked her head outside.

"They're here."

"Oh! Great. Let me grab Thomas." She set the cup down and walked out into the yard, where Thomas sat with his brothers and Jace around a firepit, watching the kids play.

"Hey, hon," he said as she got close.

An excited smile lit her face. "They're here."

He hopped up from his chair and rubbed his hands together. "This is going to be good." He looked down at the others. "Come on."

The group headed back to the house. Thomas let out a whistle to get the kids' attention and motioned them to the patio. They gave up their game and ran for the house, descending on the punch bowl and other Halloween goodies set up on tables for everyone to snack on.

"Give us a minute, then send Mason inside," Rayna told Jace as they walked toward the door. He nodded. She and Thomas left the others to wrangle the hyper bunch and went inside to greet the newcomers. A plump woman in her fifties with a kind smile that lit up her blue eyes stood in the living room talking to Lee, Jenny, John, and Izzy. A teenage girl stood quietly next to her with her arms crossed. Her face said she'd done this before and was ready to leave.

The group looked up as Thomas and Rayna entered the room.

"Hello," Thomas said, walking forward. He held out a hand to the older woman. "I'm Thomas Archer."

Rayna held out hers as well. "Rayna Nydert."

The woman shook their hands. "Constance Heyward. It's nice to meet you finally."

"Same here," Rayna said. She turned her gaze to the girl. The resemblance was uncanny. She shared a glance with Thomas, his eyes telegraphing the same thought.

"Thomas? Rayna? Jace told me to come inside and find —" Mason's voice cut off as he entered the room. He stood just over the threshold. Eyes wide, his mouth hung open as he stared at the girl.

"Emma?"

The girl, who no longer looked so defiant and bored, dropped her arms and stared at the tall young man across the room.

"Mason?" she whispered.

He was across the room in three strides, scooping the girl into his arms.

Tears spilled over Rayna's eyelids as she watched the siblings' reunion. Thomas wrapped an arm around her waist and pulled her close.

Mason pulled back and held the girl's face in his hands, staring down at her. "I never thought I'd see you again." He let her go and turned to look at the adults in the room. "How?"

Rayna swiped at the tears on her face and shrugged. "We found her birth certificate looking for yours. Seb contacted the juvenile courts, who put us in touch with Mrs. Heyward. Emma's been in foster care in Denver for the last seven years."

He looked down at his sister. "Have they been good to you?"

Emma shrugged. "For the most part. No one's really been mean. But I feel like an outsider most days."

"Well, you're not an outsider anymore," Rayna said.

Mason and Emma looked at her, confused.

"What do you mean?" Mason asked.

She glanced at Thomas, who gave her a nod. They looked back at the kids. "Thomas and I petitioned the court to adopt the two of you."

"There are still a few details to work out, but if all goes according to plan, in the next few months, you will officially be our kids."

Emma's hands flew up to cover her mouth, and she looked up at her brother. Mason stood staring at them, eyes huge.

Thomas stepped up to the young man. "I know you're an adult, but do you want to be part of our family? For real?"

The young man swallowed hard, and tears pooled in his eyes. He nodded. "I'd like that. Very much."

Thomas wrapped him in a hug. Mason extended an arm, reaching for Rayna. She stepped into their embrace. Together, the three of them turned to Emma, who just stared at them.

"Why?" she whispered finally.

"Because your brother gave us a second chance at something we never thought we'd have again," Thomas said. He glanced at Mason. "And we want to repay the favor." He arched a brow at the girl. "So, what do you say, Emma? Will you let us be your family? All of us?" He motioned to the group around them.

Emma looked at him, then Rayna, then around the room. Mason stepped forward and took his sister's hands.

"Em, I know you're scared. To put your trust in another set of strangers. I was too." He took a deep breath, hesitating. Rayna found herself holding her own.

"I was in a bad place for a long time after we were separated. I ran away from my foster home when I was eleven, then got picked up by a couple I thought wanted to help me. They were human traffickers. I spent seven years in captivity until one night I finally managed to run away."

Emma gasped. Mason looked over his shoulder at Thomas and Rayna.

Tears trailed down Rayna's cheeks. She clutched Thomas's arm and gave Mason an encouraging nod.

He looked back at his sister. "I ended up here—well, not here, here, but Rayna's ranch, which is just down the road. She and Thomas took me in and hid me until we could get a handle on things. I just wanted to get as far away as I could from the people who exploited me, but they made me realize running would just be another prison. These people—not just Thomas and Rayna, but their families too—could have refused to help me. It was dangerous—Rayna and her dad both got shot—but they did everything they could to stop the people responsible for hurting me and so many other kids. I've found a home here, Emma. Not just another foster home, but a real home. Like what we had with Mom and Dad. So, how about it? I know it won't be the same, but can we start over and make a new family with the Archers and Nyderts?"

She looked beyond him to the people around the room. The other adults had joined them midway through Mason's speech, and they all offered her warm smiles.

The girl's eyes watered, and she sniffed, looking up at her brother again. "I mean, I guess we could give it a try."

Mason wrapped her in another hug. "You're going to love it here."

Rayna stepped back, letting the siblings have their moment, and leaned against Thomas's chest. He wrapped his arms around her waist and put his face next to hers.

"You ready for this?" he asked. "We now have two teenagers."

She turned her head, smiling up at him. "Yeah. I think we're both ready."

~

Keep reading for a sneak peek at *Close Quarters*, book 4 in the *Broken Bow* series.

Thank you for reading In Plain Sight! I hope you enjoyed it.

Want to read an EXCLUSIVE and FREE book? Sign up for my mailing list. You can find the sign-up form on my website, ashleyaquinn.com. My list also receives sneak peeks of my latest work and access to exclusive giveaways. Also, please consider leaving a rating or review on Amazon and or Goodreads. It would be greatly appreciated!

Thanks again for reading!
    - Ashley

Keep reading for a sneak peek at Book 4, Close Quarters in the Broken Bow Series.

CLOSE QUARTERS

BROKEN BOW
BOOK 4

ONE

"Oh, come on!" Dr. Alex Randall looked around his pathology lab, his anger growing as he took in the mess that bloomed overnight.

Katie Mitchum, the county's chief forensic scientist, poked her head up from behind a large boxy machine, her pink-framed glasses sliding down her nose and tendrils of her colorful hair fluttering around her pretty face.

"Seriously, Katie? Where the hell did all this shit come from? I have to work down here, too, you know." He tossed his briefcase down onto the autopsy table and put his hands on his hips, glaring at her.

She rolled her hazel eyes. "Take a chill pill, Doc. Once I get it organized, it won't look as bad."

He looked around the room, which was already stuffed to the gills. "Where are you going to put it that will make it look better?"

Her eyes followed the track his took, and she shrugged. "Somewhere. I just need to shift a couple things. What are you complaining about, anyway? You don't even use all the space down here."

He pinched the bridge of his nose, a headache already forming. "I did before you showed up."

The look she leveled on him said she thought he'd grown another head. "Sure you did. That's why it was so easy for me to move in."

Alex scrubbed his hands over his face. He couldn't wait for the county to rebuild the criminology lab so he could get her out of his space. She was driving him crazy. "Okay. Sure. I don't want to argue. Can you please just—" he motioned around the room with his hands, "move things so we have more space to work? I feel like I'm tripping over everything."

She scrunched her nose and frowned, but nodded.

"Thank you." Picking up his briefcase, he walked past her toward his office on the far side of the large room. At least she hadn't invaded it too. He put his key in the lock and opened the door. Flipping on the light, he groaned. Three more filing cabinets lined the walls.

"How the hell did she even get in here?" he muttered.

"Oh, I meant to text you about those last night, and I forgot," Katie said from behind him. He turned to look at her. "They delivered the new evidence dryer and gas chromatograph. I needed space, so I asked security to unlock your office."

His jaw worked as he looked down at her. "I thought we agreed my office was off-limits?"

She shrugged. "I needed the space."

"Find space somewhere else."

"It's just a couple filing cabinets, Alex."

"Don't care. Stay out of my office. You have until the end of the day, or they're going out in the hallway."

She sighed and adjusted her glasses. "Fine, sourpuss." Rolling her eyes once more, she turned and sauntered away.

Alex grabbed the edge of the door and flung it closed. That woman was going to be the death of him. If he thought he could find a better forensic scientist, he'd fire her ass for insubordination. Her skill was the only thing keeping her employed.

He blew out a breath and shrugged out of his coat. Truthfully, she wasn't that bad. She irritated him, yes, but she was kind and funny and the best damn forensic tech he'd ever worked with. There were just some days where her tendency to take charge ground on his last nerve. Which had been much more frequent since she moved into his lab.

Hanging his jacket on the back of his chair, he sat down to filter through his email. The phone rang, and he reached for it while he continued to skim through his inbox. "Dr. Randall."

"Hey, Alex, it's Seb."

Alex focused on the conversation at the sound of the sheriff's voice coming over the line. "Hey, Seb. What's up?"

"How fast can you put together a team to scour the Paulsons' mountain property?"

He frowned. "The place where they held all those kids captive?"

"That's the one. After I got a full statement from Mason and from the kids we rescued, not to mention all the information Anne readily gave up on her husband and Judge Brandt, I have reason to believe there are several bodies buried up there. Judge Kovac signed off on my warrant first thing this morning."

"We can probably get out there tomorrow morning if we prep today. Do you have a cadaver dog? I'm not sure if Katie has a radar unit. If she doesn't, we might have to contact Denver or Colorado Springs for assistance."

"I haven't looked into K-9 assistance yet, but I will. I might be able to get a dog from the state. Why don't you find out about the radar unit, and we'll go from there?"

"Will do. I have a question, though. When you say several,

do you have a more specific number?" He wanted to make sure they had enough supplies on hand.

"Best guess, at least four. The kids came at different times, with Mason there the longest. But he said there was at least one who was there before him and disappeared while he was held captive. He said he remembers two others as well who vanished. Anne claims Jim handled most of the dealings with their clientele. She says she was just there to help kidnap the kids and keep them clothed and fed."

"Do you believe her?"

"Maybe. When I talked to her, she was in the midst of detox for heroin, so she was a twitchy mess. I'm not sure she remembers much of what went on in that house with any clarity. When I asked her specifically about any of the kids disappearing before they kidnapped Mason, she said there were a couple, but couldn't give me a specific number. I figure you're looking for four to seven, maybe eight, bodies. I tried to get Jim and the judge to give me details, but they refused to say anything."

"Jesus. That's disgusting."

"Tell me about it." Seb's voice was terse. "I can't wait for this case to go to trial. I'm going to pin every charge I can think of on all three of them."

"Okay. Let me talk to my team and I'll get back to you."

"Sounds good."

Alex hung up and sighed. He had no idea where he was going to put that many bodies with only a quarter of a lab. He glanced at the filing cabinets against the wall. Maybe a quarter was too generous.

Pushing away from his desk, he stood and exited his office. More of Katie's team had arrived, and they were busy moving things around to improve the flow of the room. He spotted his quarry, bent over a lab table, trying to reach the outlet behind it. Alex tried not to stare as he got a full view of her tight butt in her khaki jeans. Katie Mitchum might annoy the ever-loving shit out of him most of the time, but she was a knockout.

He walked over to her and cleared his throat. She glanced up at him.

"What now? Look, I'm trying to make some more space, okay?" She straightened, still holding the power cord.

"It's not about that. Seb just called. We need to prep for an excavation."

Her brow dipped with curiosity. "Okay, which cemetery?"

"Not a cemetery. The Paulsons' place."

"The human traffickers?"

He nodded. "Apparently, there are several children buried up there."

A dark frown overtook her face. "I can't believe Judge Brandt masterminded that whole thing. I hope he fries. When do we need to be ready?"

"Tomorrow, if possible."

She bit her lip and looked around. "I'm not sure that's doable, to be honest. I need to borrow a radar. Mine's on order still."

"Okay. What else do you need that you don't have?"

"That's it. Everything else I'd need for a body recovery I've already replaced."

He nodded. "Sounds good. Get enough supplies and personnel lined up for at least eight bodies. That's the high end, but we don't want to be short on what we need once we get out there. I'm going to make some calls and see about finding you that radar. I need to talk to Amanda Pressley at the University of Colorado too. I think all our remains are going to be skeletonized, and I don't deal with just bones."

"Will do, boss." Her mouth quirked as she gave him a sharp salute.

He rolled his eyes and plucked the cord from her fingers,

leaning over the table to plug it in. "Get busy," he said, straightening. Spinning on his heel, he went back to his office.

Exhausted, Katie fell into the chair at her desk and closed her eyes. It was eight p.m., and she'd been at work since seven that morning. Alex had come through with the radar and the forensic anthropologist. Both were meeting them at the Paulsons' tomorrow morning, so she and her team had launched into overdrive to get things ready.

Her stomach growled, reminding her she skipped dinner, and that lunch was the protein bar she kept in her desk. But she didn't want to move. Her feet hurt and so did her back. She was only thirty-two, but right now, she felt more like she was sixty-two.

The soft snick of a door opening made her open her eyes. She swiveled to watch Alex step out of his office. Dark stubble dusted his jawline, and his chocolate hair with its hint of silver was mussed. She bit her lip as she watched him walk. Even rumpled, the man was a sight to behold. At a couple inches over six feet, the medical examiner's muscled frame moved with a predatory grace. Intelligence sparked out of his bright blue eyes, and she knew if he smiled, they would crinkle at the corners. She'd never had a thing for older men until she met Alex Randall.

Although he wasn't *that* much older than she was. When he started working for the county, she peeked at his personnel file, more than a little curious about the handsome doctor, and discovered he had eleven years on her.

Her chair creaked as she shifted while she watched him walk to the door. He paused and glanced back.

"What are you still doing here? I thought everyone was gone except for the handful of night shift employees."

She sat up and rolled to the drawers that made up one side of her desk, removing her purse. "They are. I stayed to finish a few things. But it's time for me to leave now, too." She picked up her coat and shrugged into it.

"I'll walk you out."

"You don't have to do that. I'll be fine." She really didn't want to walk all the way to the employee parking lot with him. Part of the reason she antagonized him so much was to keep him at arm's length. He did funny things to her insides whenever he got too close. Or smiled.

"I don't mind. We're going the same way, anyway."

She searched her brain for a reason to walk alone, but anything she came up with was lame; he'd see right through her for the chicken she was.

"Fine. But don't blame me when you get annoyed by the sound of my belly growling in the elevator." She looped her purse strap over her neck and across her chest, then moved toward him and the door.

"You skipped dinner too?"

She glanced up at him in surprise. "Yeah. So did you?"

He nodded. "While you prepped equipment, I filled out forms. Excavating bodies on this scale means a lot of overtime. Among other things. But I'm done now and heading to Boone's to grab a burger." He looked down at her. "You?"

"That was my plan as well. One of their burgers with everything on it sounds amazing."

"Want to join me?"

Her eyes went wide, and she ducked her head, punching the button for the elevator before he could make out her expression. Did he really just ask her to go somewhere with him outside of work? After all the grief she gave him every day? He must be a glutton for punishment.

She pasted a smile on her face and looked up at him. "Haven't you had enough of me for the day?"

The elevator dinged, and they stepped inside. He glanced down at her, the crinkles popping out around his eyes as one corner of his mouth lifted. "I haven't seen much of you today, so I haven't gotten my quota in yet. I'm sure by the time we finish eating, I'll be ready for a break."

"Same, Doc. Same."

"So, does that mean you'll join me?"

She nodded. "Sure." Why not? She was a glutton for punishment too.

They rode the elevator up to the first floor and walked through the lobby and down a corridor to leave the hospital by the rear entrance.

"I'll meet you there," she told him as they reached the employee parking lot.

He nodded, peeling away toward the doctors' section, while she continued through the rows of cars to where she parked her little silver SUV this morning. It wasn't her first choice for a car—that would be a Mini Cooper—but a tiny British car was not at all practical in Colorado winters in the mountains. One day, she was going to buy one anyway, even if she could only drive it a few months out of the year.

She climbed inside her car, tossing her purse onto the passenger seat before starting the engine. Putting the SUV in gear, she headed for the exit just as Alex turned onto the main road in his much more expensive black SUV. They made a handful of turns before they pulled up in front of the small diner downtown. She parked out front next to him and got out.

He joined her on the sidewalk, his posture more relaxed now that they were away from work. She tried not to stare. Was she going to get a glimpse of the real Alex Randall? The not stick-in-the-mud she'd seen him be with the sheriff? Did she want to see that man? Resisting "boss Alex" was hard enough.

Readjusting her purse strap over her shoulder, she followed him into the restaurant.

Alex held the door for Katie as they entered the diner. The vanilla scent of her shampoo assaulted him as she walked past. He fought the urge to step up behind her and bury his nose in her hair. How did she still smell so good after working thirteen hours?

He planted his feet, letting some space open between them, then followed her. He should have just gotten his food to go. What was he thinking, eating with her? She drove him crazy—for many reasons, not the least of which was her desire to run *his* lab.

It was too late now to change his mind, though. She was already halfway across the diner. He followed her to a booth by the windows lining the side wall and sat down. They reached for menus as a young woman walked up, a notepad and pen in her hands.

Alex smiled at the girl, remembering her from the many other times he'd eaten at the diner.

"Hi, Becca."

She smiled back. "Hi, Dr. Randall. What can I get you to drink?"

"Iced tea, please."

She nodded, then looked at Katie.

"The same, please."

"Do you two know what you want to eat?"

Alex looked across the table at Katie in question.

"I just want a burger and fries. And a chocolate milkshake."

He smiled at her. "That sounds really good, actually." He

looked up at the girl. "I'll have the same, except make my shake strawberry."

The girl scribbled their order on her notepad. "Okay. I'll be back in a few with your drinks."

Katie put her menu away and sat back, then gazed out the window, drumming her fingers on the table.

"You know, we've worked together for over four years now, and I think this is the first time we've done anything together outside of work. Even in little get-togethers with other lab employees, we've never hung out," Alex said, leaning back.

She shrugged. "Technically, you're my boss."

He rolled his eyes. "Like that matters to you."

She giggled. "Well, if you did things my way, we wouldn't have any problems."

"Probably not," he chuckled. "But I also wouldn't have a job."

She narrowed her eyes, a teasing glint entering them. "Are you saying I'm not enough of a brown-noser?"

He laughed. "Yes. Very much."

"What can I say?" She leaned forward and crossed her arms on top of the table. "Politics were never my thing. Or people, for that matter. There's a reason I like working in a lab."

"I hear that. The dead don't talk back."

"Did you ever try to be a regular doctor?"

Alex nodded. "In med school. I went in with the full intention of becoming a surgeon. It didn't take me long to not only realize I didn't have the patience for, well, patients, but that I found forensics riveting. It was like a puzzle. Medicine is in general, really, but forensic pathology is one of those five-thousand-piece ones that are all black. There aren't many clues; just your own ability to identify patterns and things that aren't right."

"Yes!" She lifted a hand to point a finger at him. "Exactly. Being a criminalist is the same way. That's the best part of the job. Figuring out what's not right and why."

"Precisely."

"So, how did you end up here? You were in Salt Lake City. Why choose itty-bitty Silver Gap?"

"I'm from a small town in Oregon. I missed the atmosphere. Plus, I get to be my own boss for the most part. Though that does mean I have to deal with you."

She grinned. "Aren't you special?"

Becca walked up with their drinks and shakes, interrupting them. "Can I get you anything else right now?"

They both shook their heads, tearing open straws. Alex plunked one in his shake and took a deep draw.

"Cool. Your food should be up soon."

"Thanks, Becca," Katie said, putting a straw in her shake too. The girl smiled and walked away.

Alex swallowed another mouthful of his drink, curiosity getting the better of him as he watched the woman across from him. "So, are you from here? I inherited you when I took over, and I don't think I've ever asked if you're a native."

She shook her head. "I'm from Colorado Springs. I started working here right after I finished my master's, then took over as department head shortly before you arrived when our other one quit to move to Florida."

He shook his head. "You know, if I hadn't looked at your personnel file when I started, I wouldn't have known you had so little experience. You're very good at your job."

Her smile was shy, which surprised him. She had so much confidence when it came to her job, it seemed strange that she didn't when it came to herself.

"Thank you."

He picked up his shake and sat back. "That's also the only

reason I haven't fired you." He smiled around his straw, softening his words.

She pressed her lips together and glared at him. "Funny."

He grinned.

She rolled her eyes and took another drink. "What do you think we'll find tomorrow?"

"A mess." He set his glass down. "I'm just hoping for the low end Seb quoted me, which is four."

Katie's mouth pulled down, and she pushed her shake away. "I know you told me to prep for eight, but I'm really hoping there won't be any."

"Yeah, me too. Some people are sick." He sighed and picked up his shake again. "But that's why I do what I do. To bring the depraved to justice and give families closure."

She raised her glass. "Hear, hear."

Alex knocked his glass against hers and sucked down another mouthful of the thick shake. Becca walked up to their table carrying two plates of burgers and fries.

"Here you go." She set them down. "Can I get you anything else?"

They both shook their heads.

"I think we're good for now," Alex said.

The girl gave them a thumbs up. "Okay. Wave me down if you need anything." She whirled on her heel and walked away.

Both starving after the long day, they dove into their meals, conversation ceasing as they assuaged their hunger. But that didn't mean Alex didn't study her as they ate. She was an enigma. The woman was brilliant. But she didn't look like your typical brainiac. Shades of vibrant blue and purple threaded her naturally dark hair, and tattoos colored her arms. He was sure there were probably others he couldn't see. In her Converse sneakers and flannel shirts, she reminded him of a skater chick. A skater chick who would soon have a Ph.D.

"How's school going?" he asked. She'd told him about her

doctoral program, needing approval to be absent for certain days and times to attend classes, but he'd heard little about it since.

"It's good. I'm nearly done with my dissertation."

His eyebrows shot up. "Really? I didn't think you were that close to being finished."

"It's been two-and-a-half years since I started, so I would hope I'm about done."

"It's seriously been that long?"

She nodded.

He shook his head. "It doesn't feel like it. So, what's your topic?"

"The use of CRISPR as a tool for better DNA matching."

"Really?" That was an intriguing idea. "How so?"

"Using it on degraded samples that normal sequencing methods can't build a profile from because the chains are too busted up and piecing them together creates errors. CRISPR allows for the accuracy in reassembly that other techniques lack."

"Have you had any success?"

She nodded. "Seb let me use the county's DNA database. I compiled cases where DNA evidence was used to convict a subject, got permission from the convict and the victim if one was directly involved, and ran the DNA using my technique. It's confirmed the cases that were a complete match, several that were only partial, and I exonerated two others."

"And it held up in court?"

"No, because it isn't an approved technique yet. But it gave the lawyers a reason to appeal. Through that, the police reopened the cases and found additional evidence."

Alex sat back and stared at her. "How did I not know about this?"

She shrugged. "I did most of the work after you left for the day. I would stay late. Or, I went to the university and worked on it there. It was separate from my duties in the lab, so it's not really something you would need to know about."

"So, all those late nights you pulled early this year and last year, you were working on that?"

She nodded.

He glanced out over the restaurant in a bit of awe. Both at her idea and her work ethic. He looked back at her. "I think once you get your Ph.D., I'm going to have to ask the county council to take forensics out from under my purview, your aversion to brown-nosing be dammed. You're probably already better qualified to make the decisions for your department than I am."

She grinned and stuffed a fry in her mouth. "I've been telling you that since day one."

"Yeah, but now it's true."

Katie narrowed her eyes at him, but her smile spoiled the look. Alex glanced down at his plate, surprised to see all his food gone except a couple of fries. He thought he'd be in for a long, boring dinner he couldn't wait to get away from. But the opposite was true. He didn't want to go home.

Becca strolled back up to their table, pulling him out of his thoughts.

"You guys want any dessert?"

Katie patted her stomach. "I'm stuffed, so none for me."

Alex cleared his throat. "I'll pass too."

The girl nodded and tore their check off her notepad, laying it face down on the table. "I can check you out at the counter when you're ready."

They thanked her, and she walked away. Alex reached for the check, his hand closing over Katie's as she did too. Startled at the contact, he looked up at her. She stared back at him, wide-eyed.

He cleared his throat. "I'll get the bill. You are a struggling grad student, after all." He cracked a joke to dispel the sudden tension.

She laughed and withdrew her hand, motioning to the check. "Go for it." He picked it up and slid toward the edge of the booth. "Are you ready to go?"

"Yeah." She drained the last of her shake and picked up her purse, then slid out of the booth.

He paid for their meal, and they walked outside. Stopping in front of their cars, he fidgeted with the keys in his pocket, things suddenly awkward.

"I guess I'll see you in the morning." She jangled her keys.

Alex nodded. "Yeah. Um, have a good night."

"I will. You too."

They stood there for a moment longer before he backed away with a nod. As he climbed into his car, he glanced at her through the passenger window. Light from the interior of her car lit up her face as she got inside, glinting off her glasses and hair. Colorful tresses fanned over her shoulder as she closed the door. She was so far from his type, but he'd be damned if there wasn't a knot of attraction in his belly now after their dinner together. Shaking his head, not quite sure what to make of this sudden infatuation, he looked away and started his car.

About the Author

Ashley started writing in her teens and never stopped. Her first novel, Smoky Mountain Murder, came out in 2016, and she has since published two more series and has plans for more. When not writing, you can find her with her nose stuck in a book or watching some terrible disaster movie on SyFy. An avid baseball fan, she also enjoys crafting and cooking. She lives in Ohio with her husband, two kids, three cats, and one very wild shepherd mix.

Website: https://ashleyaquinn.com

goodreads.com/ashleyaquinn

amazon.com/Ashley-A-Quinn/e/B07HCT4QST

ALSO BY ASHLEY A QUINN

Foggy Mountain Intrigue

Smoky Mountain Murder

Smoky Mountain Baby

Smoky Mountain Stalker

Smoky Mountain Doctor

Smoky Mountain K-9

Smoky Mountain Judge

The Broken Bow

A Beautiful End

Wildfire

In Plain Sight

Close Quarters

Scorched

Light of Dawn

Pine Ridge

Sweetness

Loner

Shark

Katydid

Homespun

www.ingramcontent.com/pod-product-compliance
Lightning Source LLC
Chambersburg PA
CBHW021311190726
48288CB00003B/791